VIETNAM

...

Viet-Bloody-Nam

Davide A Cottone

P.I.E. Books
Australia
π

Published by P.I.E. Books
www.piebooks.net

Copyright © D.A.Cottone 2015

Legal Deposit Lodgement: (In accordance with the Copyright Act 1968)
National Library of Australia
State Library of Queensland
Parliamentary Library (Qld)

Cataloguing-in-Publication Data
National Library of Australia
Author: Cottone, Davide A., 1947 -
Title: Vietnam … Viet-Bloody-Nam / Davide A Cottone.
ISBN: 978-0-9925293-1-4
Notes: Historical Fiction
Dewey Number: A823.4

Cover design by Michael Madden: studiomadden@gmail.com
Book layout and design by Publicious Pty Ltd:
www.publicious.com.au

Editing: Paul Vander Loos: paul.vanderloos@gmail.com

I speak
For the mothers the fathers
The partners and the children
When I say no more war
And I speak for the dead
The maimed and the injured
When I ask what for.

I hear
The pipes the drums
The trumpets and the bugles
On Anzac Day at dawn
Become the rattle of battle
Of rifle and machine-gun fire
From Gallipoli as I mourn.

I feel
The deep sorrow of World War II
What they went through
And all in vain goddamn
My heart aches for all my mates
Who fought that war
In Viet-Bloody-Nam.

I see
The Flame of Remembrance
Big and bright
Like Baghdad burning in the night
And blood in the sand in Afghanistan
As the orchestra plays and the choirs sing
I see Death's bite.

Perhaps
They could play the Last Post
To mark an end to all war
Fix its flag forever at half mast
So we could pay our respect and never forget
The wages of war
In the past.

davide a cottone

Other Writing by Davide A Cottone

1965: *The Third Half.* Absurd Drama: (Eunice Hangar Lib, UQ).

1968: *Once Borrowed.* Novel (Fiction).

1978: *Bo.* Musical (Political Satire).

2001: *The Comeback Kid.* Musical (60's and 70's Rock) Performed H.K. 2001.

2002: *The Messenger.* Drama (Religious).

2002: *Generation Z: The Male Mutants.* Novel (Fiction). Pub: P.I.E Books.

2003: *Soul For Sale.* Musical (Contemporary). Performed H.K. 2003.

2005: *The Battle of the Sexes.* A Guide.

2006: *The Other World Album.* Songs (Seven songs by Sotto Ego).

2007: *Out of Control.* Musical (Rock, funk, soul, disco).

2009: *Eroica.* Musical (Classical).

2009: *Diary of a Devoted Poet.* "The Remembrance" Series. Pub: P.I.E.Books.

2012: *canecutter.* Novel (Historical fiction). Pub: P.I.E.Books.

2012: *Il Calzolaio.* (The Shoemaker) Mystery Drama in English.

2014: *Sotto il sole australiano.* Novel (Fiction) in Italian. Pub: P.I.E.Books.

2014: *Portrait of a Devoted Poet.* "The Twilight" Series. Poetry. Pub: P.I.E. Books.

To all Vietnam War Veterans and their families in Australia and overseas and in particular:

Barry William Spilsbury: 102 Field Workshop
Matthew James Coppola: 4th Field Regiment Light Aid Detachment
William "Bill" Crystal: 5th Battalion, The Royal Australian Regiment
Phillip James "Macca" McLean: 7th Battalion, The Royal Australian Regiment
Robert John O'Brien: 7th Battalion, The Royal Australian Regiment

The Australian Active Service Medal 1945—1975
Vietnam Campaign Medal
The Australian Defence Medal
Anniversary of National Service 1951—1972
Vietnam Star

Acknowledgements

A heartfelt thank you to my advisers and proofreaders: Paul Vander Loos, Elizabeth, Laurel, Louise, Jenni, Macca, Barry and Graeme for their suggestions and corrections and to Maddison for some early cover designs. Special thanks go out to Dr Michael Wilson, the ultimate 'beta reader' identifying plot holes, issues with continuity, inconsistencies and contradictions and Professor Clive Moore, both of whom gave all of the historical references a very thorough work over.

Finally, I would like to thank Barry Spilsbury, 102 Field Workshop, whose life experiences stereotype those of many of the diggers of that era. In this way, he has left a lasting legacy for the sacrifices made by the Australian diggers in the war in Vietnam. Barry inspired me to write this book so that in the words of the motto of the Vietnam Veterans Association of Australia and the Vietnam Veterans Federation of Australia, it might help in my quest to "Honour the dead, but fight like hell for the living".

Chapter 1

"You take that bloody leg off Yank and I'll hunt you down and wring your skinny neck with my bare hands."

These were the last words he said to the American doctor stationed at the 1st Australian Field Hospital at Vung Tau in Vietnam as he slipped away on a magical morphine induced slide to that special corner of 'God's Country' in Far North Queensland. His dreams always returned him there when he was in need of solace from the agony, heartbreak, disappointment and the futility of war in that foreign land.

It was 1952 and Manfred found himself in the engineering workshop at the Babinda Sugar Mill in Far North Queensland where his grandfather Bill Kammer, engineer in charge of the workshop, was boiling the billy for smoko. At sixty-six years of age, Kammer's Germanic features had been accentuated with age and by almost forty years of being exposed to the harsh tropical Australian sun. Contrary to the stereotype of the tall, fair-skinned, blue-eyed blonde German, Kammer was shorter and broad with a barrel chest, an olive complexion and hazel eyes with a full jaw that chewed continuously as he poked and stared at the flames beneath the billy.

Manfred Wright was born in 1947 as the only child of Wilfred Wright, a bridge carpenter and Kammer's only daughter Ella, a Red Cross Blood Service nurse. From the time he became aware of his European roots, he felt uncomfortable about it and avoided acknowledging it. His father was a Yorkshire man hence the boy had an English surname and the secret was safe. In later life, Manfred came to the opinion that any denial was due to peer pressure in Australian schools that were modelled on the characteristic British traits and mores of the mother country England and he did not want to be seen as different from the other children. Secretly however, he confided in his best friend Tony years later that it was also because of the horror stories of his grandparents' experiences which he had overheard them retelling and discussing with friends and family as a child. He once overheard the whole story of how Kaiser Wilhelm II of Germany wanted to conscript the twenty-two year old Kammer into the German army in 1908 and how he and his young bride Emelie had to flee the country and travel thousands of kilometres across Russia on the Trans-Siberian railway to Vladivostok in the Far East. Europeans always spoke in kilometres even though miles were used in Australia. Another time he heard his grandmother telling some friends about how her father, a Polish Nationalist involved in the January Uprising of 1863, had been hunted down and hanged by the Russian Mikhail Muravyov, who became known as 'The Hangman'. They often thanked God that they were able to leave Europe forever by travelling to Australia via Shanghai. Yet even then they could not escape their European roots, and shortly after arriving in Australia,

Kammer was interned as an 'enemy alien' in Berrima Gaol for the duration of World War I. Again, after twenty-one years of peacetime and working in Australia, Kammer was interned for the whole of World War II simply because he was German. German schools, churches and clubs were closed, their music banned, their food renamed and even place names were changed to British ones. In New South Wales, Blumberg became Birdwood and German Creek became Empire Bay. Most Germans lost their jobs throughout Australia and had their businesses destroyed. These stories left no doubt in Manfred's mind that anything to do with Europe had an unhappy ending.

In the workshop, the boy was sitting on the small stump of a log that his grandfather reserved especially for him. His chubby frame looked like a little Buddha perched on that log, apart from his straight dusty blonde hair styled in a saucepan cut above his plump rosy cheeks. He sported a wry grin that always left one wondering whether he was grimacing or up to something. It was always the latter.

"Damn it!" Kammer scowled as he took a whiff of the stench wafting up from the steaming billy of freshly made tea. "Those damn stink beetles know how to ruin a working-man's day, don't they boy?" he uttered with a blend of deep guttural sounds and nasal grunts. He fished for the pea-sized black beetle in the billy full of boiling black tea with a spoon, exercising the utmost concentration and poise and executing it with the same precision he practised on his lathe. Soon, the offending little bug found itself on its back on the dirt near Manfred's big toe.

"Don't say a word to the men," he said as he played with his handlebar moustache and smiled through the corner of his mouth. "I'd have to boil the billy again if they knew a stink beetle had taken a swim in it."

"What stink beetle, Grandpa?" asked the boy as he quickly placed his big toe on the dead bug. "I never saw no stink beetle."

"Good boy there. Now go get the sandwiches your grandma made for you this morning. You must be starving after all the hard work you've been watching us do." Kammer let out another volley of rasping chuckles acknowledging his own wit.

Manfred adored his grandfather. He loved going with him on Sundays to the workshop during the season when the mill crushed sugarcane non-stop and there was plenty of overtime for everyone. There at the mill, the sweet aroma of the warm freshly made syrup and brown sugar drifted past his nostrils conjuring up images of cupcake sized all-day suckers of translucent toffee treats.

He scanned the workshop, his eyes dancing over all the interesting shapes of the different tools and twinkled with the shining bits of twisted metal that the metal lathe gouged out and the spirals of the spinning bench-press drill. He would collect all of them and pile them up, then bring them bouncing to the ground with 'artillery' fashioned out of pieces of scrap metal.

When Manfred returned with the curried-egg sandwiches his grandmother had prepared for him, the tea was ready and the workers had all gathered around Kammer. Manfred put out a man-sized pannikin for his share of the tea that Kammer was pouring out for all the men. He loved how all of Kammer's workmates treated him like he was one of them even though he was just a child. It made him feel important as well as loved.

Blakey, the apprentice fitter, passed the sugar around and

the boy put three teaspoons into his mug. Blakey counted each spoonful with his eyes and nodded approvingly.

"You go for it boy. There's no shortage of that stuff around here." He topped up the boy's mug with milk. "Gotta have plenty of this stuff to make a growing boy's bones tough."

"Thank you Blakey." His eyes were downcast as he noticed Blakey had nothing to eat. "Do you want a bite of my curried-egg sandwiches?" he asked.

"Nah ... she'll be right mate. Had a bit of a rough night last night ... couldn't eat a thing, even if I wanted to ... not until lunchtime at the earliest. Thanks anyhow." He raised his mug and nodded towards Kammer. "Reckon this'll hit the right spot. It's just what I need."

"You're not wrong there Blakey," said the city boy, Marty, up from Brisbane. "Had a few too many myself at the Festival Queen dance last night. You country boys sure know how to have fun ... hardly!" he said. "All those beautiful girls in the dance hall and all you boys want to do is go out the back, drink grog and brawl with the out-of-towners."

"Well, it's pretty damn obvious they only came into town to pinch our girls. So we gotta defend them and make sure no out-of-towners take advantage of them, haven't we?" Blakey retorted.

"You'd have to be joking Blakey. It's a free country ... and they're not your girls anyway."

"That's what you reckon. Babinda boys have a responsibility to look after Babinda girls."

"What about Innisfail girls and Cairns girls?" Marty asked.

"They're different. It's up to Innisfail and Cairns boys to look after their own. It's as simple as that, city boy."

"Yeah ... well ... Marty's the name and this city boy

is going to show you country blokes up at this afternoon's 'Wallaby Jack' Joe Black Picnic Run."

Marty was certainly big enough to give the locals a run for their money. He had played rugby league from when he was old enough to hold a football. The Cairns District Rugby League Club had commissioned Marty to share his expertise with some of the clubs in the Northern Division of the Queensland Rugby League, including Babinda. He took the opportunity to get some work experience at the sugar mill while he was there.

"What is it with this 'Wallaby Jack' Joe Black legend anyway?" he asked. "Any relation to you Blakey?"

"Nah, he was no relation to Blakey," a voice interjected. It was the mill's old hand, Tim Green, who knew the legendary Joe Black.

"Joe was a timber-cutter way back in the day. In the early part of this century it was. He worked his way into part of the folklore of the Babinda district with an act of heroism that has never been equalled by anyone in the north since. He and his mate were cutting giant Johnstone River hardwood trees in the scrub behind The Boulders. Huge jungle vines in the canopy pulled the falling tree to one side so that it jack-knifed into a smaller but heavy black bean tree which splintered on impact and both trees came crashing down to where the boys were standing. It happened so quickly, only Joe Black was fortunate enough to throw himself behind a boulder while his mate vanished beneath an avalanche of foliage from the two fallen trees. Joe scrambled amongst the torn, twisted branches looking for his mate. Then, in front of him, he saw this pile of rags, a shattered and bloody leg, the white flesh of a forearm and the quivering lip of the lower half of a bloodied face.

"Joe could see that the Johnstone River hardwood tree had landed squarely across the black bean tree as he cleared the leaves away from his mate.

'Hang in there Ben ... hang in there!' he shouted while he checked if Ben was breathing and assessed the situation. There were broken bones on the right side of his body. The blood on Ben's face seemed to be from a nose-bleed. His right leg was pinned against a huge flat rock on the forest floor and he could see that it would be impossible to dig him out. His thoughts were blurred by the hysterical sounds of a huge flock of cockatoos circling above the hole left in the canopy of the forest where the trees had fallen. The only way to free Ben was to lift the trees off him and that meant he would need two wallaby jacks; one for each tree.

"Joe left his mate semi-conscious. He propped his head up against a log so that he would not swallow his tongue if he happened to lapse into unconsciousness. He then set off on a run through the scrub that required him to side-step, slide and scramble all the way to the swimming hole at The Boulders. He hoped somebody would be there to help him but nobody was there. The closest place of human habitation was at Saffiotti's barracks, near the double-barrelled bridge, three miles along the dirt road back towards Babinda. Canecutters lived in those barracks during the harvesting season. They always kept wallaby jacks on hand and used them to lift cane trucks back onto the loco lines when they became derailed.

"At the front door of the barracks, Joe listened as he stooped to rest his hands on his knees and breathed in deeply to catch his breath but there was no sound coming from inside. The canecutters must have been cutting on the neighbour's farm about three miles away on the other side of Babinda Creek. He called out and the Chinese cook came shuffling in from out the back and detected the sense of urgency from Joe's facial expressions and wild gesticulations.

'I need help … take that bicycle. Can you ride?' Joe said in between deep breaths.

"The cook nodded. 'Take that bicycle and get the ambulance in town to meet me at The Boulders. Tell them Joe Black … timber-cutting accident … hurry, hurry.'

"The cook was already on his way before Joe had asked him where the wallaby jacks were but he soon found them stacked against the corrugated iron walls of the outhouse. The Trewhella Wallaby Jack was made in Trentham, Victoria, by the Trewhella Brothers. It could lift six tons to a height of twenty inches and was made of solid steel. It weighed seventy pounds and had a detachable handle which was used to crank the jack up one notch at a time.

"Joe explained to me how he threw one jack up onto each shoulder and began the agonising jog back to The Boulders. He complained how the heavy steel jacks gnawed at the skin around his neck and bounced and hammered against his collar-bone, and he described how his heels jarred against the hard, uneven ground beneath his feet. He told me that on several occasions, he almost fell over as he tried to avoid potholes in the road. Then, in the scrub country after the swimming hole, he said he kept slipping on the slopes as his clothes became hooked up in the 'wait-a-while' vines in the undergrowth. Each time he fell, he clambered back onto his feet with an 'even stronger determination'. That's how he described the focus he was able to conjure up in his mind as he realised this was not about himself but about Ben.

"When he arrived at the site of the accident, he had hardly an ounce of energy left in him. He 'was like a dead man walking', that's how he said he felt, so you could imagine how much the return journey took out of him. Ben seemed to be unconscious as his eyes were closed and for a moment Joe panicked until he detected a faint movement in Ben's chest, so he knew at least that he was still breathing. I guess the realisation that Ben was still alive was enough to make every vein in Joe's body begin pumping blood into his muscles and priming him to do whatever it took to rescue his mate.

"Firstly, he placed one jack under the giant Johnstone River hardwood tree and began cranking it steadily to make sure it was on a firm footing. The spring of the timber under its own weight would have meant that the log was not lifting at all initially. After cranking the jack up twelve inches, the tree began to inch away from the black bean. At full lift, the hardwood tree was only eight inches clear of the black bean which had Ben firmly pinned to the ground. He placed two stanchions of dead timber against the hardwood tree to stabilise it and then set about preparing the second wallaby jack on a firm footing underneath the black bean. Slowly, he cranked it up three-quarters of an inch at a time and he said he could see the pressure coming off the injured limb. The blood began to flow freely and Joe knew he would have to work quickly to get Ben out so that he could stop the bleeding. He dragged the limp body out from under the black bean tree and bound the limb tightly with strips torn from his shirt. There was a bone protruding from Ben's right arm so he carefully lifted him to his feet, pulled his left arm around his neck and heaved Ben over his shoulder. That was when Joe was able to set off back towards the swimming hole and as he staggered through the forest, he said he would never forget how Ben's mangled limbs flopped around from side to side.

"When he arrived back at The Boulders, the ambulance bearers were nowhere to be seen. He had no choice but to keep going towards town and hopefully meet them along the way. He walked, talked, grunted and screamed his way towards town and the further he went, the stronger he felt. The more exhausted he became, the harder he pushed on, until at the doubled-barrelled bridge, he caught a glimpse of the horse-drawn ambulance cart coming towards him. He dropped to his knees, thanked God, and gently off-loaded Ben onto the side of the road. He remembered the relief he felt when he was able to hand over the weight of the responsibility of saving Ben to the ambulance bearers.

"It turned out the ambulance was late because they had been attending a cane-knife injury at one of the farms. They bundled both Joe and his mate into the cart, as Joe was also in need of urgent medical attention. There was no room for the ambulance bearers, so they jogged beside the cart all the way into town. That's the way it was in those days and that, folks, is the legend of 'Wallaby Jack' Joe Black," Tim said.

"Yeah … and keep it in mind when you do the run this arvo and you'll soon understand the difference between us country blokes and you pussies in the city," Blakey teased, in an attempt to re-establish his authority over Marty.

The eyes of the little boy on the stump in the engineering workshop at the Babinda mill had grown wider and wider as old Tim Green related the legendary tale that day at smoko. His jaw had dropped in awe of the mighty deed of this one man. His curried-egg sandwich just dangled half eaten and forgotten from his limp hand.

"Why did 'Wallaby Jack' have to do all of those things on his own Grandpa?" Manfred asked as they began the short walk home to Church Street where they lived.

"He had to because there was nobody else there to help him son."

"So why didn't he get somebody else from town to help him Grandpa? Or why didn't he go and get the canecutters to help him?"

"There wasn't enough time. He just had to make the decision to do it himself. Even if it seemed impossible he still had to try. He knew that his mate depended on him. We can do super-human things when we have to, if we want to. That's what 'Wallaby Jack' did that day."

Manfred thought about what his Grandpa had said. "Even though I'm small," he stated, "I would do the same thing to save you Grandpa, because I love you. I would do super-human things if I had to, because I would want to."

"Same here, boy ... so would I," his grandfather replied. "I would do the same for you too, because we are best mates us two."

After a series of grunts and chuckles from the old guy, they were soon home again.

That afternoon, the whole family went to watch the Picnic Run. It started at the double-barrelled bridge near Saffiotti's barracks and finished at The Boulders in Happy Valley. Sixteen entrants were saddled up with two seventy pound wallaby jacks each for the big event. They were allowed any amount of padding to protect them from the gnawing and bruising the jacks would inflict upon them. After the start, all of the spectators went on ahead to set up a picnic at The Boulders, where a pig on a spit had been roasting since early morning. Small bets were laid on who would take out the grand event. However, none of the sixteen contestants went the whole distance and the organisers had to send out the council truck to collect the wallaby jacks that had been discarded along the way. Many injured and exhausted contestants took the opportunity to hitch a ride back to the picnic on the back of the truck.

They still received a rousing welcome when they arrived at The Boulders, whether on foot or on the back of the truck. The local publican had donated a keg and as the beer began to flow, all the hard-luck stories from the competitors began to filter back through the crowd. There was music, singing and laughter, but nobody collected the 'Wallaby Jack' Award that year. Everyone agreed it was worth it and the event would be hosted again as usual the following year.

Chapter 2

Private Manfred Wright from the 102 Field Workshop opened his eyes to a burning bright light. He was on a bed in intensive care with an oxygen mask and tubes coming out everywhere. At first he thought it might be the bright light of the 'other kingdom' that people with near death experiences talked about. Then a cluster of faces in masks came to peer at him, fussing about, adjusting things, checking his oxygen and muttering to each other to the extent it became clear to Manfred that some type of emergency was going on.

A person in army uniform came into his line of vision. The officer looked at him, patted him on the shoulder twice and then turned to the medic beside him.

"This boy's going home. See to it that all the paperwork is in order for him to be medevaced back to Australia. There's an RAAF Hercules flight to Australia in ten days' time. If he's well enough to travel, make sure he's on that flight."

"Yes captain," the medic replied.

Manfred again relapsed into unconsciousness. Images of a whole series of events hammered at his brain and played havoc with his senses. There was a deafening blast and a sense of flying through the air, then a thud and dust everywhere, clouding his vision. He could smell cordite and smoke and he could taste blood in his mouth. A searing pain in his left thigh made him realise how it hurt to be branded by a red hot iron. His right ankle, foot and calf below the knee were numb.

He fumbled with his right hand to feel if his leg was still there and three fingers found a gap around the ankle where he could feel the bone. His shirt front was red with blood and suddenly he had a vision of himself from above, lying passed-out on the ground with the dust swirling around him.

The roar of rotor blades slapped him into a semi-conscious state of awareness. He noticed people coming to his aid through the dust storm. His brain sucked in the heavenly relief that entered his body through a hair-thin silver needle and he remembered being 'dusted off' into the blue-grey sky. Then everything blacked out again.

The next time he awoke, he was not sure whether he had dreamt it all or whether he was at the aftermath of the point in time when the landmine detonated beneath him. Was he alive? Did a real army captain come to visit him? Was he really going home? Had they amputated his leg? He was conscious of the fact that his oxygen mask had been removed. It must have being at least a few hours later because he was in an ordinary hospital bed. He shuffled himself around trying to see where he was.

"How ya feeling cobber?" came a husky voice from the bed across the room.

Manfred looked down the length of the bed to where his legs were. It felt like pillows separated them and a sheeted canopy had been placed over both legs. He thought he had feeling in the right leg and foot, but he had heard about phantom pains and sensations that could easily discount the possibility that they were still there. He began shivering and couldn't control it.

"Don't worry cobber, you've been through the worst of it now," his lifeline to humanity said.

He lifted the covers away from his chest and stomach. They were not bandaged but they were peppered with pellet-like holes and bruised as though he had been hit by rat-shot. His genitals were still intact as well and that made him forget all his other woes for a short joyous moment as the wave of euphoria washed through him.

"I haven't lost me family jewels," he blurted out across the room.

"Good onya cobber. Keep those spirits up and you'll be outa here in no time."

The days passed but whenever he was not under sedation, Manfred could not find the courage to ask about his foot and ankle. On the fourth day, the American doctor who he had threatened to strangle came to visit him.

"I've been in hiding just in case someone else took your leg off and you decided to carry out your threat to hunt me down and wring my skinny neck," he quipped.

Manfred gave a huge sigh of relief.

"You are not out of the woods yet. There's the danger of infection and it's going to be a long road back to recovery. You are to be medevaced out next week, so the war is over for you, soldier." He shook Manfred's hand and squeezed out a smile of reassurance. It was just twenty days out from the end of his tour of duty. If only his luck could have held out that little bit longer. Then a pleasant thought entered his mind. He had a woman back in Australia who he loved and they were going to get married.

The day before Manfred was due to be medevaced back to Australia, an army psychologist was appointed to conduct a trauma assessment on him. Manfred presumed the information requested would be no more than a memory check. She wanted answers to many basic questions about standard army training back in Australia, which might have been justifiable if he had suffered head injuries, but he hadn't. Then she followed it up with further questions that seemed unrelated to his physical injuries.

"Back in 1968, what were your immediate concerns when your call-up notice informed you that you had to report for duty at the Northern Command Personnel Depot at Ashgrove in Queensland?"

How was he supposed to reply to that?

"Well I have to admit that waiting to shoot crocs in the dead of night in a tin pot dinghy was far less stressful than the thought of what the business of war involved. I guess I was a little apprehensive about that, but I figured I would find out soon enough, although I had always associated the idea of war with shooting at people rather than being shot at by people. When I was issued with two identification dog tags; one to be taken from me 'in the event of my death and handed to my commanding officer' and the other to be left with my body for identification, the reality of the possibility of being killed became disturbingly clear to me."

He judged from the look on her face that she didn't have an appreciation for rhetoric, so he wound it back a little. "By the time I had completed the ten weeks of basic training at Singleton, I did begin to feel more confident about my chances of surviving the war."

"What can you tell me about your specialist training? Do you feel it was adequate?" she asked. He was tempted to ask if he could get his money back if he answered 'no' but the no-nonsense look in her eye dissuaded him from pushing his luck.

"I was granted my first choice of specialist training, which was to serve in the Royal Australian Electrical and Mechanical Engineering (RAEME) Corps and they sent me to the RAEME Training Centre in Bandiana, Victoria, for six weeks with the Army School of Electrical and Mechanical Engineering. Yeah, I was quite comfortable with the training as it was just like being back in the mill in Babinda. I worked in a sugar mill and did my trade there as a fitter and turner. After RAEME, I was posted to the Fourth Field Artillery Regiment at Townsville Lavarack Barracks and I was attached to the Light Aid Detachment for fitters, mechanics and electricians; the Artillery Regiment."

Manfred stopped talking as he sensed that he had reached the stage where his mates would have accused him of having verbal diarrhoea. He shrugged his shoulders and looked at her as if he was unsure whether this was what she really wanted to hear.

"Yes, keep going," she prompted.

"There, I found out that I would be serving under Captain JK McBride who was also from Babinda. He had only ever been known as 'Macca' and had gone through officers' training at the Royal Military College, Duntroon. It was good to be able to reminisce with Macca about mutual friends and the early days in Babinda."

Manfred hesitated again, uncertain as to why he had to be telling her this. She also fidgeted a lot and bounced one leg on the ball of her foot, up and down, up and down, as if he was making her impatient and agitated. He wasn't too impressed with her either, and all that bouncing was grating on his nerves.

"What happened after Lavarack?" She pushed as he watched the leg go into spasms and imagined it coming off at the hip and falling on the ground.

This made him think there might really be something wrong with his brain and her questioning was not as ridiculous as he first thought. Then he wondered if he was tripping on his medication.

"We went to Canungra Jungle Training Centre for a six weeks battle efficiency course where we all learnt about Heartbreak Hill and the Bear Pit." His suggestion that neither of those two experiences 'was a walk in the park' confirmed that the woman had no sense of humour and Manfred was only wasting his time trying to turn the whole assessment into a friendly conversation. "Then I was allowed to go home for one week on pre-embarkation leave. From there, some of our mob went on the *HMAS Sydney* and I went by Hercules to Sydney, Darwin and then on to this 'paradiso' here at Vung Tau."

He waited a moment in the hope she might relax the tension in her pursed lips but they were set in plaster of Paris, cold and unyielding.

"Keep going," she urged.

"Well, we started our twelve month tour of duty here in Vietnam and in that time we were granted a whole three days rest and convalescence here in Vung Tau and one week rest and recreation in Sydney. It all proved that 'no rest for the wicked' was a lie," he joked, and again she showed no emotion.

"Did your parents know you were back in Australia the time you went to Sydney?"

"No," he replied.

"So who did you meet up with in Sydney?"

That seemed a strange question as it was way off topic and he wondered where the conversation was going.

"Well actually, I arranged to meet my future wife there. She flew down from North Queensland so that we could make plans for our wedding on my return. All the paperwork has since been done."

"You noted in the marriage papers that your mother was in fact Russian. Is that correct?"

Manfred then realised the conversation wasn't going anywhere apart from what she had really come to find out, which he suspected had nothing to do with his mental health.

"How do you know what was in my marriage papers? What does my mother have to do with my trauma assessment? Mum was born in Vladivostok and came to Australia when she was five years old. Her father was German and her mother was Polish. I suppose you want to intern her like you did her father during both world wars," he growled.

"No need to get upset, Wright. This is just a general assessment. Do you have some issues with the government over your grandfather being interned during both world wars?"

"Well, I'm here fighting for my country. I wouldn't call that having issues with anyone apart from the enemy out there." He pointed out the window.

"Of course ... please understand that this is just a routine assessment. Thank you, Wright." She stood up, gathered her folders, slapped them into her briefcase and departed, leaving Manfred at a loss as to the purpose or usefulness of that so-called 'assessment'.

"Don't let it worry you cobber," said his mate from the next bed. "They're all the same those shrinks. They're the ones that should be on the couch having their heads read."

Manfred admitted he had allowed her to get the better of him and that he felt disappointed with that interview. Until then, he had never had any complaints. He felt his training for war, the camaraderie in the army, and the integrity of his superiors had all been exemplary. Even the military police proved they could be human at times but that interview was different. There was no hint of best wishes for the future or congratulations on his upcoming marriage. He could get no closure on the reason for the assessment. Why were they so concerned about his mother? Was there something in her past that he didn't know about? He was convinced his assessment had nothing to do with trauma. Was he being treated so callously because the army had no further use for him? The pain of his disappointment was soon superseded as the pain in his ankle became so unbearable that he wanted to scream. He began to convulse.

"Hey cobber, are you okay?" His room mate panicked and pressed the call button. "Nurse ... Manfred's crook ... nurse!" he called out.

The nurse made a quick assessment of the situation, rushed off and returned with a kidney dish full of clattering medicines and injections. Manfred was thankful when the pain melted away and the world inside his head was bathed in sunshine again.

* * *

Manfred described the effect morphine had on him as "The sunshine after rain, when the mist becomes a rainbow with its pot of gold that takes away the pain. It's a caress that's never-ending, if you can imagine that," he used to say. Perhaps it was because it always carried him back to Babinda with its childhood memories and pristine places where crystal clear creeks warbled down from the dark foreboding mountains of the Bellenden Ker Range and schools of black and silver bream shadowed their way downstream pecking with puckered lips at discarded brown and yellow leaves that brushed the surface of the water as they bobbed up and down with the eddying currents tumbling over rounded river rocks.

The jungle of that sacred place knew no sounds of guns or mortars. Only the calls of kookaburras, yellow-crested cockatoos, kingfishers and parrots echoed at the back of Happy Valley where the range poked out a long black tongue of basalt rock glazed with rainwater that swelled and crashed onto the forest below in a waterfall that was the place the Aborigines called "babinda" – place of falling water. He could hear the curlews lamenting and calling out to him to come home and leave that festering foreign land that was siphoning off every ounce of goodwill towards mankind and dumping it into the sewer of war.

As the curlews' calls began to fade, he was home again, pedalling his bicycle at full pelt into the mountains towards Happy Valley with his little mate Tony on his own Malvern Star. They hurtled down the hills, dodging potholes, straining against the bicycle chain as they stood on the pedals to reach the summit of each hill. They would not stop until they crossed the double-barrelled bridge, the landmark Joe Black made famous. It was just a short walk from the bridge down the road past Saffiotti's barracks and a thirty metre walk through the shallow Babinda Creek crossing, before they reached Tony's father's cane farm. The little farm on the banks of Babinda Creek was nestled among the hills beyond the forest at the base of the waterfall.

A whole new world of make-believe and adventure beckoned the two children on that side of the creek. After the cane was harvested, they used firesticks fashioned from long crisp dried cane tops which were bound at one end and lit at the other to set alight whole fields of trash remnants. If there was no other work to be done, they went fishing for bream and catfish with homemade spear guns or caught turtles in wire traps just for fun and then let them go. They heaved huge clumps of pannikin grass floating at the water's edge onto the banks and listened for the "clicketty-clicks" of the freshwater prawns and crayfish trapped in the foliage. The hapless bream they caught were grilled on an open fire underneath the giant blue quandong tree that speared its roots into the sand at the confluence of Babinda Creek and Acatino Creek. Its base was a carpet of blue edible berries that were bitter but tempting like glistening marble-sized bubble gums.

They boiled water in a discarded Golden Circle Pineapple Juice tin and cooked the prawns until they turned a warm pink colour, then devoured them in the way growing boys devoured afternoon snacks. Occasionally, they would catch a glimpse of the resident echidna crawling into its camouflaged home or their favourite platypus nuzzling the rocks and banks underwater with its prehistoric bill in search of food. For dessert, they would forage amongst the buttress roots of the giant fig tree where the ripe golden eggs of a wild bush passionfruit became trapped after being dislodged from the vine high up in the canopy. They were succulent and sweet. They then lay on their backs on the slender sand bank where the two creeks met while Tony would make up "Piggy Wiggy" stories about the smartest pig in the whole world, who like the Phantom, could never die. Feral-pig hunters were paid a handsome bounty of thirty shillings for a pig's scalp by the Pest Control Board at the mill. However, Piggy Wiggy always outwitted the best of them and outran, outswam and outsmarted every bull-terrier pig dog that was set against him.

After dusk, they piled themselves and their bikes into the back of Tony's father's Vanguard utility for the trip back to town. The wind tousled their hair and carried the aromas of toffee from the burnt sugarcane fields and the perfumes of the jungle flora like molasses grass and lantana. Sleep was the only cure for the total exhaustion that overcame them after dinner each evening. Every possible craving of their senses had been completely satiated.

In stature at least, the two boys presented as an odd pair. Manfred was tall but plump, fair-skinned and jovial, with the round Polack face of his grandmother. Tony, on the other hand, was skinny, with an olive complexion and a triangular face that beamed an infectious grin from an otherwise seemingly serious expression. He was the son of an Italian refugee who fled his native Sicily in the early 1920s to escape the tyranny of the dictator Benito Mussolini. Their possessions were few and they had no money. Their bicycles were hand-me-downs and they each had a wooden spear gun for spearing fish; a rivet gun that fired steel rivets; underwater goggles, a shanghai and a few marbles. The rivet gun was supposed to be a toy but it was dangerous. Like the spear guns and shanghais, the rivet guns were not prohibited and children as young as six wandered around the streets with shanghais around their necks and rivet guns poked into their back pockets.

Manfred always maintained that his motivation for becoming a tradesman stemmed from his woodwork and metalwork classes at primary school. The spear guns and rivet guns were projects the woodwork and metalwork teachers deliberately chose so their students could be rewarded with something useful and tangible to take home on top of the skills learned. However, Tony was only interested in the end product. As long as it worked, he was happy and making it was just a means to an end. He would rather buy a spear gun if he could have afforded it, whereas Manfred preferred to make one.

Success at making things at school gave them the confidence to try to make things at home using the skills learned. Manfred explained to the class one day how he and Tony had managed to fabricate underwater goggles from plain glass, car-tube rubber, a half inch wide strip of sheet metal, wire, a nut and bolt for adjusting the tension of the metal on the car-rubber against the glass, and some bicycle rubber strips for fastening the goggles against the back of the head. The plain glass was cut into an oval shape using a template, a steel scriber, methylated spirits and fire. A good template was an oval shaped plate that Tony produced as he proceeded to demonstrate the process. First, he used the scriber to scratch a deep oval indentation into the glass. Methylated spirits was then poured along the crack and ignited. The heat differential created along the crevice was enough to cause the glass to fracture, creating the oval looking-glass for the front piece of the mask. This impressed the other students as well as the teachers.

Shanghais, also known as slingshots, were made with forks cut from the hardy branches of the guava tree. The forks were lightweight and would last for years. Bicycle-tube rubber straps were attached to the two prongs of the fork with rubber bands also cut from a bicycle-tube. The leather tongue of any old shoe became the pouch for the projectile. Small cracked rocks called blue metal were mostly used, but glass marbles or ball-bearings were the ideal. Any projectile coming out of a shanghai was potentially lethal so the boys had to be responsible from a young age.

Apart from such obvious neglect of safety issues, the guidance their elders provided was completely devoid of any concerns about conservation and protection of the environment. Trees were there to be felled and burned. Soil was there to be tilled and sowed with seed or planted with food crops. Gardens were planted with exotic species of trees and shrubs rather than native varieties. Rabbits were introduced for food, prickly pear cultivated as hedges, and foxes were released for the sport of hunting in the great English tradition. Native animals were only there to be hunted for sport, trapped for their fur, or for their carcasses to be consumed as pet food. Most were poisoned and eradicated as pests. There was no social conscience about protecting the native flora and fauna and there were no laws enacted prohibiting the slaughter of endangered species or the exploitation of the environment.

It was not until later on in life that Manfred realised how, in the 1950s, these practices and behavioural patterns were the norm; just like going to war had been for previous generations. Social, racial and gender stereotypes were also entrenched and perpetuated. Specific religious and political affiliations were preferred, with opposing religious and political beliefs demonised at all levels of Australian society.

However, Australia was supposed to be on the cusp of a new wave of thinking after World War II. It was packaged and sold as another "war to end all wars Mark II", after World War I, the original "war to end all wars", had failed miserably. Manfred was led to believe the promised nirvana of peace that their fathers and forefathers had fought and died for was to be post-war society's reward. He and Tony had been told every year at school on Anzac Day that a "free world" would eventuate from all their sacrifices. The new wave of thinking was supposed to be sanctified through repentance and fortified by tolerance and respect for all of humanity. It was the theme that stood out in school history books and in literature on war and peace and Manfred was at first convinced about the road to redemption, until he discovered that the cycle of war and peace, like life and death, was condemned to repeat itself ad infinitum. The promise that "it would be different this time" was broken when other wars broke out like in Malaya, Korea and Vietnam. Manfred's father, Wilfred, who had a particular interest in the history of war, was a stickler for detail and had done some comprehensive research on all of them. He would go into great depth about his findings which he revealed to his captive audience one evening at the dinner table. They were all shocked to find out that there had already been sixty-three "wars" since World War II. Fifteen of those were longer than the six years of World War II, and included a host of civil wars in Costa Rica, China, Greece, Malaya, Vietnam, Rwanda, North Yemen, Nigeria, Laos and Palestine. There had also been a series of wars of independence in Indonesia, Morocco, Tunisia, Cameroon, Algeria, Guinea-Bissau, Mozambique and Angola, and rebellions in Madagascar, South Korea, Philippines, Tibet and Iraq. Then there were the revolutions in Bolivia and Cuba and the Korean War in which Australian troops participated. There was no way Manfred was ever going to be convinced that war was going to "be different this time". His father argued about war at every opportunity and especially at work but few had any interest in number crunching statistics.

One truth that Manfred discovered was during his early teens. He found out the meaning of back-breaking work. The use of child labour was a common practice in the cane fields, especially around sugarcane planting time. There simply weren't enough men around to carry out the labour intensive tasks necessary, so planting had to be carried out during the school holidays in May and August each year. When most city kids dreamt about lying in the sun on the beach or going to the movies, country kids like Tony were "sentenced to hard labour in the slave yards" as they referred to it. Tony had no choice while Manfred had a choice, but wanted to be with his mate, and he needed the money.

For planting, standing cane was cut, stripped of trash and replanted by hand in drills about one foot deep. The workers filed their long-bladed cane knives to razor sharp and walked along the lengths of cane in the drills, cutting them into billets about eight inches long. Each stroke of the knife was brought down with rhythm and preciseness, and perilously close to bare feet, like a guillotine cutting through soft butter. There was no margin for error and the work was carried out at a cracking pace. Beads of sweat rolled off their foreheads but the workers made light of it all, chatting to one another about different events in their daily lives. The young men teased each other about their cars and their girlfriends, while the younger boys were more interested in throwing the odd lump of soil at each other, and the older men muttered complaints about their worries and their wives.

At the end of each drill, the fastest workers would backtrack into the slower workers' drills to help them catch up. This was a signal to them that they were not pulling their weight and they should lift their game. The competition was healthy in that it took the drudgery out of the job and the thought of cold beer at the end of the day's work helped them tolerate the rising blisters on already deeply calloused hands. To Manfred, these sorts of experiences reminded him of what he had heard his father talking about diggers bonding in WWI and WWII and how that bond held fast after they returned home. Whereas a lot of young people thought of the RSL as a sort of secret society for old disgruntled men, Manfred understood when his father explained to him how RSLs across the country were sacred places to war veterans.

The seasons came and went and everything in the community revolved around the cane harvest season. However, for the two boys, there were many other exciting seasons to anticipate. There was watermelon season around school break-up time in early December when a huge truckload of watermelons always arrived on the last day of school. The joy of the first burst of flavour that splashed into their mouths at the first bite of the first slice of watermelon could only be eclipsed by the thrill of a direct hit of a skilfully cast chunk of half-eaten watermelon on someone else's skull. A chase would follow where the victim avenged himself by hurling a payback volley of pieces after the perpetrator.

Then there was mango season through December and January. This was watermelon season all over again, except that it was mango flavoured. The mangoes were of the turpentine variety where the stringy fibres of the fruit would embed themselves between the teeth, making the children look like troll monsters whenever they opened their mouths. The yellow juices would ooze out of the sides of their mouths and down their chins and onto their chests. The sloppy remnants of skin and seeds that remained in their hands would be thrown at their nearest adversary.

The third most battle-compelling fruit was the humble guava. The ripe wild tropical fruit consisted of a pink gum-coloured flesh textured with thousands of edible seeds the size of pinheads that unleashed a taste sensation like no other and would linger on the tastebuds for hours. The over-ripe guava yielded a mushy maggot-infested missile that was the ultimate assault weapon in any friendly fight. The grenade-sized fruit would explode on impact and completely dehumanise and demoralise any unsuspecting victim.

Women and girls were usually not so partial to watermelon, mango and guava season because of the ultimate chaos and "childish" behaviour of those who participated in the fights, and therefore they preferred to maintain a wide berth from the battle scenes. However, men became little boys again and grinned when they heard their wives and daughters admonishing the brats for their devilish deeds.

Manfred and his friends grew up with mechanisation as an integral part of the sugar industry. They learned to drive tractors and trucks and cars and railroad jiggers, and operated hay-rakes, scarifiers, planters, and reversed trailers up, down and across hill slopes. They spent weekends hunting with rifles from the back of utilities and fished off boats with nets and water skied behind speedboats. Their world was full of experimentation and innovation while the older generation shied away from the new ways of farming using modern machinery. Teenagers found themselves catapulted into the world of men and were expected to behave like men. They underwent a rite of passage that came with no fanfare or ceremony or particular timeframe; it just happened.

Many of their friends left school at thirteen, having completed the eight years compulsory part of their schooling. Some went to work on farms while others took on apprenticeships in town and at the mill. Others studied a further two years at a secondary school for their Junior Certificate and then left to take on clerical positions in businesses like banks and shops. Students who wanted to gain a profession, providing their parents could afford it, went on and studied a further two years at secondary school for their Senior Certificate to prepare them for positions at teachers' colleges or in commerce and accounting firms. A trickle went on to university to study law, medicine, science, commerce or engineering. Manfred had sometimes thought about attending university and he was certainly bright enough but the desire was only fleeting. He knew how much he loved working with his hands and he was proud to be continuing on in the tradition of his father and grandfather. Tony, however, had no intention of returning to the "slave yards" to work so he stayed on at school and kept his head down.

At sixteen, four years after his Grandpa Kammer died, Manfred was given an apprenticeship at the Babinda Central Mill as a fitter and turner. He found himself in the same workshop where his grandfather used to bring him as a child on Sunday mornings during the crushing season. His boss, Nick, had actually been apprenticed to Kammer. He said he would teach Manfred everything he knew just as old Kammer had taught him and Manfred was never allowed to forget it. Nick was a tough taskmaster but Manfred noticed Nick was prepared to go that little bit further with him to give him every opportunity to excel.

Manfred was quick to learn. He loved the trade and had already proved he was not afraid of work. Tony had gone to Townsville to study law, and Manfred began to develop a new set of adult friendships. He played football on weekends, had a few beers as underage boys did and went to the local dances. He and a few mates, "Gunga" Crane and "Muscles" Larson, bought a little humpy down at Russell Heads, at the confluence of the Mulgrave and Russell rivers, for 100 pounds each, which they used as a base for fishing. It was a typical fishing hut on local hardwood stumps and framed with local hardwood timber brought down by barge. The cladding was corrugated iron on all sides as was the roof, and even the windows were corrugated iron nailed to push-out timber frames on hinges. Those fishing humpies were built to catch the gentlest of sea breezes, yet, when in lock-down, the severest of cyclones had not been able to destroy them.

The community had banded together to bring water to the village through a pipeline from a pure freshwater source at Freshwater Creek, about one mile away. That involved digging a trench about one foot six inches deep and connecting the pipe to all the individual houses in the settlement. There was no treatment plant and no chemicals added to the water. Only a sieve was attached to the pipe at the catchment end to keep solid particles out of the supply system. Manfred used to talk about the Russell Heads community as "the salt of the earth". It was probably because he knew they could be trusted and were always there for each other and it certainly rubbed off on him. Manfred would do anything for his mates.

He, Gunga and Muscles would often sneak out the back gate of the mill early on a Friday afternoon and go fishing for the weekend. All they had to do was to find someone who was prepared to clock them off at five o'clock. That's the way it was in those days according to Manfred and he would do the same for them when they wanted to enjoy a long weekend. It probably explained why Manfred was such an accommodating character. He didn't suffer fools but he certainly was a bit of a larrikin who got up to his own fair share of mischief like the time he blew up Tom Norman's letter box on Guy Fawkes night. On the way to The Heads, they would set the barramundi nets across Harvey Creek where it met the Russell River and around Mud Island or at the edge of the floating hyacinth pads in Frenchmen's Creek. Another great place to set nets for barramundi was where the Alice River, which drained the Eubenangee Swamp, entered the Russell River. Sales of the barramundi kept them in pocket money for petrol for their outboard motors, running costs of the humpy at The Heads and the occasional carton of beer. There was an abundance of fresh crabs, prawns and fish from the reefs around High Island and North and South Frankland Island nearby. Often, they spent the weekends on the islands spearfishing, catching crayfish in the shallows of the reef or shooting pigeons.

Soon, Manfred was able to afford a small four metre bondwood boat with a nine horsepower inboard Villiers motor. This enabled him to go hunting for crocodiles where the real money was to be made. When he went croc shooting alone, he would often set nets for barramundi in Coopers Creek and Bramston Creek while waiting for the tide to run its course. In the '60s, crocodiles were in plague proportions in Far North Queensland and they were beginning to encroach on the popular swimming holes along the creeks around Bramston Beach and along the Russell and Mulgrave rivers. Crocodile skins fetched a good price from dealers in Cairns who on sold them to manufacturers of leather belts, wallets and shoes.

All the "glamour" shooters with huge speedboats and spotlights roared up and down the big rivers frightening everything in sight and catching nothing. Manfred anchored his dinghy in one of the small creeks that drained into the Russell or Mulgrave rivers and sat and waited patiently for the tide to do his work for him. The water could be as shallow as one foot at low tide and three feet deep at high tide. He had a small light on the front of his boat shielded from his own sight and facing away from him. This cast a reflection into the eyes of any crocodiles swimming towards him. Many people thought crocodiles were lazy because they appeared lethargic in their movements but Manfred figured that crocodiles were smart creatures that chose to drift silently with the tide in search of their prey. He waited patiently with his loaded .303 rifle until the shining eyes of the crocodile were at close range and he could put a bullet right between its eyes. This killed it instantly and it would sink to the bottom.

Manfred used his paddle to prod around under the water to locate the crocodile and would prod it several times to make sure it was dead before he climbed out of the boat and into the water. He then tied a rope around the beast's head and towed it back to the landing at Deeral where he enlisted the help of the Mannings family to skin the animal and roll it up in salt to preserve it. Only the belly skin was kept. Manfred left the rest of the carcass for the aboriginal elder to distribute among the members of the family as payment for their help. The local Aboriginal women took the offal away. Consumption of crocodile offal had a special cultural significance for them. Whether it was spiritual or simply culinary, Manfred never bothered to find out, but he was only too happy to oblige. Sometimes, Manfred kept slices of crocodile tail which were quite a delicacy cut thin and barbecued. With no battle scars, a two metre "cleanskin" crocodile fetched about eighty-four pounds from the taxidermist in Cairns. Compared to the seven pounds a week he received as a second year apprentice, this represented big money, and within one year, Manfred bought a new AP5 Valiant sedan for cash.

On his nineteenth birthday, the boys went down to the local pub to celebrate. The legal age for drinking at that time was twenty-one years. The local police turned a blind eye to underage drinking, subject to strict rules of behaviour. People argued if they were old enough to fight in the war at eighteen years of age, they were old enough to drink in a pub with the men. They lied to the publican and told him it was Manfred's twenty-first birthday bash, and to their delight, the publican shouted them a keg of beer on the condition they drink the keg at some venue far away from the pub so there would be no disturbance to the peace.

They decided to have the celebration at The Boulders, and on the Friday night, the boys set off with their keg of beer. They lit up a huge bonfire and set up a barbecue plate which they loaded up with sausages and steaks during the ensuing marathon drinking spree. By morning, not too many were able to remember what had happened the night before, but they all knew they had a great time. A quick head count was taken to ascertain whether anyone had wandered off into the bush and become lost or fallen into the water and drowned.

There was always the danger of drowning at The Boulders. One hundred yards downstream from the main swimming hole, The Devil's Pool had claimed the lives of several single young men. Aboriginal folklore relates that a local tribal elder named Waroonoo married Oolana who was betrothed to him. At a later dance ceremony at The Boulders, a handsome young warrior, Dyga, from another tribe, caught her eye and they fell in love. They ran away together but the two tribes soon found them. Dyga was taken away and Oolana drowned herself in the place known as The Devil's Pool. Occasionally, her spirit called out to single male visitors walking by The Devil's Pool, inviting them to dive into its mesmerising depths. If they fell or dived in, a forceful undercurrent dragged them into a deep underwater cavern beneath the rocks where they became trapped and drowned. All of the locals knew about the legend and the danger, so unless they were drunk and fell in by accident, they avoided the pool.

After the head count confirmed nobody had drowned or become lost, they all agreed that as the keg had run out, they should despatch a designated driver to purchase another one from the pub in town. Paul Higging was chosen because he had a severe case of alcoholic poisoning from the week before and was on "toast only" sips of red wine, which was not enough to hinder his ability to drive. On the way back from the pub, Paul's ute struck a huge pothole just before the double-barrelled bridge and the keg bounced out of the vehicle and rolled into the creek about five metres below. Fortunately, it did not float away, but the descent was steep and retrieval impossible and Paul returned to The Boulders empty handed. It was past lunchtime so they stoked up the fire for a barbecue brunch, and after a barrage of suggestions, it was decided they should shift the venue to the double-barrelled bridge, climb down to the creek and drink the keg dry there.

Later that day, while everyone was still partying, Manfred climbed back up the bank and walked down to check out the old Saffiotti barracks. It was January, the middle of the slack season, and there was no sign of life around the old shack. He thought he could hear someone calling out and he imagined the old Chinese cook in his slippers and gown shuffling his feet on the ground as he approached the sound of the voice. "I need help ... take that bicycle and get the ambulance ... tell them Joe Black ... timber-cutting accident ... hurry, hurry". He was so sure it was Joe Black that he hoped he could gain a glimpse of Joe Black. All he could see were shadows and as the shadows vanished into the dusk, he found himself poking around the back of the old building. It was the same as he had always known it to be and in the shed out the back beside the outhouse, he saw a pile of tools, bits and pieces of lawnmowers and motors and implements. Behind the implements against the wall of the shed was a pair of wallaby jacks.

Manfred's mind flashed back to the story of "Wallaby Jack" as he picked up one of the jacks. It was heavy. He tried picking up the two wallaby jacks and they were really heavy. He lobbed them up, one on each shoulder and felt them bite into his skin. After taking a few stumbling steps to get his balance, he juggled the jacks against the nape of his neck and walked about thirty yards back towards the double-barrelled bridge. Instead of returning to the barracks, he decided to go the full fifty yards to the bridge.

The jacks were cold but already a fine lather of sweat had begun to lubricate them so that the skin around his neck became supple and smooth. When he reached the bridge, he decided that maybe he could carry them all the way to The Boulders. He wondered if he could do a "Wallaby Jack" Joe Black. He had nothing to lose and nobody else had to know about it if he decided to give it a try and failed. It was a full moon and it seemed as though the heat had been completely sucked up into the sky. The two jacks were snuggling up to the flesh around his collarbone. They were heavy, but they were bearable so he kept telling himself he should do it. He decided to give it a try and instead of turning around, turned left and headed towards The Boulders.

He did not even dream of jogging or running with the two jacks. He just walked at a slow determined stride. He kept telling himself in his mind over and over the story Tim Green had related of how Joe Black had saved the life of his mate. Each time he came to the end of the story, he found himself a few hundred metres further down the road towards The Boulders. He gritted his teeth and was determined to keep going because he wanted to prove to himself that the story wasn't a myth. The clouds crossed under the light of the moon, making it difficult to see where he was going and he stumbled over loose rocks and in potholes. The jarring was so severe he knew that darkness could bring his quest undone. Then the clouds passed and he could see again. In just under an hour, he could see the signs welcoming visitors to The Boulders reflected in the light of the full moon. He paused on his arrival and was longing to cast off the horrendous load from his shoulders. He had made it.

Then he realised that the job for Joe Black was only half done at that point. Black still had to carry his injured mate back to the double-barrelled bridge. Manfred looked around. There was nobody to carry back and he cast off the ridiculous idea. As if anybody would agree to let him carry them back on his shoulders. He had to return the jacks to Saffiotti's barracks and so decided he would do that instead. On the way back, he psyched himself into a trance by imagining a set of scenarios. One scenario was Joe Black jacking up the giant trees. The second scenario was Joe carefully and gently dragging his mate from underneath them. Then he had him tearing up his shirt into strips and placing them against Ben's wounds to stop the bleeding and begging him to stay strong. He visualised Joe hoisting him onto his back and carrying him down the hill through the scrub and through the water to the clearing at the waterhole. Then he imagined Joe Black looking around and seeing that the ambulance had not yet arrived, so he had no choice but to kept carrying him towards town.

Each scenario brought Manfred further down the road and he figured this might have been the way Joe Black had managed to survive the ordeal. What scenarios had he conjured up? Had he imagined his mate dying and felt responsible for it? Had he thought about the man losing his leg and having to question his conscience every time he saw him? Had he dreaded the thought of having to face his mate's family and community, wondering if he had done his best and given his all to help him? Whatever it was, Joe Black's conscience would be clear; he was doing the best he could and that was what got him through.

Manfred had no idea what time it was when he arrived back at Saffiotti's barracks. All he remembered was collapsing on the verandah of the barracks and waking up the next morning with the two discarded jacks a few yards away and a collarbone that felt as though someone had repeatedly taken to it with a cricket bat. He was certain of one thing: the "Wallaby Jack" Joe Black story was no myth.

Chapter 3

Manfred was taken to the airport at Vung Tau where an RAAF C-130A Hercules hospital transport aircraft was being prepared for a medevac flight to Butterworth in Malaysia. He was sedated most of the time and the whole medevac process from Vung Tau was repeated again in Butterworth for his transfer to Richmond in Australia. His condition deteriorated during his time at the Richmond 3RAAF Hospital, and arrangements were made to return him to his home state of Queensland for treatment and convalescence.

Manfred had already accepted that his injuries would be life-changing once he left Richmond 3 RAAF Hospital. He was past caring. It was as if his enthusiasm for life, his easy going nature and his sense of wonder had been sucked out of him. He knew the larrikin in him was gone because creating mischief was the last thing on his mind. The war had changed him forever in his head as well as his body. He was going to have to accept this one lying down, which was something he had never done before. How was he going to be able to carry on life pretending nothing had changed when he didn't have the necessary skills? Where would he get the support he needed when he had always acted independently in the past? His confidence had waned although he tried to remain positive, trying to explain away his situation in terms of 'bad karma' from his deeds in the battlefield. If he recanted, maybe that would wipe his slate clean and allow him to start again. But the realist in him knew that scenario would never happen.

He contemplated if there was any reason why he needed to think any of his actions on the battlefield, except for one, were not justifiable. Even that one time, everyone else said they didn't blame him. Nevertheless, Manfred had trouble convincing himself. He could keep it his 'dark secret' and if nobody knew, then nobody would care, and therefore, why should he? It all made sense but it wasn't that easy. Someone had to be in his cage to know how he really felt.

That Hercules trip to the RAAF Base Amberley had none of the trappings of the Vung Tau to Richmond flight. Strapped into a field stretcher and unable to move, Manfred was placed on the floor in a corridor at the Richmond base awaiting transit. Everyone came to gawk at him yet nobody had anything to say to him. He was then carried to a van where he waited for space to be found in the plane. After the loadmaster had completed his weight-and-balance calculations, they hoisted him up into the belly of the plane. There, still strapped into his stretcher, he was "hooked up" on the wall like a meat carcass and abandoned. He was surprised to be the only passenger except for an Alsatian dog that was on a short leash opposite him. It didn't look much happier than he was and didn't even respond when he called out to it.

All the cargo packed around him hemmed him in. Boxes, equipment, food cartons, parts and military gear were crammed in and fixed to the walls with netting, straps and hooks. Mercifully, he succumbed to a deep sleep, where even dreams eluded him. Perhaps it was the overwhelming sense of relief that he was finally going back home to Queensland that gave him such peace.

He was transported from the RAAF Base Amberley to 1 Military Hospital Yeronga in Brisbane. There, he was again sedated and left in the corridor on the floor, strapped into his stretcher. People slowed down to look at him but did not talk to him and gave him a wide berth as if half expecting him to break out of his straps and attack them. He thought of how strange it was to be back in Australia and being stared at like an animal in a zoo. "*Welcome home,*" he thought as he dozed off amid a haze of random and chaotic flashbacks. The chaos subsided after another sedation which triggered a clear recollection of an event five months earlier when he was last in Australia.

He was on one week's Rest and Recreation leave from the battlefield in Vietnam. His plane had just touched down in Sydney. A confused sense of joy and uncertainty overwhelmed him, as he tried to anticipate the reunion with Angel. Much had happened on the battlefield in the short time that he had been away from her. The young man who had been so shy he had to be coaxed and begged by his mates to agree to partner her to a debutante ball, was returning. He knew the innocence associated with those times was all gone. Would she sense it? Would she be able to discern the changes in outlook and personality he had been forced to undergo in order to survive in Vietnam? Could she be expected to still want to marry him because of what he once was rather than what he had become? Would he become as unrecognisable to her as he was to himself? He guessed he was about to find out and he would have to deal with whatever panned out over the next few days.

He exited the plane and scanned the airport observation area for any sign of that special person in his life. Then, down at the arrivals gate on the tarmac, he saw her pushing through to the front of the crush. She started jumping up and down and screamed hysterically as she waved a long white silken scarf in the air above her head. He felt himself jogging after the first few paces, and for the last twenty yards he ran towards her. She threw her arms around him and he hugged her tightly. He felt the warmth of her body against his and soaked it all in. *"If only she knew who she is really hugging,"* he thought. He knew that every person who came back from active duty in war was damaged goods to some extent. Although the body came back at a peak level of fitness, the mind came back frail, bent and fraught with the indelible deeds of inhumanity committed against other people in the name of war. What went on "beyond the wire", which was the perimeter of the Nui Dat Camp or the Vung Tau Camp, was all relegated to each individual's conscience. Each had to shoulder his conscience alone. There was no communal or social ownership of deeds. It was all individual ownership and the individual paid the price.

Conscience, like panic attacks, was all-consuming and instilled a state of terror in Manfred that rendered him helpless at times. It surfaced when he was at his most vulnerable or unable to control it, like when he was idle and had too much time to think, in dreams or after too many drinks. That was when "Doctor Jekyll became Mr Hyde". He had to learn to bottle it all up when he was out of the war zone and he soon realised he lacked the skills needed to do that. He wondered how he was supposed to compartmentalise and set aside events like the time the SAS Regiment personnel used one particular terror tactic to demoralise the enemy. On that occasion they infiltrated behind enemy lines in the middle of the night and slit the throats of random Viet Cong at a particular camp near Binh Ba while their comrades slept. Their VC comrades awoke next day to the shock and horror of finding them murdered. That was how the psychology of shock and fear became a powerful weapon of war. It provoked a violent rage and desire for revenge that reinforced the doctrine of "eye for an eye" and thus the war became one foul deed for another. Manfred gradually became desensitised towards brutality, cruelty and death as the war continued, and feared he might remain that way. Every incident was replayed in his mind as he relived the horror of every brutal event over and over again, and he wondered how long it would take for those memories to break him.

Manfred and Angel lingered in their huddle at the arrival gate. Neither wanted to let go and be the person responsible for breaking out of it.

"All right Angel, let's get outa here," Manfred said at last. "We've only got one week and I don't want to have to share it with anyone else but you."

He was certain, that for that week at least, he only wanted to be who she still believed him to be. He collected his luggage and they wandered out to the cab rank, hugging and cuddling like two teenagers. Manfred could not imagine how he could ever feel so entirely happy and fulfilled, although it was tinged with a sense of guilt because he had kept his return trip to Australia a secret from the only other people who meant everything to him. His family in Babinda knew nothing of his return, but he guessed they would have to get used to sharing him with Angel. It was her turn now and they had marriage plans to sort out.

"Show us around Sydney a bit and drop us off at the best place to stay around Kings Cross," he told the cab driver. "Somewhere a young buck can be with the woman he intends to marry as soon as he completes his tour of duty in Vietnam, buddy," Manfred added as he opened the door for Angel to slide into the back seat.

"What's with the buddy bit, Man?" Angel asked. "That's an Americanism if ever I heard one. Don't tell me those Yanks have got to you already. Don't charge him Yank rates," she implored the cabbie. "They don't come any more Aussie than my Man."

Manfred loved her calling him "Man"; the double meaning was special.

"No worries miss, I know just the place for you guys. Enjoy the ride ... I'll take you the long way. Welcome to Sydney."

He took them to Bondi Beach, did a sweep around Darling Harbour and past The Rocks and over the Sydney Harbour Bridge, all with a relaxed and informative commentary thrown in. He really made them feel special and when he finally pulled into the kerb outside the Gazebo Hotel in the heart of Kings Cross, they knew that whatever it was going to cost, it was certainly well worth it.

"No charge, sir." The cabbie waved a dismissive hand as Manfred reached for his wallet.

Manfred and Angel both insisted but there was no way they were going to convince him to accept even one cent.

"You guys put your life on the line every day over there for us. This is the least I can do to show my gratitude. I'm proud to have had you and your beautiful lady friend in my taxi, sir. Enjoy your stay and a safe return at the end of your tour of duty mate." Then he called out as he pulled out from the kerb, "Tell them Ted the taxi driver brought you here and that should get you ten per cent off your accommodation bill."

If Manfred needed something to make him feel good, that was more than enough, much less having Angel. Her smile, the way she held his hand, the sparkle in her eyes – everything about her – made him feel good. He wasn't too sure about dying for his country, but he would die for Angel any day, and he told her as much that night. They got their discount after mentioning Ted the taxi driver and were alone at last in their executive suite. He had certainly come a long way from roughing it in a tent at Nui Dat or sleeping under the stars on patrol. They showered, changed into some light casual gear and listened to the relaxing folk songs on the radio.

"Want to do something special?" Manfred blurted out.

"Like what?" Angel asked.

That stymied him. He was hoping for suggestions.

"Like … like … like cuddle up tightly, for example," he spluttered.

She slapped his hand lightly and her eyes sparkled into his as she drew him towards her. She loved this shy and lumbering hulk of a man who couldn't help driving her crazy with his antics. She kissed him and he broke into his wry grin right on cue at the end of the kiss. He was expecting another kiss but she gave him a cheeky glance instead.

"Have you ever done anything naughty with a girl?" she said.

He wondered if it was a trick question as Angel was good at trick questions and he didn't want to get caught out.

"Come on ... ever ... like ... anything?" She shook her head from side to side and her eyebrows raised up.

"Yeah, well ... ah ... well actually, yes. I did something very naughty when I was in Grade One ... but I'm not going to tell you."

"Why not?" she giggled and prodded him. "Come on ... tell me."

"Well ..." he kept her in suspense for a moment. "It was in my second week at school and I wanted to impress one particular girl in the class so I brought a shoebox to school for Show and Tell."

"A shoebox? What was in it?"

"I'm coming to that. First, I asked that girl to come out the front and peek in the box so she could give a clue to the other members of the class as to what was in there." He paused and mused over the way Angel bit on her bottom lip when she was wondering.

"Well ... what was in there?"

"The day before, I had been playing with my friend Tony D'Italia on the sandbank beside the Russell River near Babinda. Suddenly, this batch of newly hatched crocodiles about ten inches long came scurrying across the sand past us towards the water. We managed to catch two of them and put them in an old sugar bag we had brought with us to put turtles into to take home as pets. Even at one day old, those little critters could inflict a pretty mean wound. Anyhow, I figured they could be as interesting a pet as any turtle, until I came up with the bright idea of bringing them to school for Show and Tell."

"You didn't?" Angel's eyes went wide.

"Yep ... and as soon as she opened the lid the two little crocs jumped out and onto the floor, snapping at everything in sight. Girls were screaming everywhere; kids started running out of the room; desks were tipped over; our class teacher Miss Brennan was absolutely hysterical and climbed onto the teacher's table. Everything but the fire brigade turned up at the classroom door."

He pounced on her and started tickling her around the ribs. Angel started giggling and was at the stage where she could hardly breathe. "No ... no ... stop!" she begged as she fought to regain her breath.

"Well you wanted to know," he playfully argued. He stopped and Angel breathed several deep breaths and finally regained her composure.

"That surely was naughty, Man. What a little terror you were. What happened? Were you punished?"

"Yes, I was marched down to the office by old 'Chrome Dome' and caned. One stroke was delivered to each hand. I was not even six years old for God's sake."

Angel sat on the bed and cradled his big head against her breast.

"Poor little man-child. Let me kiss you better." She kissed his head and both his hands. "Well serve you right for being naughty. At least you learned that being naughty can get you into a lot of trouble."

He felt uncomfortable knowing what he was really capable of and realising his sweetheart's naive innocence.

The rest of the week was spent making plans for their wedding. His tour of duty was supposed to end in five months' time on February 2, and they needed some time to send out invitations and organise things after he returned, and therefore they settled on April 4, 1970. They shopped and dined, swam in the swimming pool and relaxed in the spa and sauna at the Gazebo. They drank and they laughed and they went to cabarets and read the daily rave reviews about a musical called *Hair* produced by the entrepreneur Harry M Miller. The musical was on the front page of every paper and stemmed from an idea that two New York actors Gerome Ragni and James Rado developed from a script they co-wrote. The inspiration for the musical was a series of events that unfolded in Europe in 1968, where students had rioted in Paris, protesting against capitalism, consumerism, traditional institutions, values and social order. Attempts to introduce reforms towards democracy and greater personal freedom in Czechoslovakia were crushed with the Soviet invasion. In America, the escalating war in Vietnam became a focus for protestors, with hippies and drop-outs preaching peace. They engaged in almost daily protests against the evils of war fuelled by the use of mind-altering drugs and psychedelia.

Hair, the American tribal rock musical, had opened in Sydney's Kings Cross in 1969, and they decided they just had to see it. However, when they did, they were quite shocked as it challenged many established social values of the time. It contained nudity, bad language, drugs and "free love". If that was all there was, Manfred and Angel would certainly have left the theatre feeling totally liberated. However, at its core, the message was clear, unrelenting and unforgiving; to stop the war in Vietnam and "make love, not war". They left the theatre feeling totally embarrassed and devastated. The war in Vietnam was being demonised.

* * *

On the flight back to Vietnam, Manfred sensed that his heart for the war in Vietnam was no longer engaged. The only consolation he could muster up was the knowledge that it was the last time he would be going back there. The hum of the aircraft was ethereal and he allowed his eyelids to drop as he savoured every precious moment of that last week with Angel over and over again. Thoughts of what had passed since he had been away from her intermingled with thoughts of her. When he first arrived in Vung Tau on the February 3, 1969, the whole country was writhing in the shadow of the previous year's major Tet Offensive that the Viet Cong launched. The "Tet" was the Vietnamese Lunar New Year, which in 1968 fell on January 31. The North Vietnamese set upon 126 South Vietnamese cities simultaneously that year, through a coordinated attack that sent every provincial city reeling under the force of the offensive. Heavy shelling, mortars and rockets hammered the South Vietnamese Army and the allied positions. At the Battle of Hue alone, 150 US troops and 400 South Vietnamese troops were killed and hundreds more wounded. It took one month of house-to-house and room-to-room fighting for the marines to re-take the city. That year alone, 15,000 American soldiers died. Those were the statistics and reports on the 1968 Tet that Manfred heard in answer to his questions.

Despite the fact that the United States repelled the enemy, the 1968 offensive was interpreted by the media as the US not making the progress that US President Johnson and US General Westmoreland had intimated to the American people. Images broadcast by the news media to the American people of military police having to fight off rebel commandos in the US Embassy in Saigon, turned people away from supporting the war in Vietnam. The fresh memory of the 1968 Tet Offensive when Manfred arrived in Vietnam in 1969 hardly enamoured him to the place. Nevertheless, although he had never been fully convinced during his training as to why he should be fighting that war, he accepted the slogan "theirs not to reason why, theirs but to do and die" which negated any need for rationale. He just hoped he didn't have to succumb to the latter part – "the bit about dying" as Manfred referred to it.

He was posted to Nui Dat Camp in central Phuoc Tuy Province. It seemed safe enough in there. Outside the actual camp, there was a four kilometre exclusion zone where the local population was prohibited to inhabit. This was Line Alpha. "The wire" was the term given to the perimeter of the camp itself. The moment they went "beyond the wire", they were in what was potentially enemy territory. Knowing so many troops were there with him, certainly made Manfred feel quite secure but not quite so once they went "beyond the wire". Manfred's role was mainly counter-insurgency, involving "cordon and search" activities, where an area was cordoned off and searched for weapons and insurgents. This happened throughout Phuoc Tuy Province at places like Binh Ba, Long Hai Hills, The Horseshoes and Long Green. He was ranked "craftsman" and belonged to 102 Field Workshop at 1 Australian Logistics Support Group. Manfred's area of specialisation was as an armourer looking after small arms but he was also engaged as an armament fitter maintaining and repairing heavier equipment.

When he was told the Vietnamese Lunar New Year would commence on March 3 and that he should be prepared for his own "baptism of fire", Manfred felt a tingle of trepidation. The enemy delayed the Tet attack for the first time and began a week later, just as the allied troops were beginning to believe it might not happen. The offensive was launched on March 10 on 115 cities and military bases across the country. At Cu Chi base camp, Manfred learned that nine Chinook helicopters had been destroyed and four badly damaged. In that week, 453 American soldiers had been killed and Manfred expected they would be overrun at any time. Fortunately for him, that didn't happen and the offensive was suddenly called off as if the commanding officers had simply flicked off a switch.

All diggers fighting in close quarters, whether in the armoured, artillery and engineer corps or helicopter crews, were often in danger. They were deployed in mainly rural or jungle locales against an experienced and skilled enemy. In the rural areas, where there were open tracts of land, they were more exposed to enemy fire. Places like rice fields and rubber-tree plantations that the French had established during their period of colonial occupation in Vietnam, were especially dangerous. They also had to do battle with the intense heat and the heavy monsoonal rains. They were constantly out patrolling, ambushing and in pursuit of the enemy. The enemy employed mainly mortar and small arms fire but they also used landmines and booby-traps. Landmines and booby-traps were the psychological warfare facing every soldier. They were the unseen enemy, maiming and killing with ruthless efficiency. This all happened against the backdrop of the pulsating sounds and cyclonic winds and dust storms that the air force and army helicopters generated, providing gunfire support and evacuating the wounded.

During the day was fine for Manfred as he had to remain focussed and couldn't afford the luxury of reflecting on his life and where he was going with it. Interacting with his comrades, they fooled themselves that it was all a big adventure but he could see the loneliness there in each one's eyes. At night when he had time to contemplate, there was no space for what he wanted to think about like home and Angel, his mind got stuck regurgitating recent field events, vividly. He had learned to accommodate the sound of small arms fire and machine guns in the night and the smells of rice and other possessions being burned outside the villages suspected of harbouring the Viet Cong. He was accepting of the silence of the dead and the lifeless lenses peering at him at every tally. What he had difficulty with were the images of the living; the fear on the faces and their opened mouths that registered their disbelief at how everything had gone so out of whack. Their revolving heads not knowing which way to turn as eyes lifted skywards searching for their God, their bodies scrambled into tunnels searching for a shortcut to a hell of their own choosing over the inferno being rained upon them from above and from every side. It was a two way street this war, with no signs, no traffic lights and no road rules. That was how Manfred explained it to himself at night and then he was allowed some sleep.

Manfred had been involved in mostly minor skirmishes until he was assigned to 5RAR as an armourer in the Battle of Binh Ba, between June 6 and 8 a few months before his R&R in Sydney. An enemy communist force comprising the 33rd North Vietnam Army Regiment (NVA), a Viet Cong D440 Provincial Mobile Battalion, a Binh Ba and Ngai Giao Guerrilla Squad and a Chuck Duc District Company had occupied the town of Binh Ba on June 5. A rocket-propelled grenade struck a Centurion tank and an armoured recovery vehicle as they entered the town, severely injuring one of the crewmen in the tank. "Operation Hammer" went into full swing and Australia assaulted the enemy with infantry, armour and helicopter gunships. There were sixty-five men from D Company Fifth Battalion Royal Australian Regiment, troops of APC's from the Third Cavalry Regiment and a troop of Centurion tanks from First Armoured Regiment. The 105 Battery of the Royal Australian Artillery provided artillery support with pinpoint accuracy. Manfred was able to witness for himself for the first time the full force of an enemy offensive.

He had to let go completely and give it his all, abandoning all fear of dying. For the first time he felt like a warrior even a gladiator; his SLR was his sword and he was invincible. The waves of enemy troops kept coming at them. This time, the enemy seemed to be prepared to fight to the death. Three of the Centurion tanks were disabled with Rocket Propelled Grenades (RPGs) within an hour of the initial assault. As enemy troops began to feel the heat of the fire-fight, some escaped through underground tunnels, only to return again from another flank, while others discarded their uniforms and mingled with the civilians. Manfred found himself at the forefront of the attack. As the enemy vanished before him something kept telling him that he wanted more. It was as if he had become possessed by an insatiable thirst until a prolonged silence quenched it and the adrenalin of the moment abated.

Manfred and two diggers were ushering civilian groups to the rear of the battle zones as was common procedure after such a fire-fight when a Viet Cong popped up like a jack in the box from a tunnel entrance inside what looked like a makeshift thatch-walled outhouse. The Viet Cong emptied a full clip of bullets into them from his AK47, at a range of about thirty yards. The three soldiers didn't have a chance. The two sappers with him were mowed down before his eyes and as Manfred went to ground behind them, his hand grabbed a grenade from his belt and he lobbed it straight into the hole just like he had done so many times before in his youth while dynamiting fish at the Golden Hole just outside Babinda.

Manfred hadn't been hit but his two comrades were not so lucky. One was on the ground unconscious. The other was writhing in agony with one leg spurting blood, and his hand looked as though it had been blown off. Manfred called out to him.

"We gotta get outa here. That guy wouldn't be alone in that tunnel. Do you think you can walk?"

"No my leg's pretty bad. Maybe on one leg ... how's Bertie?"

"He's breathing. Can you stand up? I'm going to carry you both outa here but you gotta do what I tell you. As soon as I get Bertie on my shoulder, you stand up and lean over my other shoulder and grab his right arm above the elbow, so you guys can't fall off."

"You can't carry us both. Take Bertie and come back for me. I'll cover you." He reached for his SLR and then realised with horror that three fingers had been blown off his right hand.

"Just do what I say!" Manfred screamed. "Now ... stand up!" Manfred leapt to his feet and hauled Bertie up onto his right shoulder. Meanwhile, the other soldier did what he was told and slowly raised himself off the ground on one leg. Manfred bent his knees.

"Okay, lean over my left shoulder and grab Bertie's right arm above the elbow!"

Manfred shuffled them about, grabbing one of each of the sappers' legs in front of him. He shrugged his shoulders twice to balance them properly before he was fully erect and stepped forward with the two men's loose limbs dangling. He clenched his teeth and walked with a slow and steady stride. A group of diggers materialised by his side and encircled him, putting their bodies between him and the enemy and giving him the cover he needed to get the two boys to safety. For Manfred, this combination of events was overwhelming. It taught him that in war, they were all heroes; anyone who was prepared to lay down his life for his friend was a hero and no one could ask for more. He relinquished his charges to the medics and turned back in the direction of the fray but the immediate threat was gone.

"Gee fella, where did you learn to carry two men on your shoulders like that?" said one of the diggers.

"Just try carrying two wallaby jacks on your shoulders at the same time for a few miles," he quipped as they all withdrew separately.

Both sappers had been 'dusted off' by the time he returned that evening and he got the good news from the medic that Bertie was concussed with a head wound but had regained consciousness before being evacuated by helicopter along with the other wounded soldier.

Binh Ba was still insecure and the men and their armoured support "harboured up" with a few machine-guns set up on an area of high ground. The real tragedy of a combat zone was all captured there in one single still shot for Manfred. There were scores of dead and mutilated VC bodies all around with dismembered body parts strewn in every direction. Contorted and broken bodies piled up in one corner peered at him through closed eyes. He thought of their fathers and mothers and wives and children and they suddenly became just people. Then he rationalised it away, knowing that those people could as easily have been his own people and he recalled the comparison he always used about the two way street and it made sense to him.

Manfred heard distant screams and shouts that night, punctuating moments of serene silence. The pitch black of night was peeled open in technicolour as random flares and tracer fire went off at indiscriminate intervals. The monotonous sounds of AK47s and the occasional grenade followed short bursts of machine-gun fire. They were told that there was still fighting going on in the hamlet of Duc Trung to the north, as communist troops kept pressing towards Binh Ba.

Next day, tanks blew up the enemy soldiers who were barricaded in houses as if they were just plastic toys. Ground troops mopped up the survivors. They herded them into pens like animals and processed them like doomed men at Hell's gate. The whole village lay in ruins with hardly a house left standing, and the troops began a search of bunkers and all possible areas of concealment, like air raid shelters and underground tunnels. In all, one Australian was killed and ten wounded. The enemy's tally included 107 killed, six wounded and eight captured. Manfred realised it was a testament to the superior fire-power of the allies as there was no shortage of courage on both sides in that battle. What he could not understand was why the Viet Cong would not surrender. He knew it was un-Australian to hit a man when he was down but this was war and an adversary could kill you whether he was up or down. They had no choice but to do what they were doing. Throwing flowers and blowing kisses at the enemy wasn't going to stop the war. The only thing that was going to stop that war was a surrender.

The battle of Binh Ba was one of the major Australian victories of the war. 5RAR, the 3rd Cavalry Regiment, and the 1st Armoured Regiment were awarded the "battle of honour" Binh Ba, which meant that they could emblazon the name of the battle on their flag or uniform. It was a huge knot of anguish for Manfred that kept tightening and twisting inside his stomach, with all the images of the brutality emblazoned on his memory rather than on his flag or uniform. They had won the battle but he was losing the war with his God, his conscience, his innocence and his right to go on living. Who would be there for him when this was all over? Would his God take him back? Would he be absolved of all his "sins"? Could his innocence be restored in this life and who would convince him of his right to go on living? Had the formula been invented yet that would bring his life back into equilibrium, and if not, was anyone working on it? These were the things that went through Manfred's mind after the Battle of Binh Ba.

The moment Manfred landed back in Vietnam after his short stint in Australia on R and R with Angel, he was appointed as an armourer to the Sixth Battalion RAR-NZ, which was engaged in reconnaissance and ambush activities. It was the second fierce engagement with the enemy that Manfred was to experience after Binh Ba and in every way, just as brutal and gruesome; same disproportionate number of dead, bodies mutilated and body parts strewn in the field. During the thirty-two days of continuous ambushing and patrolling, the 6th Battalion RAR attacked and defeated 33 North Vietnamese Army Regiment in a series of company actions. They attacked and ambushed the 274 Viet Cong Regiment on three occasions and drove C41 Chau Duc Viet Cong District Company from its home base bunkers. He felt like he was a passenger on an enormous bulldozer that was sweeping everything before it and yet nobody behind him was talking about winning and no-one in front of him seemed to be worried about losing. His cognisance of the war was becoming a surreal understanding that he was participating in an absurd drama on an insignificant stage somewhere in "La La Land" that had nothing to do with the real world back home.

The war was becoming a statistics report where at the end of each day, someone ticked a whole series of boxes and the next day, it started all over again. Every morning, Manfred could hear the line from Herman's Hermits song *I'm Henry the Eighth I am* in his mind, blaring at him like a track on a broken record – second verse same as the first ... second verse same as the first ... second verse same as the first.

The patrols intensified as the months dragged on and the men were at breaking point. In WWII, the average soldier had 40 days of combat whereas in Vietnam, the average soldier had 240 days of combat in one year. The psychological impact was debilitating. The Nashos were relatively raw recruits, not career warriors who had been afforded the luxuries of time, training and conditioning to develop a conscious resilience to the atrocities of war. They were not like the Regulars who were often battle hardened by experiences in other conflict areas like Korea, Malaya and Borneo.

Above all, some Nashos had no focus on war as something that was taking them into the future. Manfred felt that war was just something that had taken him away from his past, his family and loved ones. Opposition politicians argued that Nashos were a cost-saving convenient cohort of sustainable cannon fodder but Manfred had no way of knowing this. Year after year, the "marbles" in the "lotto draw" of chosen birth dates kept falling, and wave after wave of Nashos kept coming forward. Manfred did not lack the guts; he lacked purpose. Was he fighting for his mates or for his country or was he fighting someone else's war? Did the people back home still believe in the war? Did they ever believe in it or did politicians foist it upon them for the sake of alliances? Was there the hidden agenda that conspiracy theorists always alluded to? All these thoughts echoed what he recalled his father talking about.

Ho Chi Minh, the North Vietnamese leader, claimed he wanted to reunite a divided Vietnam. Separated in 1954, the people in both North and South Vietnam had had their fill of colonial exploitation at the hands of the French and neo-colonial interference through the Americans, their Korean and Thai allies and the Australians and New Zealanders, who they referred to as "America's puppets". Were the senseless killings of soldiers and civilians really justifiable? Was the use of the lethal cocktail of 2,4,5-T and 2,4-D, known as "agent orange", too much overkill? How far off barbaric was the use of napalm to burn the flesh of other human beings? Could "carpet bombing" ever be condoned in a civilised society? All this had happened but was any of the enemy's reciprocal savagery directed towards the US and her allies acceptable or understandable? Manfred had to wrestle with these questions as he witnessed it going on all around him. He had seen his mates killed and wounded yet he in turn, had killed and wounded many of the enemy.

Terrorising all the diggers throughout their whole tour of duty were the booby traps and the anti-personnel and anti-tank mines. They had all been told that over one third of all deaths and injuries in Vietnam were officially attributed to booby-traps and landmines so Manfred and every other soldier had every right to be preoccupied with thoughts about them. The only thing that made sense for Manfred was his instinct to survive. Wherever he was, with or without the support of the personnel carriers and Centurion tanks, he became focused on only two things – the life-threatening hazards surrounding him and the thought of going home. He was convinced that the reasons for the war could no longer justify the means being employed in an effort to win it at all costs and he just hoped the enemy would surrender so that they could all go home and get the bad taste of Vietnam out of their mouths.

Manfred's skills as an armourer were his ticket to many places throughout Phuoc Tuy Province. On January 12, twenty-one days before the end of his tour of duty, he found himself attached to 6RAR/NZ (ANZAC) Battalion. It was heavily involved in cordon and search, reconnaissance and ambush activities during Operation Napier. Again, supply points were destroyed, vital lines of communications were denied, the logistics system of the Viet Cong was irreparably damaged and services groups were crippled. As they moved into position for a cordon and search surrounding the village of Ap Ngai Gao, the Vietnamese police screened the local people. The police were dressed in conspicuous white uniforms and they were brutal and arrogant and had no reservations about beating peasants to a pulp. Even the diggers and the American soldiers gave "the white mice" a wide berth.

It was nightfall and the platoon retreated to the safety of the night harbour area complete with its M60 machine-guns on patches of higher ground and picket lines of riflemen. The gunner, with two machine-gun belts criss-crossed over his shoulders, back and chest, was on full alert watching and listening for any signs of movement in the darkening night. Each rifleman also carried a 100 round belt of ammunition for the M60 machine-guns. Nothing happened and an eerie silence surrounded the camp. So much of that war was spent just waiting, which in itself was nerve-racking and Manfred could tell which soldiers had just begun their tour of duty by the levels of apprehension they exhibited when on picket duty.

Next morning, on patrol and accompanied by a Centurion tank, they came across many abandoned VC shelters made from bush materials with canvas roofs. They searched for bunkers and tunnels but the Viet Cong were nowhere to be seen. Manfred was walking behind a Centurion tank when the front left-hand track detonated a landmine which was wired in a sequence to multiple landmines, setting off a daisy chain of explosives. Seven explosions rocked the area. The track of the Centurion tank was blasted off the rollers in the first explosion and the third explosion erupted just in front of Manfred to his right. He took a massive hit on the right ankle and the inside of his left thigh. Shrapnel particles peppered his chest and he felt himself flung violently to the ground. He remembered feeling to see if his leg was still there and as he ran his hand down from the knee in search of damage, he felt the wound on his ankle. He clenched his teeth against the pain in the thigh of his left leg. The medic rushed towards him and produced a syringe. Manfred felt the jab of the morphine injection and then nothing. As he wavered in and out of a consciousness, he could hear the rotor blades of a chopper and voices shouting orders. His senses were immersed in total chaos all around him. His vision blurred and his hearing distorted, and he could taste blood in his mouth. He was nauseous and he could smell diesel. He tried to talk but couldn't get the words to come out. Soon he was airborne and another needle took away the joy of the moment of being rescued and thankfully, the pain of his wounds.

The only other thing he remembered was giving strict instructions regarding his wounded leg to the American doctor stationed at the Field Hospital at Vung Tau.

Chapter 4

It wasn't until he got to 1 Military Hospital Yeronga that Manfred learned that it was the Salvos in Vietnam who packed his gear and sent it back to Australia. Nobody from the army or the police had told Manfred's parents that he had been wounded. They eventually found out when the Salvation Army informed them in Babinda and asked if they could be of help in any way. It was as if he had suddenly dropped off their radar as far as the army was concerned. It worried him and he discussed it with several other patients at the hospital who also felt that they had become alienated by both the army and mainstream society. He imagined himself as being trapped in a foetal position in one of the many capsules he was being asked to swallow each day as part of his treatment, in that he was powerless to extricate himself from his present position and he simply had to accept his plight along with all the other medication he was taking.

It had to be a severe concern for Manfred to be like that because throughout his life he had always been a jovial, positive person whereas now he was becoming sullen and introverted. Maybe he needed someone to be there with him; someone to talk to, to help him sort out a lot of the issues that were on his mind. He needed answers to questions about what he was going to do with his life and where to turn to for help. He had no money, no clothes apart from one uniform, and it was only after he received that letter from his mother that he realised that no one up north had been told anything about him. Even then, they were expecting him to come home as they knew nothing of the extent of his injuries.

He resigned himself to the fact that he would be confined to the hospital for an extended period of time. His wounds were so severe that when they succumbed to infection, it was beginning to look like the amputation that had been avoided in Vung Tau might be necessary after all. There was a scarcity of visitors to the hospital. The atmosphere as he was wheeled along the corridors was sombre and he could feel the walls closing in on him. What he found strange was the absence of laughter; no sign of any pockets of happiness anywhere, and thus he referred to it as a "leper colony" when he spoke about it to the nurses. He was unhappy and he told them he would end up "strangling the preacher" who had never uttered anything to him other than "Bless you my son". His other gripe was that there was no games room, gym or entertainment other than the television, except for a fortnightly excursion to the cinema complex at Indooroopilly.

Manfred spent each day waiting for nobody and staring at the ceiling, wondering what would become of him. What would he do for work if he lost his leg? Would Angel still want to marry him? He wondered what it would be like to go back home again, to be among people who probably had preconceived ideas about what went on in Vietnam and no real understanding of what he and his mates had been through. Already, some of the other veterans had warned him that their friends felt too uncomfortable asking about the war and it was too hard to know where to start talking about it. Vietnam might just as well have been on another planet as far as those people were concerned. People had to have been there to even try to understand.

After two weeks, the danger of losing his leg passed and Manfred's spirits lifted. He began to walk around with the aid of a frame, but only for short distances. The place resembled a morgue and as he walked past the patients in their beds, it was so quiet, he would look to see if there was a tag attached to their big toe identifying who they were after they had died. The few visitors who did come to the hospital were inclined to meet patients in the reception rooms and it was there that Manfred first saw the front page headings in The Courier Mail about the My Lai Massacre.

The massacre at My Lai of 504 unarmed civilians in South Vietnam was committed by US Army soldiers on March 16, 1968. The casualties included old people, men, women, children and infants. Some of the women were gang-raped and their bodies mutilated. The event was so horrendous that the US military kept it under wraps for one and a half years and it only became public knowledge in November 1969. Manfred gasped on reading the report of those events. He knew that Australian soldiers would never condone such atrocities but he feared that in their ignorance the public in Australia might construe such conduct as universal and nothing could be further from the truth. Nowhere in the article could Manfred find one single statement that unreservedly exonerated Australian diggers from any such or similar misconduct. As more and more shocking evidence came to light, the daily newspapers buzzed with it. The war in Vietnam was suddenly being scrutinised from a new perspective and Manfred could sense how public opinion was turning towards universal condemnation. The papers reported that in the streets and at the airports, diggers coming back from Vietnam in uniform were often met with hostility. They were heckled and called baby killers. Gangs of anti-war protesters jostled them and spat on them. That was the hornet's nest that Manfred had to imagine he had come home to.

As Manfred perused the media and ingested the public's slandering of troops involved in the war, he was beginning to understand why the hospital resembled a morgue and why it was more like a leper colony. Nobody wanted to go near them and they were hidden away from the public eye. When he broached the issue with Nurse Vonnie who was young and the only spark of life after death in the whole hospital, she was adamant.

"It has to be true if it's in the papers Manfred, doesn't it?" she asked. Sister Heather who had two nephews fighting in Vietnam saw it differently.

"All our family wants is for our sons to be out of that hell hole. How are those poor buggers going to feel coming back to this sort of a reception?" she said gesturing towards the television set with the empty tea cup in her hand as American soldiers returning from Vietnam were being pelted with eggs and rotten fruit.

An American inquiry into the My Lai Massacre initially found and charged twenty-six soldiers with criminal offences even though two whole platoons; First Platoon and Second Platoon, had been involved in the massacre. The deed was too despicable to rest upon the conscience of the allies; it was the Americans who were to blame. Soon, it was also found to be too grave for responsibility to rest with the Americans and it became the American army's fault alone. The American army did not want to shoulder the responsibility for the crime as it was First Platoon and Second Platoon who executed the horrendous deed. The individuals in both platoons insisted they were only carrying out orders and refusal to obey orders was tantamount to a crime. When they enlisted, they took an oath to "obey the orders of the officers appointed over me". Under Article 90 of the Uniform Code of Military Justice, they argued, it was clear that "during times of war, a military member who wilfully disobeys a superior commissioned officer can be sentenced to death". That meant the blame lay with the twenty-six soldiers who were in positions to give orders. In their defence, it was argued that they too were following orders and hence they were not culpable either. Ultimately, it was narrowed down to just one guy, Lieutenant William Calley Jr, to shoulder the blame. That good old time-tried golden rule that the individual should shoulder the blame allowed America and its allies to wash their hands of the whole despicable event and Calley was given a life sentence.

Once the issue of culpability had been settled and everyone knew whose soul was going to rot in Hell, Calley's sentence was reduced by the Convening Authority from life to twenty years. Eventually he served only three and a half years under house arrest at Fort Benning, including three months in a disciplinary barracks in Fort Leavenworth, Kansas, before being paroled. He had paid for the crime; he had done the time and was able to return home because in the end, all had been forgiven.

Manfred stopped looking at the television. The screens of every channel were featuring anti-Vietnam protest marches. Soldiers returning from Vietnam were changing out of their uniforms into civilian clothing before alighting from the planes. Friends and relatives whisked them away as if they were ashamed to acknowledge them in public. New atrocities against civilians in Vietnam were presented and old atrocities revisited on screens across Australia, over and over again. War atrocities were the most talked about subject on talk-back radio. The musical Hair was offering extended sessions which were all sold out and it was about to go on a tour of the country. It had acquired a status whereby it was enjoying a cult following beyond the usual alternative communities of beatniks, bums, drop-outs, hippies and yippies. The "straights" and "squares" of mainstream society, especially the young, were beginning to line up in droves.

Australia was ripe for protest. In America, hippies had commandeered the Berkley campus of the University of California and Governor Ronald Reagan branded them as communist sympathisers, protesters and sex deviants. Violence erupted on the campus, and police sent loads of hippies to hospital with head trauma and shotgun wounds. Reagan eventually declared a State of Emergency. That same year, the Woodstock Music and Art Fair in Bethel, New York, drew a crowd of over half a million people. They rocked to the sounds of Janis Joplin, Creedence Clearwater Revival, The Who, Carlos Santana and Jimi Hendrix. To Manfred the whole idea of the war was beginning to look like an excuse for a party back home. This was followed in December 1969 when 300,000 people attended the Altamont Free Concert with the Rolling Stones, Crosby Stills Nash and Young and Jefferson Airplane. The Hells Angels even entered the equation and provided their own brand of security for the event. The hippie counter-culture spread across America and Europe and was becoming entrenched in Australia. What started off in the late fifties as a generation of beatniks, characterised by poets and sages like Allen Ginsberg, W.S. Burroughs, Jack Kerovac, Ferlinghetti and William Carlos Williams, erupted into a force to be reckoned with. That was one commentator's take on it. Manfred joked with the other patients about it.

"We're going to have to start checking our tucker in case they try to poison us after watching this sort of stuff on television."

"Or knock us off in our sleep," added another.

"Doesn't worry me," joked Mick, the shearer's son from the outback town of Bourke who had lost an arm and a leg. "I haven't got as much to lose as you guys." They all laughed but Manfred froze. As he pushed the tea tray in front of him away so that he could get up, the cup and saucer flew off and smashed on the floor. "We can laugh," he said, "As long as no other bastard laughs at you Mick. That's what worries me. You're better than them." He grasped his frame and hobbled out of the room.

The hippie craze was about being carefree and about being against the establishment and "Big Brother" which they perceived as corrupt and flawed. They rejected middle-class values, opposed nuclear weapons and the Vietnam War. They were eco-friendly, loved folk music and cherished peace, love and personal freedom and sought a utopian society. Manfred had to read about all of this and try to come to an understanding as to how the world had changed in just a few years. He often spoke about how he wanted to try to come to terms with the rationale behind the social upheaval internationally. Hippies experimented with marijuana and LSD to explore the altered state of consciousness. Manfred called all that "a load of codswallop." They wore brightly coloured ragged clothes, tie-dyed t-shirts, beads, sandals and handmade jewellery. Manfred called them "fairies." Men grew their hair long and women wore no make-up. Manfred just shook his head at that to express his disbelief. Their logo was the peace symbol of the "Y" enclosed in a circle which many wore on a chain around their necks. "Each to his own," was how Manfred saw it. Some lived in communes and they travelled in groups in Volkswagen buses adorned with colourful scenes, symbols and statements like "make love not war". Manfred could see where all that was heading but who could resist the allure of such a lifestyle? All around him, Manfred could see that Australia's youth was being sucked into the nonconformist lifestyle vortex. Even Time Magazine came up with a cover story entitled *The Hippies: The Philosophy of a Subculture.* Scott McKenzie's rendition of John Phillip's song *San Francisco* became a huge hit with its refrain of "If you're going to San Francisco, be sure to wear some flowers in your hair". Thus the followers of the hippie movement became categorised as the "Flower Children" and it was like they were envisaging the beginning of a new world just as Manfred was.

All Manfred could focus on was the mouldy cream ceiling of the room he was confined to "in solitary" as he termed it. Occasionally he would doze off under the weight of boredom and painkillers only to wake in fright when the overhead fan threw a wobbly that resembled the "whop-whop-whop" sounds of the rotor blades of a helicopter gunship. There were periods when he was afraid to go to sleep, knowing he would be waking up to some nightmare.

He tried to stay awake by thinking of pleasant events from his childhood – playing with his mates at school, or swimming in Babinda Creek with his best mate Tony at Happy Valley. It made him start wondering where they might be and what they might be doing; if they still played football, went fishing and hunted crocodiles. He missed the times when they could all enjoy a cold beer at the pub and he tried to imagine what Tony was doing with his life in the "big smoke" after he had finished his university studies. Had anyone else from Babinda been called up? The only other people he had heard of who had gone over there from Babinda were Captain J. K. "Macca" McBride, Jeffrey Kapor and David Zealot who were both Nashos, and Bobby Braid who was ten years his senior and had joined up with the regular army years ago.

Bobby led a gang of bikies in Babinda that were the closest thing Manfred had ever seen that might be categorised as counter cultural. Bobby's hair was styled into a rack which came forward to a point at the forehead but was slicked back at the sides and held together by Brylcreem. He wore his collar up to support his ears, rolled his sleeves up to under his armpits and had bell-bottom trousers over pointed black shoes. He had a tattoo and wore selective jewellery and a leather jacket. He drove his BSA motorcycle at breakneck speed and headed a bikie gang of bodgies and their female counterparts, the widgies.

Bobby's best mate was Gary Greaves who sported a Mohawk haircut and wore a black mesh shirt and herringbone jacket over a pair of tight jeans. Bobby and Gary were both in love with Linda, a dark-eyed siren of Italian extraction. She was nobody's girl and leader of the pack among the widgies. Her hair was cut short and she wore tight jeans and a denim jacket. A pair of yellow-tinted goggles complemented a set of gold teardrop earrings and matching necklace. Bobby and his gang were forever in trouble with the police and maligned as delinquents by the conservative citizens in the town. Nevertheless, one solitary act of heroism was all it took to reinstate the whole gang back into the community.

Babinda Creek was a raging torrent after twenty-four hours and twenty-four inches of monsoonal rains had hammered down one weekend in January 1957. A railway bridge crossed the flooded creek on the outskirts of the town. A road bridge spanned the creek a further fifty yards downstream. A group of ten-year-old boys, including Manfred and Tony, were dive-bombing off the railway bridge and into the flooded creek. The whole gang of six bodgies and five widgies had congregated together in the middle of the road bridge, and were making plans for the day. Four of the girls had already paired off and were sitting pillion on their partners' motorbikes. That left Linda to choose between Bobbie's and Gary's bikes. She was trying to negotiate the dilemma when suddenly they all turned to look upstream in response to Manfred's shrieks of help. A Greek boy, Micky, had jumped too early after Manfred and landed on top of him. Manfred was stunned on impact, his arms went limp and he was unable to swim to save himself. Each time his head went under as he was swept towards the road bridge, he was able to touch the bottom with his feet and propel himself upward for another breath of air. He bobbed up and down like a cork and yelled "help" each time before going under again. He dreaded what lay in store for him beyond the road bridge; he would surely drown, because from there, the water swirled away as a deep rapid current and he would no longer be able to touch the bottom.

Linda screamed at Bobby and then at Gary to jump in and save the boy but they were fully clothed and reticent about jumping in and getting soaked. The boy was halfway to the road bridge when Linda realised there was no time to waste. Fully clothed, she dived in, but was immediately seized by the current. Manfred's heart leapt for a moment when he realised he might be saved but when he resurfaced again, he could see Linda was fighting to save herself and grasping at the strands of pannikin grass dangling from the bridge.

When he resurfaced again, he could see that Linda had abandoned the rescue attempt and was swimming back to the bank. Then, as he went under for what he thought would be the last time, he caught the slightest glimpse of somebody else jumping off the road bridge. He felt himself sinking again and began to succumb to swallowing mouthfuls of water into his stomach and lungs. A cluster of fingers reached down from above and grasped him firmly under the chin and started towing him slowly against the current towards the bank.

"Are you okay, boy?" Gary asked when he was within a few yards from the bank, and Manfred nodded. "Are you sure?" Gary said, awaiting confirmation.

"Yes, you can let me go now," Manfred said, hoping to redeem some pride.

Gary loosened his grip but Manfred was too feeble and immediately sank again.

"Man, you have been totally stunned. Here, stay with me and I'll bring you right up to the bank." Gary pulled him to shore and heaved him onto dry land.

"You really shouldn't be swimming in the creek when it's in flood," Gary warned.

He left Manfred there to regain his breath and climbed up the bank to join the members of the gang who were clapping madly. Manfred didn't even thank him. As he looked up, his sense of guilt eased and he was no longer sad that he hadn't thanked Gary. Linda, still dripping wet, was thanking Gary for him with a huge kiss and a cuddle as she climbed onto his motorcycle to ride pillion with him. She placed her arms around him tightly and Manfred could see the pink blush on her face as she rested the side of her head against his back. Then they were gone. The whole motorcycle gang just rode out of his life, yet without them he would certainly have drowned. He owed them something and it was more than a simple "thank you". When he became older and thought about it, he figured that maybe he thought bodgies and widgies were delinquents and didn't deserve to be thanked. He hoped the real reason was that he was still in shock and the whole event was simply too much for him. Either way, from that day onward, Manfred was sure that Gary and Linda were good people and he didn't care to which culture or sub-culture they belonged.

Manfred could remember that day so clearly and he could also remember how the attitudes of the people of the town changed towards the members of that motorcycle gang after the dramatic rescue. Were people so fickle? If the hound dog could become a hero so easily, could a hero become a hound dog just as easily? Was public opinion really so powerful yet so shallow? Was all that he had done for his country, which he really believed to be something special, going to amount to nothing? Was he only ever going to be "nothing but a hound dog" and should he howl about it like Elvis did? Were all of the sacrifices the boys had made in Vietnam going to be forgotten?

Chapter 5

Tony had been out there somewhere, but it was hardly the "big smoke". He had graduated from Innisfail State High School and had been accepted into Law at the University College of Townsville, Pimlico campus. The straight Law subjects were correspondence courses with the University of Queensland that provided tutors who were barristers in private practice. Townsville was only about twice the population of Cairns at that time, and was no more than a of large country town. It had a population of 58,000 against 656,000 in Brisbane. Nevertheless, in terms of gender ratios, there was a plethora of teenage girls around his age, especially on campus, and Tony was ecstatic. His previous experience with gender ratios up north was one girl to every three boys at best. The only hope for boys around Babinda was to find one girl between three or four guys and book a table at a cabaret or dance venue in Cairns or Innisfail. The girl would act as a "security guarantee" in any pick-up line the boys used on other girls.

"Hey, how about joining our table over there? See the one near the band … with the girl seated there? Her name is Lucy; she's a lot of fun."

Chances were the girl or a couple of girl friends would be happy to join the table if there was already another girl there. That's the way it worked up north. The boys would then shout the girls drinks, dance with them and, with any luck, get to know them better. It was always a game of stealth and usually ended in failure.

On campus, however, there were as many girls as boys, and chances were that the girls who had left home felt more liberated and were easier to partner. Tony had never imagined that university was going to be like that. All the skills he had honed when the going was so tough with girls up north would be to his advantage when courting these girls. That year, there was a small group of exchange students from America who were keen to introduce elements of their hippie subculture to the university students in Australia. Tony, in a determined attempt to make it with the in-group, grew his hair long, wore colourful psychedelic clothing and leather sandals, sported a "peace" logo on a pendant around his neck, adopted vegetarian virtues and eco-friendly initiatives, opposed nuclear weapons, rejected middle-class values and championed "free love".

After three years of Australia's increasing involvement in the war in Vietnam, Tony felt it was time to take a stand. He became conspicuous on campus through his leadership in promoting anti-war protests and opposition to conscription. At one on-campus event, a government delegate, Mr Killin, from Canberra, offered to talk to the members of the student union about any issues regarding the war in Vietnam and conscription. The college refectory, where he was to address the students, was packed to capacity and Tony had to settle for a spot right at the back of the room.

Killin thought that by belittling the students, insulting their intelligence and ignoring or deliberately misinterpreting questions, he could dissuade them from challenging his rhetoric. He demoralised each adversary one after another, treating every interjection with such disdain that a deathly quiet crept across the audience. It was as if he had broken their spirit, dulled their enthusiasm and exploited their naivety with contempt. It was an opportune moment and Tony knew that he had to do something to rekindle their deflated egos and re-engage them in dissent. His father had taught him well that it was "better a day as a lion, than a lifetime as a lamb" and he wanted to demonstrate the power that mentality could yield in a crowd.

He removed his shoes and turned to the students around him. "Hoist me up onto your shoulders, folks, so that I can give this guy a piece of my mind!" he shouted. They willingly answered his call as boys and girls alike lifted him up high against the back wall. He looked like a messiah rising from out of the throng, resplendent in his ragged clothes and tousled hair. He thrust out his clenched fist in a salute with the "peace" necklace dangling and swaying to and fro as if to hypnotise them.

"Liberated students for the next millennium!" he shouted. "Do not allow yourselves to be dumbstruck by this deluded drop-kick delegate from the parliament of the last century!"

Total silence followed as the audience focused, anticipating the oration that was about to follow. He wanted them to be ready and he wanted them to dig deep to show their support for what he had to say.

"You may have been given the stage Killin," he fumed at the guest speaker, "but I have captured the high ground up here on the shoulders of my fellow students; the voices of the next millennium!" On that cue, the students let out a roar and stamped their feet until the floorboards began to reverberate.

"Your government is asking these students right here," he pointed down at them, "to die for their country, in somebody else's war, on somebody else's land!" he trumpeted as the stamping began to die down. "Where will your government be when the caskets draped in our noble flag are brought home?"

He waited for the stamping to recommence. "Where ...?" he asked as he prompted the audience to stamp harder and become more vocal. "Where ...?"

This time they repeated after him, "Yeah! Where ...?"

"... and where will your government be when the wounded and the maimed return from the war that nobody wanted? Nowhere!" he prompted.

"Nowhere! Nowhere! Nowhere!" the students chorused.

"Who will be there to help shoulder the burden on the families of the broken men and women veterans of the war? No-one. Not you ... Blue!" he shouted.

"No-one. Not you ... Blue! No-one. Not you ... Blue! No-one. Not you ... Blue!" shouted the crowd.

"Make love! Not war!" he shouted, punching the air with his clenched fist.

"Make love! Not war! Make love! Not war! Make love! Not war!" they echoed, punching the air in unison.

"We are the generation that will change the world ... through peace. We will build a cradle for that new civilisation. We will be the hand that rocks the cradle of the new civilisation for the new millennium. 'The hand that rocks the cradle rules the world!' " he said.

"The hand that rocks the cradle rules the world! The

hand that rocks the cradle rules the world! The hand that rocks the cradle rules the world!" they shouted.

"That's our message to Canberra, Killin. Pass it on!"

"That's our message, Killin. Pass it on! That's our message, Killin. Pass it on! That's our message, Killin. Pass it on!"

"Now, get outa here!" he yelled as he lost his footing and fell into the crowd.

"Yeah … get outa here! Get outa here! Get outa here!" chanted the crowd as they started pelting things at the people on the stage until they were forced to retire under a hail of shoes, fruit and everything else that was being thrown at them.

It was a great win for the students. They had exhibited their solidarity and Tony was had become a cult hero. At rallies, even weeks after the event, a group of students would hoist him high above their shoulders to revisit those moments in the refectory and he would call out, "We are the voice of the next millennium!"

Girl friends seemed to materialise from everywhere. They all wanted to be near him. They wanted to discuss things with him and they wanted to plan with him and help him carry the world forward to a better place. In fact, he was so preoccupied with his new vision that he missed lectures and fell behind with his tutorials and his assignments, but that was the price he was prepared to pay. Later that same year, Tony was appointed student union events organiser. There were endless parties and in the manner of the American exchange students, some light experimentation with herbs and hallucinatory drugs that many students felt helped them delve into the higher levels of consciousness necessary for deep thought and higher levels of thinking.

It was soon November and Tony had always promised himself that he would travel to Melbourne to witness the iconic Melbourne Cup race. He had developed a habit for gambling on horses at the local Cluden Racecourse in Townsville. He and two mates and three girls flew down to Melbourne on the Monday night before the cup. They joined revellers that night at their hotel in a game of two-up. Tony had trouble remembering what happened that night, but awoke the next morning to the pleasant surprise of a wad full of notes in his pocket that he had obviously won the night before. Everyone was semi-comatose from the over-consumption of alcohol but they managed to board the tram that would take them to Flemington racecourse on the Tuesday. All around Melbourne, the mood surrounding the cup carnival was electric. People were partying in the car parks, under tents and marquees, on chairs, around blankets and eskies, and everyone was in their best outfits. The women especially were a fashion extravaganza from the feathers in their hats to the tips of their high-heeled shoes.

Inside there were parades of women as well as horses, people in costume, groups in period dress, whole families, tourist groups and students in uniform on school excursions. There seemed to be every type of food and drink available to satisfy the hungry hordes but it was the champagne bottles that were everywhere, with corks popping incessantly. Everyone was welcome to rock up to any group and share in the merriment. Eskies and personal possessions were left in the care of strangers while people went to place their bets.

One particular event that made newspaper headlines for a week in Australia and overseas was the appearance at the track of the world's highest paid fashion model, Jean

Shrimpton, at that 1965 Melbourne Cup. She set a trend that day that was to reverberate throughout the world for years to come. She wore a mini-skirt that was about six inches above the knee, no hat, open shoes and what seemed to be no stockings. It was impossible that she was wearing stockings because her skirt was so short that the tops would have been visible. In fact, she was wearing pantyhose, which the English called "tights" and no-one in Australia had yet heard of them.

The other incredible thing was that everyone "knew" the winner of the cup, even before it had run, yet no two people could agree. With twenty-two runners in the cup, there were twenty-two winners and only the actual race itself was going to settle the matter once and for all. Tony backed various amounts on every horse in the race, because he was determined to be able to say to his grandchildren one day that he had picked the winner of the Melbourne Cup in 1965. The Bart Cummings trained mare Light Fingers won the cup at the odds of fifteen to one, and Tony had made a special bet on it, reaping a small fortune. Between what he made at two-up the night before and what he won on Light Fingers, Tony and his friends were able to stay for the rest of the week in Melbourne.

They visited the many historic places and museums and traversed and criss-crossed the city to see the sights on trains, trams and buses. At night they went to theatres, cabarets, nightclubs and pubs and spent their last night getting drunk at The Drunken Poet, the Irish pub in West Melbourne. It was a fitting end to a week of the best entertainment, totally funded from the proceeds of their gambling.

Tony flunked two of the subjects of his Law studies in the end of year examinations. It was unfortunate, but inevitable after a year of overindulgence in politics, partying, sex, alcohol, drugs and gambling. The following year, Tony went to Brisbane to repeat his first year subjects of a University of Queensland Law degree again. This time, he attended Cromwell College, with the intention of making a better job of it. Because he was in first year, that meant he would have to submit to the initiation games again. He was not too happy about that, but it was part of the tradition of the college and he figured it was better to go through the motions rather than be a pain and try to squirm out of it. However, students in the residential colleges were mostly conservative, with entrenched middle-class values. Tony saw no joy in hanging around these kinds of people and moved into some student digs at Hill End with a group of like-minded students.

The counter-culture scene was more advanced and pronounced in Brisbane and especially at the University of Queensland. He became involved with the Vietnam Action Campaign (VCA), which had been formed in Sydney in 1965 to organise demonstrations against the Vietnam War. On a trip to Sydney, he met up with some of the stalwarts in the movement, including John Pilger of Green Left Weekly fame, Ted and Gail Lord, and Tribune photographer Noel Hazard. It also marked a turning point in his life, because it was on that trip that he met up with the divine Cara Reynolds.

Cara hailed from Far North Queensland around Mowbray, Mossman, Port Douglas way. She was a high spirited country girl who loved riding horses and swimming and hiking through the bush. When she was sixteen, O'Malley's Show Troupe arrived in Mossman with a buckjumping, horse training and bullock riding spectacular. Proprietor Lance O'Malley challenged the townsfolk to try to ride one of his ponies that he claimed had never been ridden. He offered the princely sum of ten pounds as a prize to anyone who could stay on the pony for three minutes. Several of the locals tried and failed but old Granny Reynolds, the family matriarch, stood up and shouted, "Give Cara a go. There's never been a horse in this town that Cara couldn't ride."

Cara knew horses. She had been taught to ride horses from when she was six. Cara ambled up and talked to the horse for two to three minutes as if she was negotiating with it. Then she gave the pony two lumps of sugar and quietly climbed into the saddle. The horse bucked and kicked and swerved but Cara sat firmly, exhibiting the perfect balance that only the masters of the game could maintain. Much to the surprise of old O'Malley, she stayed on for the full three minutes and collected the generous ten pound prize.

Having heard that story, one had to be forgiven for imagining Cara was a real tomboy. However, she was a slight, delicate looking girl with shoulder-length black curly hair parted down the middle with a single signature two-inch curly lock at the front that dangled down over her forehead. A cute stub of a nose made her look forever young and that little bit cheeky. She was flirtatious, with a most alluring smile that made the boys go crazy for her, but none was able to turn that girl's head.

The Mossman and Port Douglas Catholic Church Committee ran a "Queen" competition that same year. They were raising funds to build a church in Mossman. Cara was chosen to represent the Port Douglas area and her friends and family hosted socials, dances and card parties at Granny Reynolds' rambling colonial farmhouse at Mowbray

Vale. Everybody gave generously to the fund and Cara was crowned queen at a Catholic Ball at Mossman, and the boy who had raised the most money was allowed to partner her in the victory waltz.

The best word that Tony could think of to describe her was "precious". All he wanted to do was protect her. Cara had left the north the year before she turned nineteen, because she wanted to experience city life. She chose Sydney because all the women's magazines had put it right up there with the major world cities. In Sydney, she was immediately attracted to the hippie scene, which was another reason she left the north. She wanted to be free and she wanted to meet people from all over the world with bright new ideas and big dreams. She wanted to be a part of the exciting new world that industry and technology were offering up to young people. She didn't want her world to be trapped in a time warp like Granny Reynolds' world. In fact, it was Granny Reynolds who encouraged her to "go see a bit of the world me dear. You young people ... you need to be more adventurous. You only live once".

She wanted to stay somewhere central and was told there was an old house in Macleay Road a few streets back from the El Alamein Memorial Fountain in Kings Cross. A bunch of young hippies had set it up as a type of halfway house, welcoming anyone to stay a while until they found their own digs. Access to the house was via a walkway hemmed in by blank red-brick walls on one side and chainwire fencing on the other. A group of young people sat on a sandstone block wall overlooking the walkway. The girls were dressed in ragged crotch-hugging short-shorts and tie-dyed blouses. They wore a mixture of leather plaited headbands, dark sunglasses and pendants with peace symbols around their necks. The boys were bare-chested with an array of long and short brown coloured bead pendants around their necks and they wore bohemian trousers or faded jeans. The girls had hair down to their waists and two of the boys had shoulder length hair. They were all barefoot.

There was a bit of a jam session going on, with two of them strumming guitars. One was singing and the remainder joined in with vocal harmonies. Cara was captivated by the totally mesmerising compilation of sound, particularly when they were singing The Byrds' cover version of Bob Dylan's *Mr Tamborine Man*. She could tell the boy on the jangly 12-string guitar was very talented; the sound he produced was so similar to the original soundtrack. She decided then and there to nickname him "Jangly".

"Hey babe," he called out as he brought the music to a halt with a wave of his hand. "You dig the music?"

"Yeah man … you guys are breaking it out big time. I'm looking for a halfway house, supposed to be around here somewhere, that welcomes lost souls and beaten down losers like me," she replied.

"That's us babe. You came to the right place. There's a set of stairs just over there through that gate." He pointed to an old steel gate encrusted with rust and strangled in creepers. As she began walking towards the gate, he called out to her,

"This one's for you babe." He started off on a rendition of the Beatles' song *I'm a Loser*.

Cara turned her head and cast a bashful grin at the group. She knew this was where she wanted to be and the group soon realised they were happy to have her. She was special and she didn't have to prove anything to them.

The first thing she learned was to strum a guitar and join in with their music making. They found her a job at a hippie clothing shop nearby, which sold everything for hippies including tie-dyed t-shirts and blouses, long dresses, pixie dresses and halter-neck dresses, bandanas and headbands in every style and colour, flower-power hats and ponchos. As well, they sold mushroom corduroy backpacks, tie-dyed shoulder packs and feather-fringed messenger bags. Mexican sandals and water buffalo sandals were the go for those whose feet were too delicate to go barefoot, with Minnetonka Peace moccasins for the women. Tie-dyed skinny jeans and yoga pants were also the rage along with sunglasses with rims that faded into rainbow colours of blue to brown to purple around mauve glass. They were just the type of accessory that accentuated the "super-cool", along with patchwork magic mushroom passport pouches for international visitors.

Cara loved the job in Kings Cross. She had a particular interest in sewing and a keen eye for fashion and actually created some designs of her own. Most of all, she loved the opportunity it provided for her to meet hundreds of young, easy-going beautiful people with like minds; brothers and sisters from all walks of life. The customers responded to her relaxed, informed, supportive, no pressure salesmanship and she was the top-selling sales person week after week.

It was in that shop that she first met Tony who had heard about the shop and thought it would be the ideal place to find gifts for his friends in Brisbane and catch up with the Sydney trends and fashions. He initially felt a little awkward interacting with this beautiful city girl and he feared she might typecast him as the stereotypical out-of-towner. Cara soon dispelled all such thoughts the moment she found out he was from Brisbane.

"So you're down from Brisbane," she said nonchalantly. "I'm from up that way myself," she added. "In fact, I'm from far further north than that."

"Oh, I am too. I'm from the Far North … Babinda, just south of Cairns," Tony challenged.

"Further …" Cara teased out the conversation.

"Further than Cairns?" Tony asked.

"Yep … Mowbray, Port Douglas, Mossman. This here girl is just as at home up there in the Daintree country as she is right here in Hyde Park, Sydney," she replied, adopting an American accent.

Tony was gobsmacked and at a total loss for words. She might have looked like a siren, talked like a siren and caused palpitations in his heart like a siren, but he figured "*this woman had to be human if she came from North Queensland*". In fact, if she came from further north than he did, then maybe that was why she came across as extra special. Tony was immediately smitten as he had never been with any girl.

Over dinner, they talked about all the things they had in common and reminisced about different things that they had experienced in their childhood. A person had to be a North Queenslander to talk about North Queensland because the content as well as the language was a dialect in itself. City slickers couldn't tell the difference between the smell of burnt pannikin grass and burnt sugarcane. There were no wait-a-whiles or wild pigs or crocodiles in Hyde Park. No-one would even dream about riding a horse bareback in Sydney. Who needed street names to locate a particular place? Up north, Tony reminded her, people navigated using landmarks and followed blazes on trees. She laughed at that one.

"Probably wouldn't go so far as to suggest we follow blazes on trees," she refuted, trying to keep the discussion honest.

"Well, Edmund Kennedy and Jacky Jacky did and Christie Palmerston did," Tony shot back, trying to redeem himself. "City slickers would never be able to tell the difference between the tribesmen of the Mamu, the Ngadjon, the Yidinji, the Jidabal and Barbarum tribes," he boasted, in an effort to impress her.

That one was a winner and she conceded it by grabbing his arm just below the shoulder and pulling him towards her. She nestled against his shoulder giggling.

"That is so absurd Tony ... stop it!" she insisted as she looked up at him.

Then he kissed her. She could feel herself melting in that silly man's arms and she wanted that moment to last forever. What was it about that boy that seemed so different? She had a whole life ahead of her and she had only been away from home for a year. There was a wide world out there that she had yet to see and he was getting in the way of all that.

Suddenly, Tony stood up and threw her over his shoulder. She was so taken aback, she was unsure how to protest.

"Tony, put me down this minute!" she insisted.

"Not until I've paid the bill." He shuffled around in his pocket for his wallet with one hand, opened it and approached the woman on the till. "How much, miss?" he asked. "I'm taking this girl home until she learns to behave in public."

Outside on the footpath, two long-haired girls in long white smocks were selling yellow jonquils on long green stems. He paid for a bunch and then gently put Cara down, got down on one knee and offered her the flowers from his outstretched hands.

"Please forgive me," he begged.

She looked at him for one moment with a look that Granny Reynolds had perfected for miscreant children and then accepted the flowers. She placed them against her breast and leaned forward to kiss him on the lips.

Tony could feel a wobble in his knees as he tried to stand up. He nipped one of the flowers off its stem and as he rose, he tucked it into her headband. An assembled crowd applauded as a group of Hare Krishna rattled their sand-shakers and started chanting in the background. Tony felt it was a good start and he simply could not believe his luck.

The main event that year on the protest calendar, which was the main reason for Tony's visit to Sydney, was American President Lyndon B. Johnson's visit from October 20–23, 1966. It was a thank-you visit for Australia's support for the war in Vietnam and one million people had lined the streets of Sydney for a glimpse of the president. While the NSW Premier, Robert Askin, urged Sydneysiders to "Make Sydney gay for LBJ" and chant "All the way with LBJ", the anti-Vietnam protesters lay down on the road all along the route to the state reception at the Art Gallery of NSW. Their aim was to "get in the way of LBJ". It was so successful, the presidential motorcade had to be diverted and ended up finishing the journey at high speed. Student intelligence reported that Askin was so frustrated and humiliated that he actually gave the order to his driver to "run the bastards over".

Tony and Cara were there among the throng carrying scores of placards denouncing the war in Vietnam. As the crowds cheered with "All the way with LBJ", his band of protesters chanted "Hey, Hey, LBJ. How many kids did you kill today?"

Hundreds of protesters including Tony and Cara were detained for the duration of President Johnson's stay in Sydney. Tony had been struck on the head with a police baton and was bleeding profusely. An orderly at the police station dressed the wound to stem the bleeding as Cara kept shouting "police brutality!" to the assembled journalists. Tony felt he had earned every right to exact vengeance from the "establishment" for the assault.

The events in Sydney reverberated across Australia. In Melbourne, Johnson's limousine was splashed with red and green paint. In Canberra and Brisbane, the protesters turned out in force as well. There was an air of seething discontent that was building up around the president's visit. The papers tried in vain to turn the tide of public support by publishing his 1942 near-death experience while on a routine flight in Australia. During World War II, the then US Navy commander and congressman, LBJ, was visiting US forces in North Queensland from New Guinea. His pilot became disoriented, was lost and was running out of fuel. He was forced into an emergency landing at Carinsbrooke Station in Western Queensland. The story made the front page of the Townsville Daily Bulletin, but was buried deep in the folds of all the other Australian newspapers.

Tony and Cara were released without charge the same evening of the president's visit to Sydney. Outside, they met a young French hippie couple who offered them a lift back to the Cross. The couple had just returned from a jaunt up the east coast of Australia and a two-month stay in a hippie commune at Holloways Beach, north of Cairns. The Holloways Beach commune was the first major regional counter-cultural outpost in Australia. After infusing Cara and Tony with tales of the most incredible events and people they had met throughout the whole journey, the French couple convinced them it was a journey they had to make.

They were due to return to Paris at the end of the week and they were looking for someone to purchase their old VW Kombi. It was a 1957 "splittie" or split-screen Volkswagen bus, which had such wide seats that it could accommodate up to eleven people in those days of no seatbelts. The dashboard had one gauge for fuel and two buttons; one for lights and one for wipers. The motor was in the back with a small window in the hatch for a rear view.

The real charm of those hippie vehicles was in the artwork. The rear of this particular vehicle had a pair of eyes; one a bright blue and sparkling and the other all bloodshot. Just above the rear bumper bar was a giant mauve set of smiling lips. The left side of the vehicle was sequenced with a series of flames, a solitary forest tree, an oversized starfish on an undersized beach, followed by a plumped up rainbow the full height of the vehicle. The other side featured flowers representing the earth, and stars and planets representing the sky. There was an "Om" symbol on one of the doors and a peace symbol on the other. The front had a swirl of multi-coloured streaks emanating from the front bumper bar, with two eyes showing grit and determination on either side and just beneath the headlights. "Peace", "Love", "Je t'aime" and "Ti amo" were written on the four side window panels. A huge roof rack held an esky, a spare tyre, an easy chair, a gas bottle, a water container and some camping gear. This vehicle was in a class of its own and needed a new owner who would love and care for it just like the French couple had. It did occur to Tony how cool it would have been to rock up back in Brisbane in such a classic wagon but he did not have the means to purchase it. Cara thought about it too. She could afford it, but was not so sure she had a need for such a vehicle. The French couple insisted they should give their vehicle a home and that Tony and Cara could have her cheaply. The final price was nothing short of a giveaway, but the French couple were happy to part with it at that price. Tony and Cara agreed to drive them to the airport at the end of the week, when they would give them the money in exchange for the car.

After the French couple left that evening, Tony and Cara found themselves with the dilemma about who was to take possession of the van. Cara had a job in Sydney and she couldn't see herself going anywhere anytime soon. Tony was studying at university in Brisbane. His exams were in two weeks so he couldn't see himself going anywhere anytime soon either.

"How about we just pack up and hit the road and retrace the French couple's journey up north to Holloways Beach? Jack Kerouac, the American Beat novelist, talked about a similar road journey he undertook and documented in his book *On the Road*. We could do it too," Tony ventured.

"Are you mental Tony?" she retorted with a roll of her eyes. "What about my job? What about your studies? We can't just up and leave. We've only known each other for … never."

"We could go up to Brisbane. I could sit for my exams then take a couple of years off and we can trip around Australia in '*Betsy*' here."

That was that, the Kombi now had a name. Cara just looked him in the eye for a moment and then gave him the answer he hoped to hear. "Okay, I'm in." That was how zany and spontaneous Cara proved she could be.

They packed Cara's possessions into *Betsy* and hit the open road the day after the French couple left. On the way to Brisbane, Tony dropped a bombshell.

"I've decided I'm not sitting for my exams, Cara. When we get to Brisbane, I'll pack up my gear and we just keep going."

"Tony, you must be out of your mind. Why drop out now when you could take your exams and defer your studies?"

"Cara, the truth is, next year I will be twenty years old. I will have to register for National Service. If my birth date is drawn in the ballot, I'm gone for two years in the regular army with the possibility of a further three years part-time in the Army Reserve. I'll be out there with all those other poor suckers in Vietnam. I'd rather take some time out now and follow my dreams before that time comes. My dream is to share this journey with you, whatever the price. My chance is right here and now. I don't want to have to wait for the outcome of the ballot to pursue my destiny."

Cara reached towards her shoulder to take his hand which was resting there.

"Let's do it then," she responded quietly, as she shuffled up closer to him and placed her head on his shoulder. She too was supposed to be pursuing adventure and Tony was the man she wanted to share it with.

Whereas urban-based hippies imbibed in manufactured drugs like LSD, hippies up north cultivated drugs like marijuana and "magic mushrooms". The Holloways Beach hippies were a mixture of people in their early twenties and older people who were ex-professionals and artists. The older ones generally had savings from previous working lives and took on extra jobs labouring in the community to support their lifestyle which was based on sustainability and simplicity. They preferred to be called "hairies" because the only element they had in common with the hippies was that they had long hair down to their buttocks. They were more bohemian than hippie. Conversely, hippies were younger teenager drop-outs who wanted to indulge in the more hedonistic practices of drinking, drug-taking and free love, preferring to live off welfare and the generosity of others in the commune. There was therefore this divide within the so-called hippie community.

Cara and Tony left Holloways Beach as the older "hairies" were not particularly friendly. They had become staid and more conditioned to local council demands and by-laws. The "hairies" even monopolised the other two communes of Titanic and Rosebud.

The couple decided to move to the fertile tropical forests of Kuranda on the range west of Cairns. Kuranda commune also boasted an authentic middle-aged Buddhist monk complete with shaved head and resplendent in his orange robe. He had exchanged the lifestyle of his prominent industrial family with all its trappings for a life of meditation and prayer. He was heralded as a guru and all of the communes between Kuranda and northern New South Wales were graced with his presence from time to time. He also made yearly pilgrimages to Asia ostensibly to enhance his knowledge of the faith. Teenagers flocked to the Kuranda commune, and in time, whole groups, including young children, lived together in substandard lean-to shelters without hot water or sanitation services. It was fast becoming the hub of drug activity in the north. Anything and everything was beginning to happen for people who wanted to discover the inner realms of the self through taking drugs. Some even smoked dried toad skins which were naturally infused with LSD. Hallucinogenic mushrooms were cooked in omelettes and hippies often overdosed on them because they did not realise their potency.

Tony was also "poisoned" in an overdose of a particular mushroom whose effect came on with such severity that he had to be rushed to the Mareeba Hospital for treatment. First, he started vomiting until he was dry retching. In hospital, it felt as though he had huge boils all over his body and as he became delirious, he could see himself swinging on a trapeze miles up in the stratosphere. Colourful fireworks were exploding all around him, and despite all his efforts, he had no strength to return to Earth. Cara was with him in a separate bed in the hospital but fortunately she had only taken a small amount. She was nowhere near as spaced out as he was. She heard one of the nurses call out "Cardiac irregularity here, Sister" while monitoring Tony's condition, which prompted other nurses to come running. She tried to determine what was going on but the bed had been screened off. It was fortunate he had vomited up most of the mushrooms, otherwise they would have had to pump out his stomach.

After the poisoning scare, Cara and Tony decided it was time to move on. They decided to go and visit Cara's family in Mowbray, but the sight of *Betsy* alone was enough to send the whole family into shock, including Granny Reynolds who kept insisting they call the police to arrest "this child molester" who had obviously abducted her granddaughter against her will. Tony's own family in Babinda had already disowned him for abandoning his studies at the university. They decided to stay away from the Far North completely and instead travelled south to the Whitsundays group of islands off the coast at Proserpine. There, as he had reached twenty years of age, Tony registered for National Service and waited for the ballot and the dreaded letter that would determine his destiny for the next two years at least.

Cara got a job as a barmaid at one of the local pubs while Tony managed to get work as a deckhand on the island ferry. Cara fell pregnant and when they had saved enough money, they decided to return to Brisbane. They parked *Betsy* at the Eight Mile Plains Caravan Park and Tony immediately went looking for more permanent work. There was a lot of work to be had for anyone who had completed their university entrance examinations, and Tony applied for a position as a clerk in the Commonwealth Bank. Within a week he was appointed as a clerk to the New Farm branch of the Commonwealth Bank. His mail was still being forwarded from their Proserpine address to the Central Post Office in Queen Street, and once a week, Tony would call in to collect any mail. When the official letter arrived from the Department of Labour and National Service, he dreaded the thought of opening it, for Cara and the baby's sake. He had not done the right thing by her. They were still not married. If the letter revealed that he had been called up, then she would be left on her own with the baby. Of course he would support her, but she had no family to go back to.

The realisation of the possibility of drastic consequences was too immense to contemplate. He went across to the Shrine of Remembrance in Anzac Square where a flock of pigeons suddenly leapt towards the sky as if to make way for this man with a heavy heart. There, beside the Eternal Flame, he would open the letter. He figured if he was going to be called up, he would want to find out in a place that honoured those who had done it before him and for him in the two world wars and the more recent conflicts in Korea, Borneo and Vietnam. He promised himself that whatever the outcome in the letter, he would immediately marry Cara. He carefully opened the letter and hurriedly scanned the contents. The hungry flickering Eternal Flame in the background seemed to want to consume the letter as he held it in front of him. It seemed to lick at the edges of the notice surrounding it with flame, but the flame did not claim it this time. It withdrew as Tony came to the realisation that his birth date had not been drawn.

Cara was relieved when he told her he had not been called up and he watched as the tears welled up in her eyes. The flood of tears that followed when he offered her the diamond ring brought tears to his eyes as well and he could not believe he had been so selfish not to have proposed to her a long time ago. He realised then and there what an incredible strength and courage this girl had and he loved her dearly for it. They would be married and he would provide a house and a future for his new bride and unborn child. He would stop indulging in self gratification and substitute it with the pursuit of happiness with his new family.

He was prepared to do anything except give up his stand against the war in Vietnam. Now that he had not been called up, he was determined to do his part in the war in Vietnam another way. He would do his part by fighting to bring Australians back from the war and working to stop conscription. He wanted all the diggers to be able to come home to their families and enjoy a family of their own. Above all, he promised himself he would fight for the rights of every returned soldier, because the wars that were supposed to end all wars had failed them and he feared this war was going to be no different.

Chapter 6

After more than two months of operations, infections, antibiotics, physiotherapy, psychotherapy, loneliness, despair, nightmares, disappointment, depression and abandonment, Manfred was finally cleared for release from hospital.

The loneliness was from being away from family and friends. He despaired about his future in the workforce now that he was handicapped. Then, there were the continuous nightmares about his past. He was depressed about the attitude of the nation towards returned soldiers and disappointed about the standard of the rehabilitation at the hospital. Above all, his sense of abandonment was total and he could not come to terms with it. Nevertheless, this would all be overshadowed by what he saw as the most anticipated moment in his life; his impending marriage to his sweetheart Angel. All he wanted was to be with her again and he convinced himself that his love for her would sweep the past away and he would be able to rebuild his life. What he feared was that ultimately his greatest enemy was going to be himself. Why had he withheld so much information from his psychotherapist? Was he too proud to admit that he needed help? Was his dislike for whingers and "wusses" going to be to his own detriment? His image had always been important to him and he couldn't disappoint his family and his mates by admitting that the war had got the better of him; that he was a broken man. He considered that he had no choice but to tough it out.

It was April 1, 1970 and he had three days to get back to North Queensland and get himself to the church on time. He would still be officially in the army for two of those days, as his discharge date had been set for April 3. His only possession was his army uniform which had come over with him from Vietnam. He had no money or access to money, as any paperwork relating to his discharge was to be effected from his discharge date, which was in two days' time. He had phoned his mother from hospital and she had to organise for the local newsagent to issue a plane ticket for him to fly back to Cairns.

He went out to the road on crutches and was able to hitch a ride on a garbage truck which was in transit to the army barracks at Enoggera. Because they had not completed his discharge papers at the hospital, the personnel at the army barracks gave no support other than a ride to the airport, . On board the commercial flight to Cairns he hoped someone would be there to meet him and no placard wielding protesters. It was early afternoon and as he disembarked and felt the warmth of the North Queensland sun, the first thing he thought of was Vietnam. He thought coming home would be uplifting but strangely with the heat and the smells of the tropical vegetation, it was the opposite and he found it hard to compose himself. He looked around hoping not to see anyone he knew so he wouldn't have to make conversation or engage in small talk about where he had been, what he had done, his wounds or his plans for the future. Fortunately, his mother, still in her Red Cross nurse's outfit, was there to pick him up in the family car, and as they pulled out of the car park, his sense of relief was like being evacuated from a skirmish by helicopter. This confirmed for him that the problems in his mind were not going away. He could feel a cold sweat breaking out all over his body. He tried to focus on positives and felt himself drawing strength from the mere presence of his mother beside him.

It was an inexplicable feeling having her alone to himself. There would be plenty of time for Angel. That journey home was a special time for him and he gleaned a joy from it that he had not known since he was a child. His precious mum had always given her all and asked for nothing in return. He reminded her of that, because he wanted her to know how he felt.

"Oh Manfred, if only you knew how much I have asked for in the last two years," she confessed. "It was only one thing, but I asked for it every day, on my knees in prayer; that God would bring you back safe to us."

That brought tears to her eyes and he cried invisible tears from the heart. She had hundreds of things to tell him on the way home; about Wilfred and Grandma and everything that had happened in the last two years in Babinda. She even told him about the strange interview from army intelligence about her birthplace of Vladivostok.

"They certainly are thorough when it comes to matters of national security," she observed.

"Yeah, pity you had to hear from the Salvation Army that I had been wounded in Vietnam," he said.

"Yes ... and it was the Salvation Army also that sent all of your gear back from over there. I would have thought the army would have organised that."

Angel and the rest of the family were there to welcome him home, and for a brief moment, he imagined he had never left. But that feeling was fleeting as he could not pretend that nothing had changed. He had nothing in common anymore with all his old mates at home. He had found new mates in his comrades in arms, and together they had stared death in the face. Manfred knew he had to leave Babinda, his friends and even his family. After his wedding, he would ease himself out of that cocoon of suspended animation all around him and go in search of another life.

He glanced through the wedding list and was surprised to see so many of his old mates on it. There were mates from his school days, work mates from the cane farm and the mill, his shooting and fishing mates, and drinking mates from down at the pub. A second glance confirmed that his childhood mate Tony D'Italia was not on the list. Tony had left Babinda five years before and they had not heard from him since. If Angel had thought about it, she could have tried to get Tony's address from his parents who still had the farm at Happy Valley. He had no way of knowing that Tony D'Italia had married a Port Douglas girl two and a half years earlier and already had two children. The eldest was a girl, Linda, and the baby was a boy, also named Manfred. If only he had known that Tony and Cara were only a stone's throw from him at Graceville throughout the whole period of his ordeal at 1 Military Hospital.

* * *

At the time Manfred and Angel were married, Tony had become entrenched in his job at the bank and had finally been promoted to teller. His job at the bank involved taking and giving out money to clients, issuing cheques and receiving cheques, counting coin and answering client queries. In the mornings, he helped with posting the ledgers, and after the bank closed he would balance the cash holdings and spend any extra time calculating interest on savings accounts. It was only a small branch with a bank manager, accountant and two juniors who were fifteen years old and did the menial chores like exchanging cheques with other banks, running errands, calculating interest and posting letters. If it became too busy, the accountant would help out as a second teller.

Hodges, the accountant, was an arrogant private person who didn't see eye to eye with Tony. He followed AFL and became upset when Tony referred to it as "aerial ping-pong". He also insisted that "football" was played with a round ball despite Tony explaining to him that the round ball was for a game called "netball" that girls played. Hodges had no sense of humour. Soon, Hodges began having a dig at Tony about his political activities on weekends and the street marches and protests in which Tony participated. Tony ignored his taunts and accepted that Hodges was entitled to his own point of view providing he didn't overstep the mark.

His major fault was that he was a bully. He loved making the lives of the two juniors a living hell and they were petrified of him. Tony began suggesting to the two juniors that providing they did their work, they did not have to suffer the insults and degrading language Hodges was dishing out to them. Hodges must have sensed the mutiny in the ranks and came down heavier on young Peter and especially Jill. He would hang over her like a vulture while she was calculating interest and pounce on her the moment she made an error. He sometimes brought her to tears with his nastiness. Tony and the two juniors each had to finish calculating interest on a quota of fifty ledgers a day. In an attempt to alleviate the stress on the two juniors, he finished his quota quickly then helped Peter and Jill with their quotas. The accountant raised his eyebrows and on the third day summoned Tony to his office.

"Why are you helping the clerks with their quotas when you should be checking your own ledgers to make sure you have not made any errors?"

"I have checked my ledgers and there are no errors," Tony assured him.

"Well, check them again."

"I can assure you there are no errors, but if you wish to check them, then I would be prepared to do another full quota in my own time for every error you find, to make up for it. I would rather spend my time helping Peter and Jill who could do with a bit of support at the moment."

"What sort of a smart-arse comment is that, D'Italia? If you don't want to keep checking your ledgers, then pretend to be checking them. I don't want you helping those two juniors."

Tony just stood there,

"That's all; you can go now," Hodges said, dismissing him.

Tony went straight over to Jill, sat down and kept helping her with her ledgers. He could feel Hodges creeping up on him like a hyena.

"D'Italia, if you are not prepared to do what you're told, then maybe you should leave the bank and get a job in a fish shop," Hodges growled.

"I beg your pardon?" Tony retorted in a measured tone.

"Why don't you get a job in a fish shop or a fruit shop like the rest of your mob?" Hodges repeated.

"Oh, I see. Can we discuss this matter further in your office?"

Hodges turned on his heel and strutted into his office and Tony followed him in, and swung his head around and winked at Peter and Jill.

"Hodges ..." Tony began, "I figure you're about thirteen stone in weight. I'm nine and a half stone in weight. If you ever talk to me like that again or threaten me in any way, or even suggest anything about 'my mob', I will take you out the back and give you the bloody hiding of your life. If you think I'm kidding, let's do it now. You and me ... out the back ... now!"

Hodges looked up at Tony who punched his thumb towards the door and glared at him. He shrivelled back into his chair and was lost for words.

Tony's eyes flashed wide and he slammed the palm of his hand on the desk, causing Hodges to shrink back. "In fact, if you've got something to say to me in future, go in and ask the manager to come out and tell me. Tell him you are having trouble handling your own staff."

Hodges gaped without saying a word. Tony cast a look of disdain towards him, turned around and walked back into the front office. Jill and Peter stared up at him with wide eyes and expansive grins. Tony returned a cheeky smile, realising that they appreciated him for putting his job on the line for them. Hodges had been humiliated into submission and he never gave them any trouble from then on.

On the more serious issues regarding forcing the withdrawal of Australian and foreign troops from Vietnam and repealing the National Service Act of 1964, a lot of progress had been made and a lot of organisational matters had been initiated. Tony had worked his way up the line to Queensland state representative for the Vietnam Moratorium Campaign (VMC) that Jim Cairns MHR had initiated at the national level and was its president. Church groups, trade unions, students, pacifists, socialists, communists, anti-war groups, professionals and politicians were all campaigning for change.

On November 15, 1969, Tony was astounded to find out that the Americans had held a massive Moratorium March on Washington, D.C. which attracted 500,000 demonstrators against the war in Vietnam. Pete Seger sang John Lennon's new song *Give Peace a Chance*, addressing President Nixon and Vice-President Agnew between the choruses. The VMC set three Vietnam Moratorium dates for Australia soon after the great success in America. Jim Cairns led the first on May 8 and 9, 1970. In Melbourne, the moratorium drew a crowd of 100,000 marchers with 200,000 participating across Australia. The crowds again came out in force on September 18 with 200 people arrested in Sydney. Tony had been appointed the Queensland representative on the National Co-ordinating Committee and was proud to have been a part of putting so many people onto the streets across Australia who supported bringing the boys home from Vietnam.

He believed that the moratorium marches had proved to be a great victory for participatory democracy and the idea of people power. What he had not realised was that the pendulum had swung too far and was continuing on a trajectory that was leading to the vilification of Vietnam War veterans, just as had occurred in America. The Moratorium Movement had succeeded in stopping the war and bringing the diggers home but had that success provided the justification and the opportunity for the public to place the blame for the war on the shoulders of the veterans and to vent their frustration on them? If that was so, and Tony was conscious of the fact that it was heading that way, then he had to decide if he wanted to be a part of society's abrogation of responsibility for the war. Had the whole rationale behind the protests gone awry and was it about to self-implode and take those veterans down with it? He found himself wrestling with that dilemma.

Chapter 7

Manfred was trying to get on with the business of living and re-establishing his working life in North Queensland. He also had to adjust to the "politics of difference" that was becoming a part of his new reality. As a Vietnam vet, he was perceived as different from the rest of mainstream society. He had been to war and he was a "killer" as far as they were concerned, whether he had killed someone or not. That was the difference from the perception that had been built up of veterans from other wars, who were perceived as heroes. This new reality was constructed in parallel with what was happening overseas, especially America, and perpetuated throughout society by the media.

Manfred went to Vietnam in the prime of his youth as a fit self-assured young man and with enough spark in him to make him popular without getting into trouble. He had a career, was relatively well-off financially, had great mates and was socially well adjusted. On his return two years later, his mates were able to maintain a view of life that was basically the same as when he had left them, but his attitudes, values, beliefs and even his faith had altered markedly. He was unfit, unhealthy, unhappy, physically handicapped and had developed a low self-esteem. He was not sure about who his mates were, and his social standing was bordering on outcast. He had no career and was worse off financially than when he left. In his first year of National Service, Manfred earned about half the salary he earned at Babinda Mill. In his second year, his tax-free salary with all the allowances including his war zone allowance only equalled what he received when he first left the mill two years before. He had no doubt why Gough Whitlam, himself an RAAF navigator in World War II, argued that conscription had been used to keep down the pay and conditions of regular defence personnel. Nashos were "cheap to keep" compared to regulars and were naive enough not to complain, yet they did the same job. Above all, they were young and carefree and gullible within every shade of meaning of the word; they were more credulous, trusting, impressionable, unsuspecting, unwary, ingenuous, immature and ultimately easier to control.

Fresh out of their teenage years, these twenty-year-olds had no immediate "baggage" like a wife and children to whom the government might be held responsible and accountable if these men died. The lasting memory of so many diggers was miniscule; a photo, some fragments of letters home, a name on a war memorial somewhere, a tree planted in their honour or, at best, a mention in despatches for some act of heroism or bravery. Those who returned could only hope that the government and the people who had sent them to war would acknowledge and appreciate their sacrifice.

What diggers like Manfred saw, what they had to do to survive, what they endured and compartmentalised was embedded in their psyche during their engagement with the enemy. What nobody realised and what society refused to accept was that in time those experiences often returned as demons that were soul destroying and irreversibly traumatic. Manfred, like so many other diggers he knew, said he finally understood the difficulties refugees had re-settling in another society. That was how he saw himself as he tried to re-engage with the old norms of life-long work, marriage and children, and his psychological wellbeing deteriorated as a consequence. Those difficulties festered just beneath the skin and in his mind, before becoming painful and eventually breaking out. They manifested themselves as nightmares and were triggered by everyday things that were otherwise harmless. Things like the sound of a helicopter became a helicopter gunship that was coming in with all guns blazing to support soldiers on the tipping point of defeat and death. Choppers usually meant casualties and came on the scene to "dust off" their wounded comrades. Their sound was synonymous with chaos and destruction. The smell of a burning match became the smell of gunpowder. A balloon bursting at a child's birthday party became a sniper's bullet buzzing past their ear. There were enough daily reminders out there for every scenario in Vietnam to be revisited again and again.

At first, a drink or two and then a drink or twenty-two did the trick to help ease the pain of remembering. Then prescriptions helped to stem the pain that never went away. Nothing was prescribed to alleviate the suffering of the families, wives and children who bore the brunt of that diggers' disease. After he was married, Manfred looked for work in Cairns where Angel was working as a hairdresser. He applied for a couple of jobs and was unsuccessful. By the time he had applied for a further three jobs unsuccessfully, he began to wonder what he was doing wrong. Every time he filled out the mandatory job application forms, the inevitable "Vietnam Vet eh?" comment, or a variation of it, was mumbled. Some asked whether he had killed anyone over there and one wanted to know whether he had anything to do with the My Lai massacre. Didn't the ignoramus know that the soldiers involved in the My Lai massacre were American? Did he look or talk like an American? Pisshead! Manfred actually asked him those two questions and called him exactly that. The guy had the hide to pretend he was offended.

Then Manfred saw an advertisement for a job as foreman with ammonia compressor and general machine maintenance qualifications at the Northern Australian Brewery in Cairns. He had always wanted to work in a brewery; it seemed such a privileged position for a person who enjoyed a beer as much as he did. When he went to ask for an application form, he saw that the person behind the window at the administration counter was old Babinda boy Max Brentwell.

Max was about two years older than Manfred. He was also the pay clerk at the brewery which employed about forty workers, and was given the job of assessing the applications. Manfred got the job, entirely on the strength of his application Max assured him.

Manfred offered to buy him a beer but Max winked and smiled at him. "Why buy a book when you can join the library? Come on up to the first floor. It's free sample time in about ten minutes and you need to get familiar with the quality control processes they have in place here at Northern Australian Breweries."

They drank on late into the evening, and throughout the whole time Max never asked one question about Vietnam. Mostly, they talked about Babinda, because they had both shared similar experiences; the same reason most diggers only talked about war to other diggers.

After a year at the brewery, Manfred felt it was time to move on. He had heard a lot about the hippies at Kuranda and the way those guys just bought a van and headed off in one direction and didn't stop until they felt it was time to stop. The idea of getting out onto the open road really appealed to him. He and Angel had not seen anything of Australia together, apart from that week in Sydney during his R and R. It would also give him the chance to get away from everyone he knew. He wanted to start afresh, find new friends and try different jobs. He thought it would be a good way to help him to forget if he became involved with new places and was alone with Angel as his soul mate. Angel was thrilled and they bought a caravan and hitched it up to a truck and headed straight for Mildura. It was January 1971 and the fruit picking season was about to get into full swing.

They answered to nobody on the road and it was the first time that Manfred had felt totally relaxed since his return from Vietnam. He still had pain, but it was just pain from his war injuries. His head was in a good space and he knew he could live with his injuries as long as Angel was there with him. Sometimes he couldn't believe how lucky he was to have her and he chided himself for ever doubting her that time before he was to meet her in Sydney on his R and R. The trouble had to be just in his head as she had never expressed having had a problem with him. He had the problem with himself and having acknowledged that, all he had to do was come to terms with it.

Grape picking in Mildura was just what Manfred needed to help get him fit again. His injuries reminded him that it was going to take time but it felt great to be out in the sun in the open air among the vines and it reminded him of his labouring days on the cane fields around Babinda and the tobacco fields around Mareeba. There were mostly itinerant labourers on these farms too. Some were illegal immigrants like the Greeks and the Yugoslavs who came over as cabin boys on tourist ships from Europe and then jumped ship in Australia. Each one had a story to tell and each one was running away from something. The Greeks were running away from poverty, the Yugoslavs were running away from the dictator Tito, the Spaniards from Franco. They all wanted to come to Australia, just like Tony D'Italia's father who had run away from Benito Mussolini, and Manfred's grandparents who wanted to escape war torn Germany. They were people who took everything at face value, who didn't judge others and who treated others like they wanted to be treated themselves; with respect.

Manfred soon realised that there were still challenges out there in the workplace. His flair with anything mechanical had him scratching his head about the painstaking process of stopping stalk rot on the grape vines using a potash treatment while they were being dried on racks. Before the season was finished, he had worked out a way to mechanise the treatment plant using electric motors, which gave him immense satisfaction. After the grape-picking season was over, he and Angel heard about Labor Opposition leader Gough Whitlam's plans to decentralise industries away from the major coastal cities. Albury-Wodonga on the Murray River was mooted as the site for an ambitious proposal to create a huge inland city with more than 300,000 people.

If Labor came to power at the next election, Whitlam promised Federal Government incentives to workers who were prepared to resettle and work in Albury-Wodonga. This was the place where Manfred and Angel wanted to start a new life. They would have children there and the family would grow together with the new city.

It was 1972 and Manfred secured a highly paid job, with opportunities for plenty of overtime, as a mechanical fitter with the firm of Borg Warner that manufactured automatic transmissions for Mercedes, BMW, Peugeot, Renault and Chrysler Valiant. Prime Minister Whitlam was true to his promise and offered generous incentives to industry to move to Albury-Wodonga after he won the election. In 1973, Manfred and Angel still had no children but Manfred had progressed to the position of foreman at Borg Warner on the generous salary of $8500 a year.

The war in Vietnam had already been relegated to history since Australia's withdrawal. Communist leader Ho Chi Minh's dream to unify North and South Vietnam was fulfilled despite his death before the war ended. So many lives were lost and many more lives were ruined as a consequence of two conflicting ideologies. Already, Manfred was beginning to wonder whether the allied effort amounted to something or whether it was all for nought. He asked himself whether anyone was any better off as a result of it, and how many were beginning to feel they were better off dead.

* * *

Throughout his time at the bank, Tony was having doubts as well. He had difficulty achieving much job satisfaction.

The work was monotonous and routine, and prospects in the profession were all long-term. He had no particular interest in any opportunities the bank had to offer and was fortunate that much of his time was taken up with his political pursuits, which gave him a purpose that was meaningful.

Any other spare time he had was spent writing poetry. He derived a lot of joy from that and from a book he had been writing on and off about his love affair with Cara and their experiences on the road as hippies. It was titled Daintree Girl. He would read a portion of the book to the family every few nights after dinner just before Linda and Manfred were put to bed.

Cara would cuddle up to him and peek over his arm to sneak a look at the text. Occasionally, she would correct some small statement of event, place or time, but other than that, she would just give him a slight squeeze to let him know she was enjoying the memory of it. He would also get the occasional poke if she thought he was getting too cheeky. Little Linda usually giggled through most of it and was more cognisant of any of her mother's reactions than anything in the story. As for Manfred, a few bubbles and the occasional burp were his only responses to his father's deep voice.

"I love *Betsy*, Daddy," Linda said trying to get some attention. "Can we play in her after you come home from work tomorrow night?"

"Of course, darling," he assured her. "One day, Mummy and I are going to take you and Manfred up to the Daintree Country where Mummy comes from," he promised.

"In *Betsy*?" Her eyes lit up.

"Yep, in *Betsy*," he confirmed. "That's why we have kept her in tip-top condition, locked up in the garage out the back."

As it panned out, there were greater plans afoot. Around that time, Tony had been reading about how the Australian Government, under the auspices of the United Nations Security Council, was commissioned to set up a framework to prepare Papua and New Guinea for self-government and independence. The country was becoming a major focus for all Australians. The media was beginning to report on many significant events involving both countries. During World War II Japanese forces occupied much of New Guinea, including the islands of Bougainville and New Britain. It was the scene of many a hard-fought battle between the Australians with their American allies and the Japanese Imperial Forces.

The islands of Bougainville and New Britain fell easily to the Japanese, and for the first time, the shores of northern Australia were threatened by the advance of the "yellow peril". The Japanese established a major base at Rabaul in 1942 but the US Navy thwarted their attempt at a naval assault on the capital Port Moresby in the Battle of the Coral Sea. The newspaper stories glorified the diggers' heroic deeds when the Japanese attempted a land invasion of Port Moresby through the Owen Stanley Ranges via the inhospitable leech infested and malaria ridden Kokoda Trail. It was on that track that the indigenous "Fuzzy Wuzzy Angels" helped save the lives of many Australian soldiers. All this had happened before Tony was born and he enjoyed the history lesson he was getting from the articles he was reading on the topic.

Tony found himself talking to his colleagues about the heroism of the 39th Battalion comprising 500 diggers and a few mainly Australian Reserve battalions and how they held over 6000 Japanese at bay along that track. Mostly young and largely untrained, the Australians suffered heavy casualties while maintaining a courageous rearguard action to halt the Japanese advance. With reinforcements from the Second Australian Imperial Force, those diggers were eventually able to defeat the Japanese including at the Battle of Milne Bay. Tony had heard all about the holocaust with the Jews but it was only from those daily newspaper reports that he was beginning to hear about the horrendous and barbaric atrocities committed by the Japanese, where Australian soldiers and citizens were executed on the beaches by decapitation and nurses, missionaries and locals were all subjected to sadistic Japanese cruelty.

Under the command of US General Douglas Macarthur and Australian General Thomas Blamey, the bitter fighting continued until the Japanese surrendered in 1945. He was surprised at the scale of the conflict when he found that more than 200,000 Japanese soldiers, sailors and airmen perished during the New Guinea campaign, while the Australian and American forces each lost about 7000 service personnel in that conflict.

After the war, Papua and New Guinea returned to the administration of the Australian government. In the early seventies, the Department of External Territories supervised the establishment of a judicial system, a public service and a system of local government. Scores of Australians were seconded from the Australian Public Service to help effect the changes. Others were trained as teachers and local government officers at the Australian School of Pacific Administration (ASOPA) at Mosman Junction, Sydney. Indigenous participation and training were principal goals, with those Australian public servants mainly employed as intermediaries and mentors. Consequently, emphasis was placed on training Australians to work in cross-cultural situations. They were provided with the sociological and anthropological knowledge and skills required to bring a predominantly primitive culture into the modern world as quickly as possible. The timetable had already been set. PNG was to become self-governing in 1973, and independence was to be achieved by 1975, under Michael Somare, a Sepik national, as Chief Minister.

Tony saw an opportunity to re-launch his career and applied to be admitted to a secondary school teacher training course at ASOPA commencing in 1971. The pay was quite lucrative and tax-free in Papua New Guinea. Departmental accommodation was also provided, and employees were entitled to return airfares to the place of recruitment every year paid by the Education Department in Konedobu, Port Moresby. At the end of the four-year contract, employees gained return airfares as well as transportation of their household effects to the place of recruitment. The whole package was almost double that of a teacher in Australia so competition for the positions was frenetic.

Tony was granted an interview in Brisbane. He knew that to have a chance, he would have to perform well in the interview, as well as have something different from what the other applicants had to offer. Because he would be trained to teach English as a second language, he figured that he needed to show some quality above and beyond matriculation English qualifications. He decided to bring along a spare copy of his completed book Daintree Girl and argued that the book showed he had a love of literature, which went beyond just qualifications. Also, he pointed out that in completing such a task, it showed he was committed and that he was capable of finishing things he had started.

The interviewer was impressed and asked if he could borrow the book to read. Tony left the interview confident he had a reasonable chance of being granted the scholarship.

The interview had been in November 1970 and he was notified that he was successful and his training would start in late January the following year and would last for two years. Cara was stoked in that she was going back to Sydney, the old haunt that had changed her life so dramatically. Tony was being paid to study by the Australian Staffing Assistance Group, a subsidiary of the Department of Australian Territories, and he looked forward to the opportunity of an extended stay in Sydney. *Betsy* was back on the road again.

ASOPA was on the site of the HMAS Penguin Naval Base in Military Road at Mosman Junction, Sydney. The school overlooked Sydney Harbour with its pristine waters and was perched on a hill above magnificent rock platforms. Tony and Cara and the two children settled into a unit in Balgowlah Road, Balgowlah, opposite the Manly Golf Club, a twenty minute drive from the school.

Whatever the selection criteria for the trainee teachers, it delivered a motley crew from incredibly diverse backgrounds in Australia and Papua and New Guinea. They were the kind of colourful characters Tony felt could teach him a lot as they were intelligent lateral thinkers who showed initiative and a maturity gleaned from their life experiences. Among them were a PNG patrol officer, riot policeman, league front-row forward, bookmaker, shearer, street vendor, paymaster, assembly line worker, beauty consultant, firefighter, singer-songwriter, actress, Hari Krishna convert, two teenage university drop-outs, a refugee artist from Mauritius and a pastor from South Australia. Tony had the least intriguing background of all of them as a bank officer. It confirmed in his mind that it was a good thing he decided to bring his book along to the interview as it was obviously the clincher. Then again, those trainee teachers were to be immersed into a political maelstrom over the next few years, and maybe the selectors considered his Italian background and valued his cross-cultural experience.

As it turned out, Tony's only political foray during the whole two years of his teacher training was to participate in the June 30, 1971 Moratorium March in Sydney. It was the ultimate success of all of his political involvement to date. Hundreds of thousands of people turned out throughout all of the capital cities. The Australian people had spoken with one voice. On November 25, 1971, under Prime Minister William McMahon, Australia ended its combat role in Vietnam. Tony felt that an end to conscription was inevitable and he was pleased with the contribution he had made.

He was ready to forge a career for himself as a teacher and studied hard at ASOPA. His studies in sociology, psychology and anthropology helped give him a better informed understanding of the individual, the group, the community and the society at large. They also gave him an appreciation of other cultures and of the importance of law and religion in any society. He became empowered by an awareness of the role of authority and the existence of a distinct hierarchy within each society. In particular, his studies of "primitive" or "developing" societies proved enlightening. These provided examples of the process of socialisation in its purest form. The ground breaking studies of the Melanesians on Manus Island by anthropologist Margaret Mead, and Professor Bronislaw Malinowski's studies of the Trobriand Islanders inspired him. He became engrossed in a private study of the Siwai people of the South Bougainville district, to put all their theories to the test and they held true.

Even in economics, he could see that the systems among the primitive tribespeople of Papua and New Guinea had been operating successfully for centuries. The Hiri, for example, was a system of seaborne trade whereby the Motu people would trade with the people from the Gulf of Papua around Central Province. They would wait for the south-east trade winds in October and November to carry their fleet of twenty to thirty lakatoi canoes westward, laden with clay pots and shell artefacts. In exchange, the tribes in Central Province would prepare tonnes of sago for the lakatoi to transport back to the Motu villages on the wings of the January north-west monsoons.

When the time came for the teacher graduates to be posted to schools throughout PNG towards the end of 1972, a political imbroglio was unfolding on the island of New Britain. The Mataungan Association, inspired by the outspoken and well educated John Kaputin, was threatening to derail the carefully prepared plans towards PNG self-government and independence over indigenous land rights issues.

The Tolai tribes around Rabaul in East New Britain district were deadlocked in talks with the central administration represented by the District Commissioner Jack Emanuel. The land rights issues had the Tolai Mataungan Association demanding the abolition of the Multi-Racial Local Government Council. The Tolais wanted independence from the central government over land rights and what followed was like the Mau Mau Uprising in East Africa revisited. In a carefully planned rendezvous, the Mataungans were able to lure Jack Emanuel away from his police escort and stab him to death with a World War II Japanese bayonet. The region became a flashpoint and every aspect of diplomacy was employed to expedite a resolution to the dilemma brought on by the murder because of the broader agenda involving self-government and independence. Anticipating a possible bloody massacre of the expatriate population, there was a sudden exodus of Chinese trade store owners, plantation owners, civil servants and business people from Rabaul.

Instead of being posted to places like the swamplands of Kerema, the end-of-the-earth outpost of Vanimo in the Green River district of the West Sepik, or the rugged highland towns of Goroka and Mount Hagen, fourteen of the seventeen graduates of Tony's class were sent to the five secondary schools in the East New Britain district to replace the teachers who had asked to be transferred out because of the danger of violence.

The chosen ASOPA graduates as well as Cara and the two children arrived in Rabaul in the late evening. They decided they would all travel together to the five schools in the one bus. The deserted trade stores were ominous places. Shops had been looted and remnants strewn all over the floors. The streets were empty and the houses were in lockdown. As they approached the outskirts of Rabaul, scores of bush-knife wielding highlanders were returning to town from work on copra plantations. They were all indentured work labourers who were brought in from the highlands to work on the coconut, coffee and cocoa plantations. They included the dreaded Chimbu tribesmen, stocky "stone age" people, and the Kukukuku pygmy people from the Upper Watut area of the highlands who had a propensity for consuming human flesh. "Kukukuku" in the local language meant "wild", "blood thirsty" and "untameable". There were also a large number of the quieter and friendlier Sepik indentured labourers in East New Britain.

The bus continued on along the narrowing road towards Kokopo, and with every pothole, the headlights bounced over the jungle vegetation, seemingly exposing a painted face here, a skulking body behind a tree there, a spear wielding warrior in full battle dress rising out of a ditch on the side of the road or a "duk-duk" tribesman in a grass skirt about to leap out of a tree. They were all imaginary, borne of the fear of the unknown, the pungent smell of the tropical foliage, a touch of xenophobia and the recent history of violence in the area.

Three teachers, all men, alighted at the Kerevat National High School. The pastor, Phil, was from South Australia, while Marty, the oldest member of the group and a patrol officer, was originally from Ballarat and had previous experience in PNG as the first white man to patrol the Green River area. Al, the riot policeman, also had experience in PNG and was originally from Darwin. Two indigenous teachers greeted them and they were asked to locate the expatriate headmaster. Soon three shadows emerged from the gloom.

"Glad to see you guys," was his welcome. "I thought you'd never make it. Want to come in for a beer?"

The three teachers were thrilled but the rest declined as it was late and they still had four schools to visit. The bus driver turned the bus around and headed back towards town. The next stop, Malabunga High School, was about three kilometres off the main road down a narrow jungle track along the Warangoi River. One woman and three men had been posted there – Kellie the teenage university student from Condong in New South Wales, Lance the street vendor from Mackay, Barry the assembly worker from Wedderburn in Victoria, and Jean Desire Harold Louis, the French refugee artist from Mauritius.

The bus then returned to the outskirts of Rabaul to Malaguna Technical College. Christine, the beauty consultant from Murwillumbah in New South Wales, Paul, the rugby league forward from Beagle Bay in Western Australia, and Roy, "the Boy", a political strategist from Canberra, had been posted there. Nobody was at Malaguna Tech to meet them so the bus driver accompanied them to the principal's residence at the rear of the college.

They then drove past Rabaul High School which was the dual-curriculum New South Wales/Papua and New Guinea school. Tony and the bookmaker from Byron Bay, Geoff, had been posted there in the centre of town. Beyond the town and into the heart of Tolai territory was Boisen High School. Dave, the shearer from Blackall, and Sandy, the stockbroker from Wahroonga, joined the staff of the original "wild colonial boy" Val Doonan who was the headmaster.

Tony, Cara, Geoff and the two children were hauled off the bus there and told they had to have a beer with Val and several other staff members from Boisen. The staff were all quite drunk and singing *Peter, Paul and Mary* songs to the creaking sound of a clapped-out guitar. Their indigenous driver was given half a carton of beer to share with the local staff members who were chewing betel nut outside the houseboy quarters at the back of the school.

They had several beers there before Val gave them permission to leave the party but that was only granted with the proviso that they meet again the following day after school at the yacht club in town. It took a while to find the bus driver after an hour of drinking but they eventually dragged him out of the bush where he had gone to relieve himself. From someone who had not said a single word for the whole of the trip, he came out chattering non-stop in Pidgin English.

"Me lukim yu behain!" his mates kept calling out after him as the group walked towards the bus.

"They're saying goodbye to him in Pidgin English," Val translated as he patted Cara on the backside. "You get it? 'I look at your backside'... that means he is going away from them ... so 'goodbye'. Isn't Pidgin English a brilliant language?"

"Very neat," Cara replied, brushing his intrusive hand aside.

"You know the word for God?" he continued, and Cara shook her head.

"Bikpela papa em stap antap ... get it? ... 'Our big father who lives upstairs'," he laughed. "And the expression for helicopter is 'baloose bilong Jesus Christ', with 'baloose' meaning an aircraft and the Jesus Christ referring to the resurrection and rising vertically from the dead."

Everybody laughed. "See you guys at the yacht club in town tomorrow. Don't forget," he reminded them.

"Me lukim yu behain!" Cara called out to him as the bus spluttered a bit and hobbled forward.

"Me lukim yu behain, meri," he shouted back.

They were on the last leg of their journey back into town and on to Rabaul High School. There would be no-one to meet them. The headmistress, Jean Saracen, had given Geoff and Tony the keys to their houses which were built on the campus of Rabaul High School. They were new administration houses and had the added luxury of being steel reinforced, making them earthquake "guria" proof. Rabaul was susceptible to quite severe seismic activity as well as volcanic eruptions from the foreboding Tavurvur volcano, which spewed out plumes of smoke and ash sporadically. It was on the southern end of the South Bismarck Sea plate and part of the 1000 kilometre Bismarck Volcanic Arc or Bougainville Trench, which was part of the Pacific Ring of Fire. The Pacific Ring of Fire included Krakatoa in Java and Mount St Helens on the west coast of North America.

On the ten kilometre track back to Rabaul High School, the effect of the stubbies of South Pacific Lager was beginning to take effect on their driver. He was madly chatting away to them in Pidgin English and swerving along the road and obviously enjoying the ride. Coming out of one of the bends in the road near Namanula, he over-compensated and lost control of the vehicle and ran into a ditch. They were not travelling at high speed and because everyone was so relaxed, nobody was hurt. Fortunately the two children were asleep on their parents' laps and only woke up after the jolt.

Tony and Geoff joined the driver at the front of the vehicle to assess the damage. There was no visible damage, but the vehicle was hopelessly bogged in the ditch. They needed a tow truck to get out of there. The bus driver muttered something about "Ela Motors", and the word "wantok" came out several times. He then pointed towards town and headed off in that direction, leaving them nonplussed. They assumed he was going for help, and while Cara settled the children back into the bus, Tony and Geoff sat down on the road in front of the bus, hoping for a passing motorist. It was one o'clock in the morning and there was an eerie silence crowding around them.

A crescent moon was enough to cast a gentle light over the crippled bus in the ditch and create a long shadow of the two men against the encroaching jungle. Their eyes soon adjusted to the light, enabling them to see quite clearly. There was movement in the jungle surrounding the bus and Tony was sure he could hear a disturbance in the vegetation. He told Geoff he was having visions of Mataungans leaping out of the bushes and attacking them with World War II Japanese bayonets.

"Can you hear anything?" he asked Geoff.

"Nah ... you're dreaming," Geoff reassured him

A group of about fourteen men, two brandishing bush knives with long blades, materialised out of the jungle and circled the bus.

"Then again," he muttered with a quiver in his voice, "Chances are they're probably just a bunch of friendly villagers come here to help."

Geoff saw everything as a matter of chance, which was to be expected from a bookmaker.

They looked like plantation workers. Their mouths, lips and teeth were covered with the red stain from the betel nut which they would dip in limestone powder and chew with green pepper, causing them to salivate, and they would spit it out in a continuous arc onto the ground. The men in the group were spitting every four to five seconds, which prompted the pair to grimace in disgust. The betel nut had a narcotic effect that reduced stress, highlighted awareness and suppressed hunger.

One of the men, brandishing a bush knife, approached Geoff who was bigger than Tony. He started jabbering in pidgin and making motions that appeared to indicate they were willing to help push the bus out of the ditch. In fact, when they listened carefully and used a little common sense and stayed calm, the similarity to the Queen's English was remarkable. Tony jumped into the driver's seat of the bus and started the motor. He signalled to Geoff to give the order for the natives to put their shoulders to the bus. The children had begun to stir, with Cara wide awake and apprehensive.

Geoff gave them the cue with what sounded like a Roman trireme slave driver urging the oarsmen to put their backs into their rowing.

"One … two … three … Hup! One … two … three … Hup! One … two … three … Hup!"

The natives lunged forward with each "Hup!" and the bus edged a few centimetres back towards the road. The men soon adopted his rhythm and began chanting, "Wanepela … tupela … tripela …Hup! Wanepela … tupela … tripela … Hup! Wanepela … tupela … tripela … Hup!" giving them that little bit extra recovery time before the next push.

After much heaving, the bus, with Tony steering, was back on the road again. The men clapped, cheered and jumped around on the spot like excited children. Geoff started shaking their hands and thanking them in English when the leader approached him and demanded, "Mani (money) … mipela laik mani!"

Geoff was quite taken aback and came to driver's window. "What do we do now?" he asked Tony. "You're the social-anthropologist with the Pidgin English major."

Tony was still considering when a second native ran towards Geoff and began pounding his own chest with both fists. It was not too unlike the scene in *Gorillas in the Mist*, and Tony would have chuckled if it wasn't so serious.

"Mi algeta laik mani … givim mani!"

They all began to chant and pound their own chests with their fists. "Mipela laik mani … givim mani!"

The children in the bus had woken up and were starting to cry.

The leader confronted Geoff, his red teeth and lips seriously close to his face.

"Mi Sepik." He then included all of the others with a wave of his huge hairy arms, "Algeta Sepik ... algeta Bikpela Man ... Michael Somare Sepik ... Michael Somare Bikpela Man!"

He was obviously trying to tell Geoff that he was from the same district in as the Chief Minister Michael Somare who was an important person and they wanted Geoff to know that they were entitled to money. The group then surrounded the bus and started to rock it up and down, back and forth and side to side. Cara and the children shook and clung to each other. Tony jumped out of the bus and stood beside Geoff, and the natives abruptly stopped rocking the bus.

"What do we do now, Godfather?" Geoff muttered under his breath, his mouth twisted as if he didn't want them to hear his voice or read his lips. "If you ask me, I figure there are fourteen of them and two of us. Those are odds of seven to one, without counting the two bush knives. Not good. Other thing is, that if we give in to them now, who knows how much this is going to cost us," he said.

An idea came to Tony and he took two steps forward to confront the leader. He then proceeded to tell them, in the best Pidgin English he could muster, that he and Geoff were both school teachers and that they taught a lot of Sepik children. He explained how on many occasions at school, Sepik children had asked him and Geoff for help and they always helped them. Then he drove his point home by saying that if they were truly "Bikpela Men", they would not ask for money from people who helped Sepik children for free. It was tragic to see how quickly such proud grown men could go to water when faced with shame. The men turned their heads away from the two teachers and after a pause the leader approached Tony with downcast eyes.

There was no pounding of the chest this time.

"Sori (sorry) Masta ... sori Masta," he said, and beckoned to the others to follow him as he disappeared with his head hung low into the jungle.

"Good old reciprocity," Tony said. "It worked for Margaret Mead; it worked for Malinowski; it worked among the Siwai, and now it has worked for us right here in good old Rabaul." Tony smiled at Geoff.

"Go Corleone," Geoff enthused with a clenched fist, making reference to *The Godfather*. "Talk about amazing. That's what I would rate a hundred to one chance of coming off."

"Not really," Tony retorted. "The form was already on the board for that one and I study form ... good old reciprocity," he chuckled, repeating it softly to himself.

Tony drove the bus back into town. They didn't realise that the Ela Motors tow truck approaching from the other direction was the bus driver coming back to retrieve the bus. No doubt the bus driver would have had no qualms about waking up his wantok after at that hour and asking him for a favour. That's the way it was in PNG. It was all about reciprocity. When you did something for someone as a favour or as an obligation, you didn't ask for money. The act, no matter how noble, no matter how arduous, no matter how costly, was simply referred to in pidgin as "wanpela samting I nogat samting" (something nothing).

What the teachers hadn't realised and had no way of knowing was that before the new recruits had arrived in

Rabaul, a negotiated settlement with the Mataungans had already been reached. Emanuel's murderers were arrested and convicted, and peace was restored again to the peninsular. The fourteen ASOPANS who went to Rabaul and surrounding high schools ended up being the luckiest of all the recruits. Rabaul, with its lush tropical rainforests, its idyllic lifestyle and its "jewelled sea" as the poet Coleridge would have described it, was truly a paradise on Earth. It was like winning the lottery.

A bad draw in the "lottery" would have been the wetland areas of Kerema or Kikori, with their grasslands and swamp forests of betel nut and sago. These hot wet lands crawled with leeches and spawned the mosquitoes that carried the deadly malaria and dengue diseases. Hookworm, trachoma, leprosy, scabies and encephalitis were all endemic to the area. The highland areas were even less desirable, inhabited by warlike tribes of people where it was customary for women covered in pig grease to suckle piglets on one breast and their own babies on the other. Places like Kainantu, Goroka, Mendi, Kundiawa and Mount Hagen were just outposts; habitable only to natives who had adapted to that hostile rugged country.

The third possibility of a bad draw was any of the isolated outposts on the Green, Sepik and Fly River areas. These included places like Ambunti, Angoram, Aitape, Telefomin and Vanimo. If the saltwater crocodiles or bull sharks didn't claim the inhabitants in the mangrove waterways, the tropical diseases claimed them on land. Thousands of oxbow lakes were the breeding grounds for host mosquitoes carrying malaria and dengue fever and the jungles were impenetrable. Transport was mainly by river.

* * *

Manfred's destiny was also determined by a "lottery" draw. He often joked "It was the only lottery I ever won" where the prize was a one-way ticket to Vietnam. People had to qualify for that prize by being killed in action. Those who were only wounded or lost limbs failed to qualify and were given a consolation prize instead, which was a return ticket to Australia and a "handicapped" sticker for their car windscreen. That was how Manfred described it when he was trying to be funny.

If they came back unscathed, they still had the "lucky door" ticket that gave everyone a chance to take home a "stalker" who never left their side. He got inside their head and haunted and harangued them until the day they died. No amount of alcohol, home-grown remedies or over the counter pills could insulate the booby prize winner from the curse that was the "stalker". Alcohol and drugs, like painkillers, were used to try to quarantine the "stalker virus" in a makeshift holding pen somewhere in the back of the brain. But the "stalker" was the ultimate Houdini. He always escaped and ensured that, on the ebb and flow of their loneliness and despair, he was always there to torment them. On a good day they lost sight of the "stalker" but he never lost sight of them. Unseen, the parasite plotted his next move and pounced the moment the host became vulnerable, like during a fireworks display, at the flash of a camera, with the touch of someone's hand upon their shoulder, the sound of a creaking hinge or a sudden deluge of rain.

Tony had no idea of any of these scenarios because he wasn't "damaged" like Manfred. Tony's "lottery win" hadn't exposed him to the carefully laid booby traps and "jumping jack" mines, roadside bombs, rocket-propelled grenades, shrapnel, bullets, bayonets, "friendly fire" and the dreaded herbicide agent orange. Tony didn't have to worry about facing "savages" armed with AK47s intent on taking his life, the lives of his friends and ridding the country of colonial invaders. The only blood Tony would ever have to draw was when he swatted the occasional mosquito. The only watch he had to keep was the one on his wrist. He didn't have to have a rifle with him twenty-four hours a day, including when he went to the toilet.

Tony probably could have imagined what it might have been like to be under heavy artillery fire or engage in hand-to-hand combat; he'd seen it often enough at the movies and on TV. What Tony would not have been able to imagine was the smell of cordite and blood and urine on dead bodies, the sight of severed limbs hanging out of trees, and skulls hollowed out like empty coconuts. How could he have imagined what it felt like to put three fingers into a wound in his ankle and feel the bone?

The shock of battle lingered on, long after the deafness, the blinding glare, and the resonance in the brain subsided. It was a sense like the sense of touch, or taste or smell. It was real but how was one to explain a sense to someone else who had never experienced anything like it? To them it was only nonsensical. How could Tony conceptualise the horror of war from behind the walls of his secure administration house where the greatest threat of any intrusion was a gecko squeezing in between the door jamb and the flyscreen behind the locked door.

Manfred, on the other hand, did not have to imagine anything about war. Chances were that he had already been there and done that. It had been right there on tap in the forefront of his mind. It was a tap without a washer that could not be turned off. Every scene he'd ever known in battle kept on pouring out from that tap. Often the images flooded out at night when he couldn't sleep and Angel would ask him, "Are you okay Man?" to which he would reply, "Yes dear ... just thinking about tomorrow."

He knew he wasn't lying. He was thinking about tomorrow all right; thinking if it was so bad today, how was he going to get through tomorrow. He was beginning to wonder how long he was going to be able to put up with all the headaches and how long Angel was going to be able to put up with all his sleepless nights, his lack of patience and his inability to control his temper or how much he drank. He often came home late and brought drunken army mates home with him. They understood him whereas Angel couldn't. They understood him because they'd been there in the trenches, the mud, behind the plastic sandbags. They had seen the fine grains of sand trickling out of where the bullets had pierced their plastic skin. If others could not experience such simple things, how could they appreciate the complex side of coming back to a world of know-all, know-nothing civilians?

He managed to hold his job down at Borg Warner, and Angel figured it was because he was good at it and he loved his work. He was a perfectionist and he would not compromise his work. After the first two years, he ended up foreman and was on a generous salary. He never drank at work but he always promised himself that if his body and mind worked hard for him all day, he would reward them with a few drinks after work while he wound down.

Angel returned to her old trade as a hairdresser. She needed to interact with other people to put her mind off her concerns for Manfred's restlessness. In early 1974 he started talking about wanting to move on again to try something new, and before the year was out, Manfred was thrown a lifeline when he was head-hunted by Cedric Jamieson. Cedric was the former mill manager of Babinda Sugar Mill during the time Manfred did his apprenticeship. Cedric knew that Manfred had learned his trade well and that he had gained valuable experience overseas during his tour of duty in Vietnam. He offered Manfred the position of assistant chief engineer at the Marian Central Sugar Mill near Mackay. The salary was $12,500 per year with a rent-free house and electricity.

That offer did a lot for Manfred's self-esteem. He was also pleased to be heading back to his beloved North Queensland where he had so many fine memories as a child and as a young adult. He was sure it would do him good and he promised Angel that he would try to ease back on the drinking and try to spend more time with her. Initially he was so busy that he didn't have time to think of anything else but work. Then, just as he began to have everything under control at the mill, the "stalker" edged his way back into his subconscious. The "stalker" was always looking for new opportunities to taunt Manfred. In the past he had come dressed as Viet Cong with a floppy jungle hat or reinforced cardboard sun helmet, rubber sandals made from car tyres with straps cut from inner tubes and green or tan khaki fatigues. He had flashed still shots of the mutilated enemy in black pyjamas lying dead on the ground beside the bullet riddled bodies of his mates. He had turned up as a chopper or as the rattle of tank tracks and had left him alone in darkness in the jungle surrounded by booby traps and landmines.

Those things had become secondary to the nasty surprises the "stalker" was able to manifest against Vietnam Vets locally. In Mackay, he emerged with a new strategy to add to his repertoire. He appeared in "civvies" as a professional, a politician or a student in uniform. Then he became a girl in love-beads and a headband, or a barefoot long-haired male in bohemian pants tied at the waist with hemp rope and a scarf dyed with earth-friendly colours. Those were the new personae that the "stalker" used to terrify Manfred after he arrived home in Australia. He had substituted the horror and shame of the Vietnam War with the horror and shame of their homecoming.

The stage had already been set in America where veterans of the Vietnam War were referred to as social delinquents, baby killers, rapists and murderers, and were considered unstable and dangerous. They were portrayed in movies like *First Blood* as killing machines and stereotyped as locked into bad marriages and hooked on drugs and alcohol. They were discriminated against for jobs, and no publisher wanted to publish any books of their war experiences.

Some diggers repatriated from Vietnam were discreetly hidden from the public to avoid the hostile reception awaiting them back home. In America, those who were not sneaked back into the country were confronted by angry crowds from a broad cross-section of the community. They were bombarded with hate and insults, and they were pelted with rotten tomatoes and eggs. They were spat upon, called "dope-heads", ridiculed and blamed for the war and the killing of women and children. Some Aussie diggers were left dumbfounded, ashamed and depressed after their homecoming.

This was all done against the backdrop of images of war – children burned by napalm, the My Lai Massacre and pictures of summary executions of Viet Cong in the streets of Saigon. The final straw was when US General Westmoreland uttered the ultimate faux pas in a 1974 interview about the war in Vietnam. Westmoreland was Commander of American Operations 1964–1968 and US Army Chief of Staff 1968–1972. In the interview, he candidly stated, "The Oriental doesn't put the same high price on life as does a Westerner. Life is plentiful. Life is cheap." The premiere of the anti-war documentary *Hearts and Minds* that featured Westmoreland's comment was released at the Cannes Film Festival and subsequently won an Academy Award. Such a flippant comment served to cement the resolve of the anti-war lobby.

Some veterans of the war did as the American vets did and refrained from wearing military uniforms; they grew beards and long hair in an attempt to fit in with the new norm and hide their "shame". When they retreated to their place of last refuge, seeking the comradeship and understanding from among their own, the vets found they were rejected both in Australia and America. Some Vietnam veterans sensed that the Returned and Services League in Australia spurned them, especially in the capital cities. Soldiers from earlier conflicts suggested the Vietnam War was not a real war and the shame was so great that many Vietnam vets refrained from marching in the yearly Anzac Day parades. In America, the Veterans from Foreign Wars Association refused Vietnam veterans membership.

The community reinforced those prejudices in socially alienating the Vietnam vets surreptitiously, creating the perfect storm for psychological or psychiatric issues and illnesses to fester. Yet the stigma of admitting to any trauma from battle stress or experiences was as daunting as trying to survive the illness. Many preferred to closet their trauma. Others vented their frustrations on friends and family. The government for its part remained in denial, insisting the conditions in the Vietnam War were no different from conditions in other conflicts. They upheld that they were no different from the experience of shell shock or battle fatigue that soldiers experienced in the two world wars. The medical profession had already defined all types of war neuroses with terms like "soldier's heart", nervous exhaustion, neurocirculatory asthenia, trauma phobia and "survivor's syndrome".

They could not conceive of the possibility that the Vietnam War was different from all the other wars. They ignored the fact that in Vietnam there was no real battlefront but all individual skirmishes. There were no heroes proclaimed among the returned soldiers; there was only a derogatory stereotype that the media promulgated. Vietnam vets were neglected the moment they returned. There was no official nationwide welcoming parade and there was no memorial in Canberra for the Vietnam War. How were the vets supposed to interpret these omissions other than as contempt for their services? They were left to curl up in their "kennels" like dogs, with no respite or hope of redemption in the foreseeable future.

When friends began suggesting that Manfred might have one of the forms of war neuroses, Angel always made a point of correcting them.

"No," she said, "Manfred doesn't have 'war neuroses'; we both have 'war neuroses'. You have to try and understand that we are in this thing together. If we had kids then they would have 'war neuroses' as well. Families get 'war neuroses', not individuals. It's about time our society started getting 'war neuroses'. Until people understand that, these guys will never get any support from those who should be taking responsibility for sending them to war in the first place. Everyone expects that people should take responsibility for their own actions. Well, by their own logic, they should expect that governments take responsibility for their actions as well. People in government, through their mouthpieces who are the doctors, social workers and psychologists, are trying to make people believe that the Vietnam 'holocaust' didn't happen; that it was all just happening in these guys' minds. Well, I'm telling you it did happen and no amount of denial, cover-up or downright lying is ever going to change that."

Angel's voice was just another voice in the wilderness that was ignored because of interference. Nobody understood it, nobody wanted to understand it and most people who had it, didn't want to admit it because of the stigma attached to any psychiatric disorder. Thus the "stalker" always got off scot-free. There were too few out there with enough determination or true grit, like Angel, to take him by the horns and shake him out of the veterans' lives. That could have been done in so many ways. There had to be acknowledgement that a government as representative of a nation of people, had made the decision that led to events which were the cause of the veterans' dilemma. Enacting legislation for conscription to compel people to go to war was no different from forcing Aboriginal people to hand over their children to white folk to be raised. Sending young people to war by decree, where there was every chance of being harmed was no different from putting people into institutions without the proper safeguards to ensure they would not be sexually abused.

The government refused to acknowledge that specific psychiatric disorders were a direct result of the unique situation and experiences of the war in Vietnam. They even refused to acknowledge that exposure to Agent Orange, the defoliant and herbicide had caused major health problems to military personnel and their families. Named after the orange-striped barrels in which they were stored, this mixture of 2,4,5-T and 2,4D was manufactured in the US by Monsanto and Dow Chemical. More than three million Vietnamese suffered major health problems from the dioxin contaminated product. When Australian veterans from Vietnam began developing health problems like blood diseases, skin diseases and cancers in the lungs, larynx and prostate, the government denied any link. It appeared that when it was convenient for the government to acknowledge that smoking caused cancer, they put a heavy tax on it, whereas there was no tax incentive in acknowledging the health hazards of Agent Orange, only the fear of liability and compensation payments.

Since Manfred's return from Vietnam, Angel went to great pains to point out all of these issues in her correspondence with the Department of Veterans Affairs. Her pleas were ignored. She was told that the headaches, nightmares, mood swings, alcoholism, and psychosis were all unrelated to anything that might have happened specifically in Vietnam. The doctors told Manfred that they were nothing that a couple of painkillers wouldn't fix. She formed a women and friends' action support group to support the wives and families of other vets who had been suffering from psychiatric disorders. Some vets were becoming violent and abusive, especially when they were drunk or when things went wrong at work. Others were suicidal. Marriages were breaking down because of irreconcilable differences. Psychiatric disorders were becoming everyone's nightmare.

The support group observed that so many Vietnam veterans suffered from similar problems. They felt rejected, unloved, ashamed and misunderstood. Apart from any physical pain, they were subject to various ailments like rashes, twitches, cold sweats and nightmares about dead mates, dead Vietnamese soldiers, dead women, children and old people. The trauma of combat situations seemed to surround them. They became withdrawn, distrustful, unapproachable and aggressive and had issues with anger management, were impatient and often rude. Their demeanour was one of hopelessness, emptiness and frustration and they lacked self-confidence, were uncommunicative and preferred their own company. They were loners and felt uneasy in most social situations. Memories of a dismal homecoming depressed many of them who felt the RSL, government and even family and friends had betrayed them. The whole picture was bleak and as marriages began to break down, they became immersed pathologically in a downward endless spiral of despair. Some committed suicide while others were taken into psychiatric care.

Manfred had Angel. She was his life raft and he wanted her to have the children she always spoke about and deserved. Then, one day while he was at work, Manfred received news that Angel had been in a car accident. He felt as if he'd been shot in the head at point blank range and collapsed to the floor. He later described it as "no more and no less than that; no pain, nothing, a void, the end of everything". The ambulance men came and couldn't revive him so he was placed on a respirator and rushed to hospital.

When he was admitted to the Mackay Base Hospital, he could remember dreaming of being on a search and destroy mission with Angel in Vietnam. She was dressed in an Australian Army camouflage outfit and was driving an army rover. He was manning a machine gun mounted on the chassis behind her. Her long hair was flowing in the breeze and as she turned her head to smile at him, the vehicle hit a landmine and Angel disappeared before his eyes. Manfred awoke in shock and was so relieved when he realised it was only a dream. In reality, he was connected to tubes and strapped into his bed.

He called out at the top of his voice and when a nurse came rushing to his bedside, he kept asking her, "Was it a dream, nurse? Was it only a dream, nurse?"

"It's only a dream, Manfred," she assured him.

"I'm not in Vietnam? Am I in Vietnam, nurse?" he implored.

"No, you are in the Mackay Base Hospital. You had a turn at work but you're okay now," she reassured him.

"And Angel ... is she in Vietnam? Is she okay?" He was all confused.

"Mr Wright, Angel has been in a car accident. She passed away two hours ago. I'm sorry," she told him.

All the air just kept draining out of his lungs as if a giant vacuum cleaner had been clamped over his mouth. His eyes bulged and his body arched upward. The nurse gave him a sedative and talked quietly to him until it slowly took effect. Then his body collapsed back onto the bed sheets and the air came streaming back into his lungs. When he awoke again, it was dark and he was in the intensive care unit. Manfred was still groggy but he could remember everything the nurse had said clearly. Could Angel really be dead? Just like that? What about the children he had promised her? Was that never going to happen? If she was dead, he decided he didn't want to live either. He grabbed at the tubes connecting him to the life support equipment and tore them out of his body, then jettisoned his oxygen mask and waited to die.

"Go stuff yourself 'stalker'," he spat in a voice audible only to himself, glaring at the image lurking in the bright white light at the head of the bed. Alarm bells started ringing in the background as a merciful dark cloud crept over him and he was at peace with himself at last.

Manfred did not die, although he desperately tried to kill himself. When he regained consciousness again he was still in the intensive care unit, except his wrists were tied. He recalled how lonely and abandoned he had felt in the Military Hospital in Yeronga on his return from Vietnam. At least he had Angel then. He was numb. The hospital staff had concerns and he was placed on a twenty-four hour suicide watch. Counsellors came to visit him at first and then, a day later, his parents and grandmother came to visit him. Angel's parents came and workmates from the mill and Angel's friends came to visit him. He was so grief-stricken he had lost the will to live, much less talk to anyone. He stayed mute, inconsolable, unresponsive and ashen, as if life had abandoned him.

Manfred's mother stayed with him for a week after the funeral. He finally convinced her to go home and she left reluctantly, shattered by the events that had befallen her son. Manfred resigned from his job at the mill, even though the mill manager refused to accept his resignation.

"Just take as much time as you need, Manfred," Cedric begged him. "Whenever you're ready, your job will be waiting for you here; I can promise you that."

Manfred thanked him but assured him that he wouldn't be going back.

"I have to go somewhere far away. I can't live here anymore; too many memories Mr Jamieson," he explained. "I have promised my mum I would be going home for a while but I won't be. Everyone up there would feel sorry for me and I don't want that. Advertise the job please, so that I do not have to live with the guilt of betraying your faith in me as well. I will vacate the mill house in one week." He shook Cedric's hand and walked out of the office.

Manfred went to Townsville where he found a dilapidated rambling old house advertised for rent on Magnetic Island. It was right on the beach on Marine Parade at Arcadia. When he saw it, he felt that if he had to die, he was happy to die there. He told nobody where he was staying as he didn't want any visitors. He had to decide firstly if he still wanted to live and if he happened to decide against it, he didn't want any heroes rescuing him. He drowned himself in alcohol. He thought a lot and had several visits from the "stalker", but the salt air and the beautiful blue waters of the Pacific Ocean swept Manfred away from the "stalker's" evil eye and transported him in his dreams to his little beach hut at Russell Heads. Strangely, the "stalker" never followed him there. Manfred never shaved or cut his hair for three months. He wore shorts, no shoes and no shirt. He hadn't had such a great tan in years. He looked like a real beach bum and he was beginning to think the "stalker" had disowned him as well, as he rarely visited anymore, and when he did, it was only in passing as if to check if Manfred had snapped out of his feral torpor.

Manfred read the Townsville Bulletin every day and that was the extent to which he stayed in touch with the outside world. There was a lot in the news about Papua New Guinea. The country already had its own currency, the kina, which replaced the Australian dollar in April 1975. There were daily updates on the progress of PNG towards independence and on September 16 the same year, the country was granted independence.

Bougainville was an island located within the Solomon Islands group but remained part of PNG after independence. But Manfred read that the Bougainville people were unhappy with the state of affairs on the island. Bougainville Copper Limited operated one of the world's largest copper and gold mines there and the local villagers were concerned that the company, a subsidiary of Rio Tinto, had poisoned the entire length of the Jaba River with tailings from the copper mine. This river was the lifeblood of the local subsistence farming community. The villagers asserted that the marine life was being poisoned and reported incidents that suggested a major ecological disaster was happening due to erosion and sedimentation. The PNG Government reaped 20% of the profits from the mine which was its largest non-aid revenue stream. The Bougainvilleans were only receiving 0.5% to 1.25% of the total profits.

The Interim Bougainville Provincial Government voted to secede from PNG, maintaining that it really belonged geographically to the Solomon Island group and had nothing to do with PNG. Negotiations were in a continual state of flux, with Bougainvillean Father John Momis heavily involved in mediation with the central government. Towards the end of 1975, the two parties had reached a stalemate over Bougainville.

After the first three months on Magnetic Island, Manfred wanted to stay on, and he signed a new lease for another three months, expiring in December 1975. He wrote to his mother to let her know that he was well but he gave her no return address and posted the letter from Townsville. Each day, he walked the full length of the golden beach enjoying the feel of the fine sand between his toes. He swam and he fished but sometimes when he was feeling quite relaxed, inquisitive thoughts began entering his mind about PNG.

That huge tropical land mass was a new frontier. In the mid 1930s gold prospectors in the highlands had discovered more than a million "stone age" people living there. Other people who had never seen a white man were discovered in 1954. The terrain was so inaccessible and rugged that most travel was restricted to areas around the great river systems. Through articles written about the Kokoda Trail during World War II and the adventures of missionaries and traders throughout the country, Manfred was able to imagine the possibility of losing himself there for the rest of his days. It gave him hope.

In November he saw an advertisement in the Townsville Bulletin for a manager/chief engineer position in Rabaul. It clearly stressed that university studies were not a requirement but that trade experience in tropical countries was preferred. New Guinea Engineering had offices in Port Moresby and Rabaul. The Rabaul position had become vacant and the job offered accommodation, a tax-free salary well above that of his previous job at the Marian Sugar Mill, and return flights to Brisbane each year. His role would be to manage the operation of the general office in Rabaul as well as initiate, oversee and organise engineering contracts throughout the northern part of PNG and the Bismarck Archipelago.

He would be responsible for East and West New Britain districts, New Ireland, the islands of Bougainville and Buka, the Admiralty Island Group including Manus, Karkar Island and the northern coastal towns of Vanimo, Aitape, Wewak, Madang and Lae. There was a heavy demand for engineering services throughout all of these coastal areas because of the shipping trade and port handling facilities. It would involve a lot of flying and a lot of time out of the office which suited Manfred because he was not partial to office work as it was far too sedentary for his liking. The outdoor work was an opportunity to see a lot of places without having to get too involved with people in any one of them. He applied for the job and was accepted for an interview to be held on December 15 in Port Moresby.

Chapter 8

The Fokker F100 passenger plane that Manfred boarded to take him to Port Moresby took off and headed due east from Townsville. Manfred could see the outline of the Great Barrier Reef snaking northwards as the aircraft banked slightly to follow it across the Coral Sea. He knew his history and geography well and he could imagine the fierce World War II naval and air battles being fought there. The Americans were at full capacity in the New Hebrides group of islands and the Japanese were ensconced at Guadalcanal. After their successful attacks on Pearl Harbor, the Philippines and on the Indonesian archipelago, the Japanese moved on to their next task to occupy Port Moresby. This objective was thwarted as the Americans defeated them at both Guadalcanal and in the Battle of the Coral Sea.

Manfred realised that this was the first time he had left Australia since returning from Vietnam and he recalled the horror of the event that cut short his tour of duty there. He particularly remembered being strapped to the hull of an RAAF Hercules plane with an Alsatian dog on the flight from Richmond in NSW to Amberley in Queensland, and this was beginning to make him feel claustrophobic. Fortunately, the passenger next to him interrupted his thoughts.

"Are you going up to PNG on holiday or to work?" the passenger asked him, trying to strike up a conversation.

"Neither actually," Manfred said.

"Oh, then you must be running away from something ... like the rest of us," the passenger concluded.

"What's that supposed to mean?" Manfred asked.

"Hi ... I'm Jack Schultz." He put his hand out towards Manfred. "Nah nothing. It's just that everyone assumes that people who go to PNG have a shady past and are running away from something. It's the one place you can go where nobody cares enough to even want to ask any questions. Most of them are troppo up there anyhow." He tapped his head. "You know ... not a full quid up here."

"Yeah Jack," Manfred shook his hand. "I know what troppo is. So what are you running away from?"

"Nah, I was born up there. I got nowhere to run, nowhere to hide. I've got a copra plantation up in Rabaul. You probably heard about Rabaul. The Mataungans assassinated our District Commissioner a few years ago over land rights. Good thing they sorted it out. It was looking a bit hairy there for a while. All the Chinese trade store owners took off outa town like greased lightning. Most of the public servants took leave or left the country altogether. Only ones left were the half-castes and us mug plantation owners," he chuckled.

"They finally got everyone back and now all the expats are leaving town again because the vulcanologists reckon old Father volcano, Mount Tavurvur, is about to blow its top again. Wankers ... wouldn't know if you were up 'em, those guys ... not till you rang a bell," he suggested.

"So, I take it you're not expecting fireworks anytime soon?" Manfred queried.

"Nah … no chance. All the locals know. They reckon the tremors aren't anywhere bad enough. That's how you tell. Those vulcanologists, they don't know jack shit."

"Well, I'm pleased to hear that because I'm hoping to get a job with New Guinea Engineering in Rabaul. I'm having my interview in the Port Moresby office tomorrow morning."

"Oh great," Jack beamed. "I'd be happy to show you around when you get the job. I'll give you my address and phone number."

"You mean *if* I get the job," Manfred corrected him, not wanting to sound too cocky.

"You'll get the job alright. Like I said, half the people have left town. Why do you think they advertised the job?"

"That's nice to know. I'll really be able to relax during the interview now. Thanks for the tip, Jack. When I get to Rabaul, I'll owe you one. Any good drinking spots there?"

"Yeah, they're all pissheads in Rabaul. You gotta drink to keep sane or you go troppo," Jack warned. "The RSL's okay but they're all geriatrics in there. Only go there on Anzac Day to play two-up. The whole town goes there on Anzac Day to play two-up, including all the banks. They set up tables with bank clerks to give you more money to gamble if you run out of funds. Even old Father Franke from Vunapope Mission goes there on Anzac Day. The RSL gives him a cut of the takings for the mission. He was a coast-watcher during the war, old Father Franke … top bloke.

"Yeah, well … as I was gonna say, most people go to the yacht club if they're white or the Kuomintang Club if they're Chinese." Jack scribbled an address and a phone number on the back of an airline drink coaster and handed it to Manfred.

"So, give us a call and I'll show you around. What's your name again?"

"It's Manfred; Manfred Wright."

The air hostess offered them both a tray of food which Jack rejected.

"Nah," he said, pushing the tray away. "I'll just have another beer when you're ready."

"Not eating?" asked Manfred, accepting his tray with a thank you nod to the hostess.

"Nah, aeroplane food always makes me sick."

When they arrived at Port Moresby Airport, Manfred could feel a panic attack coming on. He hoped for Jack's sake that he was going to be able to contain it. The oppressive tropical heat was like being plunged back into the jungles of Vietnam and he could feel the waves of heavy heat beating against his body as he walked into the wind. The acrid scent of betel nut and lime at the arrival gate brought him back to Vietnam. The locals were all chewing it and spitting it out onto the tarmac. The saliva swamped into his mouth and he knew he was going to vomit. He let it all out right there on the tarmac until he was dry retching. Jack stayed with him and offered him a couple of airline paper towels from his coat pocket.

"You're like me, mate," Jack consoled him. "It's that bloody plane food. I told you it always makes me sick."

"Yeah mate," Manfred said. "I should have listened to you."

Outside Port Moresby Airport, Jack arranged Manfred's transport to his motel with a local driver, who he spoke to in Motu.

"Okay, this bloke will take you to your motel. The cost

will be one kina. See you in Rabaul soon, Manfred. Let me know a couple of days before you get into town so I can come in to meet you."

"Sure thing, Jack. Nice meeting you," he said as he opened the cab door. "Thanks for arranging the transport."

Next day, Manfred turned up to the job interview. Mr Jantz was the manager of the Port Moresby office and apologised for not being able to meet him at the airport the day before.

"I only got back from the Rabaul office late last night. I had expected to be back early afternoon but the flight was overbooked. It seemed there were a lot more people leaving town than usual. Hope you slept well last night. We made sure we booked you into an air-conditioned motel as it can get pretty stifling this time of year."

"No, it was all good." He would have liked to add something about any impending eruption but avoided the temptation.

"Look, I checked all the paperwork you sent me. Everything's in order. I was thinking we might go up to the club and have a chat over a few beers."

"Sounds good to me," Manfred said. "It's certainly the right weather for it and I thought you'd never ask."

"What'll it be, the RSL or the golf club? You choose."

"The golf club sounds great, Mr Jantz," Manfred said.

"Oh, it's Ted by the way. Call me Ted. We're both top of the dung pile now, you and me. Me here and you in Rabaul," Jantz insisted. "Golf club it is then. Well chosen." He ushered Manfred out to the footpath and waited for the company car to collect them.

It all sounded to Manfred as if he already had the job. Jack certainly knew what he was talking about. When they reached the golf club, Jantz sorted out some housekeeping business relating to Manfred's appointment to the position in Rabaul. Then they drank, had lunch, and drank some more until 3pm.

"Look, you're heading back to Townsville tomorrow morning and I figure I ought to show you around a bit before you go," Jantz said.

"Oh, no worries ... if you've got to get back to work," Manfred said, "I can just take a bit of a stroll around town on my own."

"No, I didn't mean to show you around town. I was thinking of taking you out of town a bit to show you some of the real culture of PNG. It's about an hour out of town but it's really worth seeing. Cargo cults only spring up once in a while and they don't usually last very long, so you are going to be one of the privileged few to see one in action."

Manfred wasn't even going to try and guess what they might be like. He thought he'd just enjoy the adventure. He certainly enjoyed the beer. On the way, Jantz explained to him everything he thought Manfred needed to know about cargo cults, so when Manfred arrived there, he would have all the background knowledge needed to fully appreciate it. Jantz said a cargo cult mentality had been instilled into the folklore of the Melanesians throughout many of the Pacific islands, including Papua New Guinea, from the late nineteenth century. The Milne Bay Prophet Movement of 1893 was one of the earlier cults. Jantz continued with the history lesson, explaining how in World War I, after the takeover of the Pacific colony of German New Guinea by the Australians in 1914, the indigenous population of parts of Papua New Guinea, especially around Rabaul, experienced a series of phenomenal events brought on as a result of the war. The subsequent process of securing and maintaining a foothold in PNG required bringing in what the locals thought of as an endless supply of cargo to its shores. This cargo included the treasured trade store goods like canned beef and fish, rice, flour, eggs and milk. The ships also landed building materials, and wartime equipment such as arms, artillery and transport vehicles. Again, in World War II, the next generation of locals was able to witness the experiences related to them by their parents. This time it was on a far grander scale throughout the Pacific, with the Americans, Australians and the Japanese becoming entrenched in certain areas. The Americans built an advanced naval base on the island of Efaté and an air force base on Espiritu Santo in preparation for the invasion of Guadalcanal. Over a period of six months, the New Hebrides island chain was able to accommodate 250,000 US soldiers. There were six airfields, eight hospitals and nineteen cinemas. The Japanese occupied most of New Guinea and the Australians clung to their major foothold in Port Moresby. As a result, the cargo truly was something to behold. There were aeroplanes, ships, trucks, bulldozers, jeeps, heavy artillery, light artillery and all the associated paraphernalia of war. Most of all, the volume and variety of cargo was bewildering. Sawn timber and corrugated iron for housing, steel and sheet metal for runways and hangars, and what seemed like an avalanche of foodstuffs poured off the ships and aeroplanes from the other world beyond the horizon. This was the paradise that belonged to the white man and the place that the natives believed the spirits of their ancestors migrated to after death.

Manfred was astounded at Jantz's depth of knowledge and attention to detail. He went on to explain how history had already prepared these people, through their folklore, for the magnificence of the goods that were being rained down upon them. Every cult promised cargo that their ancestors would bring back from the paradise of the "other world". What they weren't prepared for was the extent of this "kago," as it was called in pidgin, from heaven.

The company driver dropped them off at a Public Motor Vehicle (PMV) depot on the outskirts of Port Moresby. PMVs were much more suited to the rugged terrain, with roads often detouring through the scrub to avoid the occasional fallen tree or massive pothole. They drove haphazardly in the general direction of the Owen Stanley Range, climbing and weaving their way through dense jungle until they were near Owen's Corner, the official start of the famous Kokoda Trail. They dismounted and climbed up a steep narrow track on the razorback for about 100 yards. Fortunately, the day was overcast and there was a strong northerly breeze blowing from across the mountains, thus keeping the temperature down. The terrain opened out at the top of the track, revealing a jungle clearing resembling a landing strip. At one end of the strip was a fifty foot model of a single-wing aircraft with a twenty-five foot wingspan. It was constructed with bamboo struts and reinforced with bamboo webbing. Pandanus leaves were stretched tightly over the hull for cladding and the plane was complete with a wooden propeller, bamboo wheels and accessories in the slightly raised cockpit. On both sides of the strip, seven foot high bamboo poles served as markers as well as torches that could be lit to delineate the landing site at night. At the other end, a viewing platform, doubling as a control tower, stood perilously close to the edge of a cliff that gaped out over the dense tropical jungle in the valley below. Scores of cockatoos rose periodically out of the mists and swarmed up the valley as if gathering pace in an attempt to scale the heights towards the landing strip on the mountain top. Each time, as if acquiescing to its insurmountable height, they winged away in unison and plummeted back down into the valley and vanished into obscurity beneath the canopy of the giant buttress-rooted trees below. Bird sounds echoed up and down the canyons on both sides of the razorback behind them and Manfred felt the sensation of being at the top of the world.

A tribe of painted faces with pierced noses, and holding weapons of war and billum bags with possessions including babies in them, twisted in unison toward the two white intruders, as the word of their presence filtered through the assembled multitude around the landing site. Bearded ceremonially-scarred males held spears, axes and bows and were dressed in lap-laps and scarves. They wore hawk feathers and bird of paradise plumes in their hair. Long-fingered hair combs made from bamboo or bone and decorated with black, red, yellow and white twine binding were stabbed into their thick tightly curled and wiry hair. The younger women wore bright red and yellow flowers in their hair and the older women wore headbands of twigs with dried leaves or possum fur. The heavily laden billum bags were strung over their backs and tugged against the hairline of their foreheads. Thick armbands above the elbows matched the colours of the black, red, yellow and white ochre painted on their faces. Coloured beads and shell necklaces adorned their bodies. The men wore six inch long half-moon turquoise sea shells through their pierced noses and a select few had bronze decorated discs hanging from there as well, hence covering the upper lip.

"These people believe that the planes which fly over these hills have been built by their ancestors and are laden with cargo from paradise. They are worried that white pirates have hijacked the planes and are landing them at the airport in Port Moresby," Jantz explained. "By building this landing strip, the villagers hope their ancestors can trick the pilots into landing the planes here and delivering the cargo to its rightful owners."

As dusk began to fall, the villagers continued to gaze out towards the empty darkening sky beyond the Owen Stanleys. Some began to light the torches that would guide the planes in if they happened to land at night. Another day had passed with the villagers waiting faithfully on the mountain landing strip for their promised cargo to arrive. They would wait again the next day at this doorway to the sky, and the day after as well.

"It's like *Waiting for Godot* in our culture," Jantz remarked. "Even though it's never going to come to pass, these poor devils at least know what they are waiting for."

Manfred was impressed with the little adventure and commentary. The trek down the mountain was easier but more dangerous because it was dark. They both half slipped, half fell all the way down and it was a relief to be sitting in the PMV and on the way back to Port Moresby.

"It's sad, you know," Jantz mumbled as he hung onto the overhead strap in the PMV and rocked from side to side. "These guys were all hunters and food gatherers living in their own utopia before the white man found them. Their time was measured in terms of day and night, sun and moon, the seasons, birth, rites of passage and death and even the coming of the birds and insects and frogs. They passed the test of time by surviving for thousands of years.

We abolished slavery in Europe and America only to legalise bondage by recruiting these poor devils as indentured labourers on our plantations. The Chinese, the Indians and these Pacific Islanders were all tempted by western goods and industrial trinkets. First we took them away from their lands then we moved in ourselves. In the end, they returned from abroad and found out they had all been dispossessed. We are so good at destroying other cultures; what with our religion, social organisation, our economies and our politics." He stopped, having said his piece.

Manfred waited a few minutes before he responded. "You're not wrong, Ted. We are even good at destroying ourselves. We take the flower of our own youth out of their Garden of Eden and plunge them into a cauldron of horrors in a strange war in a strange land. We keep them dangling on false hope and ultimately, when they wake up to the reality of their non-existence, we abandon them to their own suffering. They talk about choices. Huh, I call it 'blackbirding', just like they did to those Chinese, Indians and Pacific Islanders you referred to. Of course, nobody wants to take responsibility so they call it choices. We all make choices, they argue. Bullshit ... some have choices thrust upon them."

"Yep, Manfred," Jantz agreed. "I know exactly where you're coming from. I fought in Vietnam too."

Chapter 9

It was Saturday, January 10, 1976 and Manfred walked into the airport at Rabaul, wondering if Jack Schultz would be there to meet him. He had contacted him two days earlier to let him know, just as he promised he would, but there was no white man in sight. Jantz had also told him that a Steven Magro, from New Guinea Engineering, would be there to meet him too, but again, no white man in sight. He waited patiently for his bags to arrive while several younger natives kept circling him and looking him up and down. They had a pungent smell about them like the smell of smoked crushed banana leaves. Manfred had smelt it in Vietnam and it triggered a rush of saliva into his mouth. Betel nut chewing was as bad in Rabaul as it was in Port Moresby, and the locals were busily spurting mouthfuls of the red liquid into litter bins probably put there for that purpose. This was despite signs everywhere saying "No ken kaikaim buai", meaning that betel nut chewing was prohibited. Manfred guessed that if they couldn't read, the signs would be futile. He also assumed that anyone who could read wouldn't chew buai, so why have signs in the first place?

"You Masta Manfred?" asked a young man who had been sidling up to him and looking him up and down. He was lithe and jovial and juggled his body from side to side; shy and uncomfortable about approaching the big white man who towered over him. His skin was smooth as silk and so black it looked like charcoal. "I'm Steven Magro. Mr Jantz asked me to meet you here. I work for New Guinea Engineering."

"Oh good, I'm Manfred," he said, a little surprised. "Steven Magro; that's a good New Guinea name," he added.

He offered to shake hands. "Pleased to meet you and thanks for coming to meet me."

Steven took his hand and shook it vigorously with both hands.

"Do you have a car?" Manfred asked.

"Yes, I'm the driver for New Guinea Engineering. I drive the company car. I also run errands and do odd jobs around the place," Steven told him. "You new 'bos man', eh, Masta?" he asked, with a smile that exposed a magnificent set of white teeth.

"Yep, I'm the new 'bos man', and none of this Masta shit; just call me Manfred."

His bags were wheeled in on a trolley and Manfred asked Steven to give him a hand.

"Here, give us a hand with these bags and let's get out of here. That betel nut habit makes me sick in the stomach."

When they were in the car, Manfred initiated some idle chatter with Steven who had gone silent. He suspected it might have had something to do with his comment about the betel nut.

"Tell me Steven, how come you speak such good English? Did you go to school here?"

"Yes Mas ... Manfred," Steven corrected himself. "All 'pikinini' they go to school here. Papua New Guinea was an Australian protectorate so the Australians introduced compulsory education here. We have a PNG curriculum and a New South Wales curriculum. All little kids can speak English but they prefer pidgin. At home, they speak their tribal tongue and some pidgin. Amongst themselves, the kids prefer pidgin because a lot of them come from different tribes; highlanders, mainlanders, islanders, Chinese and half-castes."

"I see, but you speak particularly well. Words like 'errand' and 'odd jobs' suggest a pretty good knowledge of English."

"Ah thank you Man... ah, can I call you bos?" he asked. "That is the proper way to address you here," Steven suggested with a sagacious tone that made it clear to Manfred that he knew what he was talking about. "I actually went to Rabaul High School, the New South Wales curriculum school. We had to dress in school uniform and had to wear shoes and a school tie. Some locals were being selected so they could take over the running of the country after independence. I was one of them."

"Congratulations, Steven. How ridiculous is that; having to wear a school tie in this tropical climate. How did they go about selecting you?"

"It depended on your primary school results; especially English. I was good at English because my father was a 'hausboi' who worked for an Australian school teacher. She was a very nice lady and would only allow me to speak to her in English. She gave up trying with my father. He was smart but he was hopeless at English. Well, he pretended to be, because he only wanted to speak pidgin. Also, he knew he could play dumb by pretending not to understand when she asked him to do something he didn't like doing. I told you he was smart, bos," Steven chuckled as he pulled the car into the kerb outside the New Guinea Engineering office.

"So, how are they preparing you to run the company, if you're driving a car?" Manfred ventured, encouraged at the young man's pluck.

"That's your job, bos," Steven said. "You have to teach me everything I need to know so that I can run the office here in Rabaul. Already, Mr Jantz has given me four promotions. The first time was when Mt Tavurvur started smoking and the Sepik worker got scared and went back to Sepik. Mr Jantz gave me his job; fourth in charge of the office. Then the half-caste who was third in charge, he left a week after when his parents sold their trade store and went to Australia. Mr Jantz made me third in charge. Then he made me second in charge when Mt Tavurvur started becoming very active and the assistant manager decided it was time to 'go pinis'. That means to leave the country. Then, when the earthquakes started opening up cracks in the road on the way to Kokopo, the manager's wife said she would leave him if he didn't leave Rabaul, so he went pinis too. That was when Mr Jantz made me manager and gave me the key. I open the office in the morning and I close the office at night. Anyhow, it all turned out to be a false alarm."

"So you're manager now, is that right?" Manfred asked, enjoying the banter that was developing out of this conversation.

"No, you the manager now, you're the bos man ... I'm second in charge."

"But, I thought you were the company driver," Manfred reminded him.

"Yes, I'm the company driver; I run errands and I do

odd jobs. Assistant manager is one of my odd jobs," Steven elucidated. "The company is not making any money bos. Maybe that's why Mr Jantz gave you the job. If we don't make money, then we don't get paid."

"So who do we have left in the office?"

"We have Nancy. She's the telephonist and she does the postage. Then we have Pauline. She's very smart. She went to Rabaul High School too and was dux of the school. She does all the accounts, the banking and writes all the letters. The other workers left, because there was no work. Mr Jantz said you can employ whoever you want because you the bos man. I'm your assistant manager, so I can help you find anyone you need. That's all." Steven shrugged his shoulders.

"So how long is it since you and the two girls have been paid?" Manfred queried.

"No, we have been paid. Mr Jantz flies up every two weeks with our pay. He checks the office and tells us we are all doing a good job even though there has been nothing to do. Pauline has been offered many other jobs by local business but she likes her job here."

Manfred just shook his head and tried to conceal his amusement.

"Your house is at the back of the office," Steven told him, pointing to a narrow cobbled path. "I'll put your bags in there bos. Then we can go and meet the girls."

The house was a three-bedroom weatherboard building on low blocks. Inside, it looked as though the last manager did leave in a hurry. It was furnished, clean but untidy. Steven put the bags down and gave Manfred the key, then motioned for Manfred to follow him outside.

"Come bos," he gestured. "Come and have a look at the 'boi haus' out the back. This is where your 'hausboi' will live."

"What hausboi? I'm not having a hausboi. I'll do my own laundry and washing up thank you. What do you think I am a cripple or something?"

"No-one's gonna think you're a cripple Manfred, just because you have a hausboi," came a familiar voice from behind the bushes a few yards away.

"Hey Jack!" Manfred exclaimed. "How you going mate? Jeez, I thought you must have gone troppo or something and forgotten all about me."

"Nah, sorry mate. I was over on New Ireland looking at this plantation and we had a bit of trouble getting back. Engine problems … had to do the last few kilometres under sail," Jack apologised.

"So what's this about a hausboi?" Manfred asked as he looked over the boi haus at the back. It was about the size of a typical Australian laundry or bathroom, built from concrete blocks with an iron roof. It had a toilet and shower recess inside and on the outside there was a lean-to that housed an ancient washing machine, some laundry troughs and an ironing board and iron. Cooking was done outside on a small open fire, and a copper was used for boiling clothes.

"Shit, I wouldn't want this as a tool shed, let alone expect someone to live in it," he said, frowning.

"It's not a matter of what you want, Manfred," Jack explained. "Housing is a premium to these people who have come from all over PNG to get a job in the city. A boi haus like that is gold to someone in need. It's a status symbol as well and it would be a waste and a crying shame not to let someone use it. A hausboi is going to cost you seven to nine dollars per week. The whole expatriate community is going to think you're a tight-arse if you don't give some guy a job, and the locals will be devastated. The hausboi will look after the place when you're away and he has a whole tribe of wantoks; people who speak the same language, who will make it their responsibility to look after you."

"I don't give a stuff about what the expatriate community thinks about it, but the rest of what you say makes total sense," Manfred conceded. "Okay, Okay, how do I go about finding a hausboi then?"

"Just ask this fella here." Jack indicated Steven. "Hey, yupela gat save long ..." he started before Manfred interrupted.

"It's okay; Steven speaks English as well as you or I. Steven, this is Jack Schultz. Jack, this is Steven, my assistant manager."

They didn't shake hands, but Steven acknowledged him with, "Pleased to meet you, Masta."

"I told you Steven, none of this Masta bullshit. You call him Jack or Mr Schultz; whatever he prefers. What do you prefer Jack?"

"Jack's fine." Jack put his hand out to Steven. "Pleased to meet you, Steven." Steven shook his hand vigorously. "You got a wantok who would be a good hausboi for Mr Wright?" Jack asked.

"Yes, my father's friend is looking for a job. My father will train him up well. He's been a hausboi for ten years. He's trained hausbois before."

"There you are, all settled then. You organise it all for Mr Wright, okay Steven?"

Before Steven could answer, Jack turned to Manfred. "Right Manfred, you and me, we got an appointment down at the yacht club. You reckon the assistant manager can give you a leave pass?"

"Too right, Jack. I thought you'd never get around to that. Just give me two ticks while I go into the office to meet the staff. Come on Steven, do your thing."

Jack waited outside as Steve and Manfred went into the office. He sensed he might be up against another do-gooder. He suspected it would be "poor native" and "we're all equal" and all that nonsense. "Call me Jack ... blah, blah, blah" and other things were going through his mind as Manfred left the office on his own and indicated he was ready to go.

As they drove down to the yacht club, Manfred sensed something and put in a half-apology. "Shit mate, I hope you didn't think I was overdoing it back there. It's just I think it's un-Australian to expect blokes to call you Masta and that sort of crap. I've been around long enough to know that life's a bitch whichever side of the fence you come from."

"Nah, furthest thing from me mind Manfred," Jack lied. "Hope you've worked up a thirst. We just did a thirty mile trip over all that water in the Saint George Channel today with not a drop of grog to drink. Bloody idiot swashbuckler, Rob De Werter, forgot to collect the carton I left to cool in the fridge on Balangot Plantation over on New Ireland. You'll meet him soon enough. He's a Dutchman; top bloke, but don't try to tell him anything because he knows it all."

Manfred spent half the night meeting people. The main topics of conversation were about what they did, where they lived, what they liked, what they hated, political persuasion, religious persuasion, sexual orientation and the list went on and on. At the end of the night, nobody's character had survived assassination. However, true to form, nobody was interested in anybody else's past. The people here lived only for the present and they drank as if there was no tomorrow. The most interesting character of the whole gathering was Rob De Werter. He was forever sailing the seas around Rabaul in his 13.6 metre *Lagoon 440* – a resin-infused fibreglass twin-hull catamaran equipped with sails and two 56 horsepower Yanmar engines. He was master over all the waters from the Admiralty Islands and the St Matthias Group of Islands in the north-west to the islands of Bougainville and Buka in the south-east. Whether it was the Bismarck Sea to the north or the Solomon Sea to the south, his trusty barque would deliver him safely from one adventure to the next. He knew every channel, every passage, sanctuary, reef, shoal and coral island in that north Pacific wonderland. From Karkar Island in the south-west to New Ireland in the north-east, he would deliver cargoes of foodstuffs, parts, machinery, fuel, building materials, alcohol and spirits, tobacco, clothing, passengers and mail to outlying plantations and missions.

Rabaul was his hometown harbour. After every cruise buffeting the waves into the unknown, there was always the excitement of knowing he had a place to go to that he could call home. At night, the lights around Simpson Harbour from Kokopo to Rabaul were his beacons, and by day, the omnipotent Father Volcano, Mt Tavurvur, with its earth-cracking eruptions and smoking caldera.

A group of businessmen and bookies, mainly Chinese or mixed-race, reserved one corner of the club on Saturday nights. They would meet after the day's horse racing events in Brisbane, Sydney and Melbourne to settle their debts and collect their winnings. The rest of the venue was abuzz with members spruiking raffle tickets in meat trays, cooked chickens, seafood trays and everything from decorated dolls to carved Sepik and Baining masks. Indigenous craftsmen lurked in the shadows outside the club where they had been relegated and were selling their meticulously carved wooden wares in the shape of turtles, dolphins, seahorses, spears, shields, masks and the universal smoothly polished carved penises complete with life-size appendages. These objects created much fascination for the foreigners and were in such great demand the locals were able to make a living from the sales.

The yacht club from a distance was like an oasis of endless happiness. Celebrations marked by singing, hollering and wave after wave of mass hysteria must have left the locals huddled in their boi hauses and squatter settlements on the fringes of the town in awe of the power and wealth of these "wailpela waitpela pipel" (wild white people). Only the silence of the dawn could offer those party animals of the night any hope of absolution. They would wake up, put their noses to the grindstone and go about their work with a renewed enthusiasm, knowing that at nightfall the happiness would return again like *Groundhog Day*.

Manfred woke up in his bed in the house behind the office. His head was throbbing and his mouth felt like he'd buried it somewhere in a grease trap. He had no recollection of going home or how he got there. He was fully dressed. His wallet, watch and glasses were on the little table beside his bed and his suitcases had all been emptied and clothes folded away in drawers or hung up neatly in the wardrobe. Any papers were carefully placed in piles on the kitchen table. It was there that he recognised the writing on a beer stained recycled piece of cardboard with the lyrics to the song about what the bar girls in Vietnam thought of the Australian diggers who earned much less money than the American soldiers. Manfred recoiled in shame as he recalled writing them out for the drunken chorus he had assembled in his drunken stupor at the club. As he perused the lyrics, sung to the tune of "Knick-knack Paddy-whack, Give a dog a bone", all the indiscretions of the previous evening came flooding back:

Uc-dai-loi, Cheap Charlie,
He no buy me Saigon tea,
Saigon tea costs many many P,
Uc-dai-loi, he Cheap Charlie.

Uc-dai-loi, Cheap Charlie,
He no give me MPC,
MPC costs many many P,
Uc-dai-loi, he Cheap Charlie.

Uc-dai-loi, Cheap Charlie,
He no go to bed with me,
Bed with me costs many many P,
Uc-dai-loi, he Cheap Charlie.

Uc-dai-loi, Cheap Charlie,
Make me give him one for free,
Mamma-san go crook at me,
Uc-dai-loi, he Cheap Charlie.

Uc-dai-loi, Cheap Charlie,
He give Baby-san to me,
Baby-san cost many many P,
Uc-dai-loi, he Cheap Charlie.

Uc-dai-loi, Cheap Charlie,
He go home across the sea,
He leave Baby-san with me,
Uc-dai-loi, he Cheap Charlie.

He ventured outside. It was 6am and there was a fresh scent of frangipani in the air. Outside the boi haus, a small fire was gently being coaxed with a broad leaf from a pandanus palm. Someone had obviously moved into the boi haus. He initially thought the black hand of the person with his back to Manfred might belong to Steven but a closer look revealed it was a stranger, who almost jumped out of his skin when he saw the giant white man leaning over him.

"Masta, Masta," he screamed as he leapt to his feet and froze with his back to the wall of the boi haus. "Nem bilong mi, Peter. Wantok bilong Steven," he added. "Me nupela hausboy bilong you Masta."

"Shit, here we go again with the Masta crap," he mumbled as he turned around, shrugged his shoulders and walked back to his house. "*Steven can sort that one out later,*" he thought. He was saddened at the ingrained servitude of the natives, which seemed so at odds with what he had seen in Port Moresby of their vibrant traditional culture. He had a long relaxing warm shower and he thanked God for that. He really needed it badly and was actually feeling remarkably refreshed after it. He took his time, shaved and trimmed a few overgrown hairs here and there in his nostrils and around his ears. After all, he had to face the staff again that day as the bos man and they would have certain expectations of him.

When Manfred emerged from the shower, he found a freshly ironed starched shirt and ironed trousers laid out on his bed. It was like living in a house with "the ghost who walks". Things seemed to appear from nowhere and disappear to nowhere. Peter was nowhere to be seen. After a while, he emerged from the kitchen with a steaming hot plate of porridge, milk and sugar and two pieces of toast and Vegemite. Manfred could not believe this guy. If this was what hausbois were capable of, he thought, then "*bring them on!*"

He was sitting down to his breakfast when Steven arrived and waited at the door until Manfred gave him permission to enter.

"What are you doing out there, Steven? Come on, come in; take a seat. Have you had breakfast?"

"Yes, bos." Steven examined Manfred's face as if he was looking for bruises.

"Don't tell me I got into a fight last night. Did I Steven?"

"No bos," was the curt reply.

"Well, any idea how I got home?"

"Yes, bos; the Dutchman and Mas ... Jack, they carried you home. They put you to bed and then they left."

"How do you know?" he wondered.

"All my wantoks, they look after you. They slept all night in the boi haus to make sure no 'raskols' would try to rob you."

"Shit; good idea of yours to have a haus boi." He waved over the food on the table. "Who paid for this stuff? Where did they get the money?"

"Haus boi borrowed the money from wantoks," Steven said. "He will have to pay the money back today."

Manfred pointed to his wallet on the bedside table. "Tell him to take the money from my wallet. Also, he can take whatever other money he needs to buy some groceries."

"No bos. That's not the way it's done here. He never touches your wallet. You give him the money and he gives you the change," Steven explained.

"Okay. It doesn't look like Peter there needs any training. The Queen's butler would have trouble keeping up with this fellow."

"Peter's not your haus boi. Peter's my father. He will train your haus boi."

"Bummer," mumbled Manfred. "I thought it was too good to be true." Manfred stood up and went over to his wallet and took out forty dollars. "Here, give this to Peter and tell him to let me know if he needs any more money. What time do we start work?"

"Seven o'clock, bos. But you can come later if you want. I've already opened the office and Pauline and Nancy are already at work waiting for you. Pauline took a phone call from Mr Jantz who wanted to know if you had settled in and she told him you had already fitted in well and had made lots of friends."

"Thanks Steven. I don't know where I'd be without you. You look after the office. I'll be there in about half an hour. If Mr Jantz rings again, tell him I'll call him in thirty minutes, then come and get me."

It was time for Manfred to get his game plan together before he rang Jantz. He would sit and come up with a sensible plan of action. No doubt Jantz would have a pile of work lined up for him. He needed to find out what hired help was available and what level of skills they had, and so he decided he would take Steven everywhere with him. The best place to learn the ropes was on the job. Steven would be his interpreter and procurer as well as assistant. He needed to inspect the workshop they had access to here in Rabaul, and the extent and quality of the tools and equipment available. Further, he needed to determine how the transport of tools, equipment and materials was to be organised, especially to the outlying isolated places like mine sites or ships at sea.

Once he had all of his thoughts collected, Manfred felt he was ready to put in his first day at the office. Pauline, the secretary, was a tall statuesque woman with the traditional plumped-out "fuzzy-wuzzy" hairdo straight out of the musical *Hair* that he had seen in Sydney. Her tribe was Tolai, the tribe of the local area. They were a proud intelligent people with a long tradition of self determination and a strong cultural heritage. All the cultural rites of passage were strictly adhered to and the village elders were fearless and protective of their rights, their land and their women. Manfred had been told all about the Tolais the previous night and he was surprised he could remember it all so clearly. He had heard about the faceless male dukduks and the female tabuans of the Tolai tribes and the firewalkers from the Bainings Mountain area. It was all exotic and beyond any of his past experiences; he was looking forward to learning more about these people.

Nancy, the telephonist and postage clerk, was from the island of Buka. Like all Bougainvilleans, the Bukas were pitch black with small round faces and short trim bodies. Their hair was kept shorter but was still characterised by the wiry miniscule tight spring-steel curls that clasped on to any embedded object relentlessly. He greeted them cordially and told them he was ready to start making some money for the company so "they could all get paid"' as Steven put it. His only wish, privately, was that Angel could have been there to share this whole new world with him.

Chapter 10

In Brisbane, Tony and Cara were in a quandary. Tony had one year left of his four year contract still to serve with the Education Department in PNG. Young Linda had attended one year of pre-school in Rabaul, but the system of schooling for expatriates was not very satisfactory. Expatriate pre-schools were private individually run meeting places rather than schools. Students were baby-sat rather than taught and they were poorly supervised. Linda had even managed to leave the premises and walk half a mile home from school in the middle of the day without anyone realising she was missing. Now her brother Manfred was due to start school and they felt any decision to waste another year on both children in Rabaul would not be a prudent one. They decided Cara would stay back in Brisbane and Tony would return to Rabaul alone. Cara and the children would go to Rabaul in the May and August school holidays and stay for an extra two weeks each time. The amount of schooling lost in Australia would be minimal. Compared to the negligible amount of learning going on at the private school in Rabaul, both children would be far better off in Brisbane where they would be continuing their studies. The year would be over before they knew it.

It was the first time Tony and Cara had been separated from each other, and that was their main concern. They knew the children would be fine and it was not unusual for spouses to be required to leave home for work related reasons. If others could do it, then they could do it too. Tony hated being responsible for the look of devastation on Cara's face as he was boarding the plane to Rabaul. He knew she was hurting deeply inside despite her brave face. She was like a child in so many ways. He wanted to run back down the stairs from the plane and hug her and tell her he was not going, but that was too ridiculous to contemplate. After all, he was hurting too.

By the time the plane was in the air, Tony had already accepted that they had no real choice in the matter. He had an interesting year ahead of him and this last year was to be the culmination of the special four-year project that he had implemented at the school. When Tony arrived at Rabaul High School in 1973, the Department of Education had just issued a directive to certain schools in each of the district capitals. They were to enrol local students in their NSW curriculum classes in preparation for the push towards localisation prior to independence in 1975. The plan was to foster an elite stratum of well-educated young people into the PNG society who would eventually take important positions in the running of the country. Those students were hand picked, and they were required to possess a good level of English. However, students from influential families in the local community were also given preferential treatment during the selection process.

Tony noticed there was a divide between the expatriate

students and the locals enrolled in the school. It was essentially a cultural divide brought on through years of domination from people of Western cultures. The locals had long been subjugated by plantation owners, traders, missionaries and patrol officers in the usual way that colonial powers ruled people under their influence. Consequently, there was a sense of not belonging and the two groups tended to cluster in separate social groupings around the school according to their ethnicity.

In the first year of his contract in PNG, Tony approached the principal with a plan to offer the subject of Agriculture based on the New South Wales curriculum, as a compulsory subject for students in Forms 1–4. These were students in the thirteen to sixteen year age group. He thought the outdoor practical nature of the subject would encourage the students to try harder to integrate with one another. The plan was to start with Form 1 and within four years to have the whole school involved in the project. The principal provided a small grant to kick off the project with the proviso that it would have to be self-funded within two years.

There were three acres of land at the back of the school available for school use. It needed to be fenced, and until the project reached the stage where it was self-funding, Tony used the school truck to take groups of students into the villages after school to obtain bamboo and other bush material to build it. The village elders welcomed them and were pleased to be included in the activities of the white man's school. This was the first time that expatriate children were becoming immersed in village activities. They used bush-knives to fell the tall bamboos and trim them back. Many of the expatriate students had never held a bush-knife, which provided an opportunity for the locals to teach them something. The bamboos were split and woven into a four foot high fence which served to keep feral pigs, pests and squatters out of the makeshift farm.

Young green coconuts, "kulau", were hurled down from the tops of the trees for the students to drink as refreshments afterwards, and often a village supplied food to the children from underground earth ovens called "mumus". Chickens were covered in coconut juice and grated coconut and herbs, and wrapped in banana leaves. Preparations for the earth oven were begun the day before. A hole was dug into the ground and hot round river rocks from the Worongoi River were placed into the hole with wooden tongs. The wrapped chickens were placed on top of the hot rocks and more hot rocks placed on top of the wrapped food. The earth oven was filled in with fresh earth and the chickens left to cook for about eight hours. The aroma and the taste of the chickens when the oven was unearthed were to die for. School had become a place of fun and practical experiences as well as learning.

An old disused bicycle shed, about twenty-five yards long, was dismantled and re-erected on the farm site. It served as a roof over batteries of caged chickens that provided the eggs to fund the development of the project. There was a huge demand for fresh eggs by the expatriate population, who previously had to rely on preserved eggs brought in from Australia by the grocery supplier called Steamships. Day-old chickens were imported from Australia to stock the cages and students spent hours up at the farm watching them grow, turning the farm into a centre of activity.

Tony approached Vudal Agricultural College about supporting the project. They appreciated the fact that

Rabaul High School, with its accredited course in Agriculture, would become a feeder school and as such was well worth supporting. Just as the chickens were on the point of lay, Vudal Agricultural College donated a prime Berkshire pig and four Muscovy ducks. The whole town was beginning to buzz with the excitement of a mini-farm in the middle of town. Primary schools and pre-schools in the area organised excursions to the farm and the project was becoming a resounding success. However, news of the farm prompted a visit from the town health inspector, a crusty old overweight German called Karl Schneider. He insisted there was no way the school could keep pigs in the middle of town. Health reasons, especially at a school where the health of so many children was in jeopardy, were cited in the order issued to remove the pig from the premises. He was prepared to allow the chickens and the ducks but the pig had to go. The school community was devastated as they had all become attached to Annabelle the pig and begged Tony to do something to save the pig.

Tony came up with a plan to try to entice Schneider to waive the order. He invited Schneider to come up to the school to consider a proposal on how they might save the pig. The sweetener was two dozen fresh eggs that the children wanted to give him as a thank you for sparing the chickens and ducks. When he arrived, they examined the shed that had been built to house the pig. Both agreed the size and location of the pen was not a problem, but the earth floor, covered in excrement and mud, was a health hazard. Tony suggested that they concrete the floor of the pen but Schneider stubbornly claimed that concrete would not solve the problem of the waste. Tony agreed and said he would build a septic tank to council specifications; the concrete floor would be hosed down daily and the waste from Annabelle would be flushed into the tank.

Schneider's fingers tapped the lid of the cartons of eggs that had been presented to him and thought for a moment. While Schneider was thinking, Tony gave the predetermined signal to bring in the children. A group of the cutest kids in the school, black, white and mixed-race, were primed to beg Schneider to let them keep the pig. They suddenly appeared with their faces pushed up against the chicken wire wall of the pig pen with their fingers clutching at the wire.

"Please Mr Schneider, don't take away our pig; please Mr Schneider. Annabelle is happy here and we love her," they pleaded in chorus.

Tony pretended to "raus" at them which was what adults did when they wanted to tell kids to go away. They froze, remained silent and refused, with bottom lips quivering. That was all that was needed to make Schneider crack.

"Wary vell," he blurted. "You 'ave two veeks to build ze floor and ze septic tank." Then he turned to the kids and spluttered. "You can keep ze pet pig, children."

The chorus was on fire. "Thank you Mr Schneider for saving our pig!" they shouted.

There were 200 birds in cages in full production at the end of 1974, and the money from sales was rolling in. Economics student Pauline Tobubu, a Tolai girl, was appointed chief bookkeeper, responsible for all the recording of income and expenditure and the banking. She had two assistants. Sales from eggs were complemented by the sale of chickens which were slaughtered for meat. While the girls among the local students were particularly enthusiastic about that task, some of the expatriate girls were horrified and refused to participate in the slaughtering. The piggery was completed on time, with concrete floor and septic all built to specifications. Annabelle was about ready to give birth to a litter of pigs so a farrowing rail had to be installed in one corner of the pen.

An area of about two acres was fenced off between the farm and the teachers' housing on the campus the following year. Improved pastures had been sown and they were in the process of building a cattle yard complete with crush and milking bale. Vudal Agricultural College had negotiated with a plantation owner to purchase a Jersey cow in calf, which the farm paid for out of savings from the project. She was named Frangipani. Meanwhile, the Muscovy ducks had multiplied to twenty and frolicked around near the caged chickens in a deep litter of wood shavings from the local sawmill. Each class had an agricultural plot allocated to it and the students chose which particular crop they wanted to grow. Some chose vine crops like granadilla or passionfruit; others chose root crops like sweet potato, carrots or yams. Some planted leaf crops like cabbage, lettuce and broccoli while others chose to plant a pumpkin patch, a watermelon patch or a rockmelon patch. One class had a plot of corn, and another planted papaws. Another class had a banana patch and one group planted sugarcane. Surprisingly, the greatest success and money-earner was the rosella patch. The principal took a special interest in that class and organised for the bumper crop of rosellas to be made into jam and sold at the school fete.

Students experimented with a variety of fertilisers. They dug chicken manure into the ground before planting their crops and used liquid chicken manure to nourish the plant seedlings. They experimented with chemical fertilisers as part of a study to try to determine their effect on plant growth. Compost was placed over the bare ground to help control weeds and retain moisture in the ground.

Annabelle had six piglets. Two were sold to local villagers and three were farmed out to students who brought them back to their villages where they were mated with the village pigs. The goodwill this generated proved useful when it came time to get posts for the cattle yard. Those same villagers were most obliging and helpful in providing them to the school. The sixth piglet, a male, was exchanged for a boar from Vudal Agricultural College. That boar would be used to mate with Annabelle.

In the three years to 1975, Tony had three full-time student helpers who came before and after school to manage the running of the farm. They ensured that water and food was available to all the animals, the pig pen always washed out and that the fences and gates to the farm were shut. They also made sure the security lights were turned on at night to dissuade chicken thieves. Soft music was played to relax the caged chickens, and as a result of the lights and the music, egg production increased by twenty-five per cent. The three helpers were Steven Magro, a Bougainvillean, Petrus Bila, a Sepik boy, and Gabriel Kama, a Tolai boy. Oliver Lote and Leo Loho were part-time helpers. A volunteer Canadian teacher, Bernie Hurlahen, from the University of Alberta, also joined the team.

Tony couldn't wait to return to the school to see how everything had gone up at the farm during his absence. Petrus, Leo and Oliver were now the students in charge and they were paid a small wage over the holiday period to look after the farm, the pigs, the ducks, the cow and the caged chickens, and deliver eggs to the retail outlets in

Rabaul. Frangipani was close to calving and Annabelle was due to have another litter anytime soon. Steven Magro and Pauline Tobubu had both been offered jobs at New Guinea Engineering in Rabaul and they had been gone one year.

Tony left his bags at the house and walked across to the cow paddock to check on Frangipani. She was close to her time, just as he had suspected, guessing she was only a few weeks off, which would be opportune because the school children would be back by then. They would all be able to share in the joy and experience of the new birth. He did a quick tour of the rest of the farm, and was pleased everything seemed to be under control. As the boys did not seem to be around, Tony went back to the house and opened the windows to give it a good airing. It was 4pm and he figured he would go down to the yacht club for a few beers and catch up on what had been happening in town while he was away.

It was only a fifteen minute brisk walk from the school to the club, but at that time of the year, mid to late afternoon, it brought bubbles of perspiration to his forehead, face and neck. The humidity was beginning to build up and the rain clouds were trying to get the jump on the weather forecaster who had forecast rain at five o'clock. Tony knew they wouldn't. Anyone could be a weather forecaster in Rabaul at that time of year as the rain always poured out of the heavens at 5pm. It was so reliable that people set their clocks by it.

Outside the club, people were skulking around, labouring under the weight of the heat, the air and the stillness, as if it was about to crush them to death. Some edged around a bit, trying not to expend too much energy, as they scanned around furtively for some shade under a tree or a bush, rather than under the buildings with their corrugated iron roofs. Even the stalwart woodcarvers, squatting down on their haunches with their dolphins, turtles and carved penises overflowing from the billum bags between their legs, were feigning sleep. They were trying to fool themselves that sleep would help make the heat go away.

A couple of sellers stirred at the prospect of a customer as Tony approached. They knew that these "pipel bilong longwe ples"; these foreigners, were real suckers for the kind of wares they had on offer. That move reverted back to their mood for slumber the moment they recognised him. They knew they would just be wasting their time trying to flog their wares to someone who had been around the traps for so long.

"Mi tingting Masta he go pinis," said one hawker who thought Tony had left Rabaul for good.

"Mi kam bek wanpela mo yia," Tony replied, explaining he was back for one more year.

"Ah ... yu gutpela tisa ... yu skulim algeta picinini," said the hawker, softening him up. Then he shoved a plastic raincoat towards Tony with one hand and pointed at the sky with the index finger of the other. "You laikim kot ren (raincoat)?" he asked, brandishing a broad smile full of red betel nut stains and two solitary teeth.

Tony shook his head and kept walking. He climbed the three steps leading into the club. It was deserted inside and Tony moved over to the bar, pulled up a stool and ordered a beer.

"Nobody here yet, eh Betty?" he asked the barmaid. "Everybody still on holidays I suppose, eh?" he guessed.

"Yeah, how come you're back so early, Tony?" she asked, as she began pouring a beer. "Where are Cara and the kids? Up at the house?"

"Nah, they're not coming back … too many hassles with school. Thought we'd bite the bullet and make this the last year. I've come back alone but Cara will be up for the school holidays. Jeez, I'm missing them already, Betty, and I only got back a couple of hours ago."

He could see someone coming out of the toilet and as he glanced around to see who it was, Betty introduced them to each other.

"Tony, this is Manfred. He's new in town … and Manfred this is Tony, school teacher from just up the road at Rabaul High School."

They both looked at each other and Manfred was the first to speak.

"Well, well, look at what the cat's dragged in. Tony … Tony D'Italia!" Manfred crushed Tony in a big bear hug. "Where've you been all these bloody years mate? Shit, it's been ten years at least," he said. "Bloody school teacher. Last I heard, you were a big shot lawyer in the city somewhere."

"I'll be buggered Manfred, I thought you were dead or something. I've been trying to track you down for the last five years, you mongrel. You simply don't exist in Australia. You're not on the electoral roll, you're not in the phone book, you don't have an address and nobody in Babinda has a clue where you are," Tony said.

"Yep, that's the way I like it, Tony. The less people know where you are, the fewer questions you got to answer."

"What are you doing up here?"

"I got a job with New Guinea Engineering, just last week."

"Oh yeah, a couple of my ex-students work there – Steven Magro and Pauline Tobubu."

"Yeah, top value that Steven. He still hasn't worked out that they promoted him to manager a month ago because everyone else had left town when they thought the volcano was going to blow its top," he laughed. "He's a good kid ... another two beers there please, Betty."

"Did you do Vietnam?" Tony asked.

"Yeah, but we'll talk about that another time."

"Are you married?"

"Yeah, but we'll talk about that another time too. That leaves you one more question," Manfred warned.

Tony thought about it for a few seconds.

"Did I name my kid after you or didn't I?" Tony proclaimed.

"You didn't, did yah? Ya silly bugger. What would you want to do that for?" Manfred was bewildered.

"Well, I figured we had a lot of good times together, you and me as kids, and if I named my kid Manfred, the good times just might keep on rolling on."

"Shit ... Manfred D'Italia." Manfred thought about it for a few seconds. "What sort of a wog name is that?" he asked.

"It's Germanic-Latino man. You can't get any more wog than that," Tony joked.

"You're a legend, Tony. So you intend to keep teaching up here?"

"Nah, this is going to be my last year. The kids have reached school age. I have a little girl too. She's called Linda."

"Good on ya mate. I'm happy to hear it and thrilled to see ..."

A huge clap of thunder snuffed out the sound of his voice, along with the rain that drummed down on the roof like a thousand galloping horses. Tony glanced at his watch; it was five o'clock sharp. A few expats rushed into the bar with their hats in one hand and wiped the raindrops off their clothes with the other. Tony and

Manfred huddled in their corner as the group pulled up some stools and sat at the bar. Betty moved across to serve them and started talking to them as she poured out five beers. Manfred and Tony left the bar and went into the beer lounge.

"Bring us a jug, Betty, when you got a minute," Manfred called back over his shoulder. "Tony and I got some catchin' up to do."

Later that evening, Jack Schultz and Rob De Werter arrived at the yacht club. They had done the rounds of all the other clubs and arrived at the yacht club just before 10pm. Jack spotted Tony in the beer lounge with Manfred.

"What are you two buggers doing in here? Shouldn't you be in the bar? Or are you waiting for some women or something?" Jack hiccupped. Then he eyeballed Tony.

"Jeez Tony, it's you. What are you doing back here? Are the holidays over already?" Jack was the plantation owner who sold the cow to the school.

"Tony, meet Manfred," he swaggered, "Manfred, meet Tony." Then he turned his head back towards the bar and called out to Rob. "Rob, over here, I'm in the lounge with the ladies."

"Ladies, what ladies?" Rob asked as he entered and scanned the room in earnest. "Jesus Jack, you must be hallucinating. I don't see any ladies. Have you been on the happy herbs or something?"

Rob had obviously had a few too many to drink as well. "Hell, I'm starving Jack. We've got to bloody-well get something to eat. I'm half pissed from drinking on an empty stomach. Let's go over to Chung Tai's and get some Chinese. We can always come back here later."

"Maybe we should all go to Chung Tai's," Tony suggested. "We haven't had anything to eat either. We can still drink grog there if we want."

They all agreed and stumbled out of the club in single file like blind men groping around in the dark. They piled into Jack's utility with Rob in the front and Manfred and Tony on the tray at the back. Jack took off, and in the space of fifteen seconds had already put it through all four gears and was caning it down the main street of Rabaul at close to sixty miles an hour. He had already arrived at Chung Tai's before the ute had fully revved out. He then hit the brakes and threw the vehicle into a complete spin to face back in the direction of the yacht club. Manfred got out of the car, poked his head into the driver's door window and said calmly, "Bloody hoon."

The two in the front seat were laughing hysterically.

"I'll tell you what, Tony; brings a bloke back to when we were kids riding in your old man's Vanguard ute," Manfred remarked.

"Sure, Manfred, the old beast was never driven faster than twenty miles an hour. Everyone in Babinda knew that."

"Yeah, except the time you cracked the ton in it down the Eubanangee straight on your seventeenth birthday," Manfred reminded him.

Chung Tai prepared a banquet for the four men and by the end of the meal they were all talking sensibly and were beginning to talk civilly to one another.

"I gotta go back to Balangot plantation on New Ireland tomorrow," Jack mentioned to Tony. "Looks like I'll be buying it but need to sort out a few more things. Rob is taking me over. Reckon I've had enough to drink for tonight."

"What are you – man or mouse?" Manfred teased.

"Aw, look at who's talking, Tony. This is the bloke who on his first night in this town disgraced himself by getting pissed to the eyeballs. Rob and I had to carry that big lump of lard home and put him to bed like a little boy, and he's asking me whether I'm a man or a mouse."

"Guilty," Manfred admitted. "I take it back. You're all man Jack, but you're not Man Fred," he laughed.

"Aw shit, we're really starting to scrape the bottom of the barrel now," Rob said. "Hey, if you guys can get the afternoon off tomorrow, why don't you come over with us on the cat? The mission house at Ulu Island is vacant this weekend and every weekend. You two could get off there and Man Fred here can experience what it feels like to live in paradise. We go across to Balangot and return to Ulu on Saturday night. We can have a few beers on the beach and leave Sunday around noon. We'd be back in Rabaul around six at night. What do you say?"

"We've got to do it, Manfred," Tony said. "Rob's not joking. That place is paradise on Earth. Can you leave work at noon tomorrow?"

"Whatcha mean, can I leave work at noon? I'm the bos man, Tony. My second-in-charge, your ex-student, can run the show blindfolded. Just ask him. Looking forward to it Rob."

"Done then," Rob said. "Meet you both here at twelve noon tomorrow."

Tony was up early the next morning and went on to the verandah of his house to check if Petrus, Leo and Oliver were at the farm. His house on campus gave him a view of the entire perimeter of the farm, although parts, like the area behind the pig pen, were obscured. Frangipani was happily chewing on her cud in the early shade of the fig tree near the cattle yard. There was a rattle of noise coming from the caged chickens which suggested to Tony that someone was within earshot of the birds. He guessed the boys were probably behind the pig pen making preparations to wash it out and feed the two pigs. The drake then started trumpeting and Tony knew that somebody had to be there.

He descended the stairs and made his way down towards the pig pen. The grass was long from the summer rains, and the previous night's downpour left droplets of water trapped where the leaves clung to the stems of grass. The cuffs of his trousers were soon soaked and his feet began to lose traction inside his rubber thongs. He tempered his pace to a stork-like walk as he picked his way around the taller patches of grass. Petrus was the first to come into view, and Oliver was not far behind him carrying a bucket full of chicken pellets.

"Mr D'Italia, you're back," Petrus said.

"Hello sir," Oliver chimed in as he lifted the pail high and balanced it on his head. The solid mass of steel wool that was his hair cushioned the base of the bucket perfectly, so that he could let go of it at any time and not have to worry about it slipping off. "How was Australia?" he enquired.

Oliver especially loved spending time with young Manfred and they would often play cowboys and Indians all over the farm. "I carved a pair of pistols for Manfred while he was away."

"He'll love that, but he won't be coming up until May." Tony peered over their shoulders. "Where's Leo?"

Petrus's mouth grimaced as he cast his eyes away from Tony's gaze.

"Ooh, there's been a lot of trouble with Leo," Oliver told him.

"Yes, a witchdoctor from the Baining Mountains performed "puri puri" on him because his father had not paid the second bride price payment that was due to the parents of his future bride. Leo's right leg swelled up and he has big boils all over it," Oliver said. "It's very scary sir."

"We think he might die," Petrus added. "His father has gone to find another witchdoctor to perform stronger magic to save his life."

"Where is Leo now?" Tony asked.

"He's over in the squatter settlement behind the teachers' houses." Petrus pointed at the settlement directly behind Tony's house.

"You go and find him and tell him to come here immediately," he ordered. "I'll wait here."

Petrus bolted off towards the village.

"You feed the chickens and then come back," Tony instructed Oliver.

As the boy left, Tony pondered on what to do with Leo.

The locals believed strongly in magic. Sometimes it was performed to produce good outcomes, like bringing rain to their crops or fish to their nets. Other times, the purpose was to inflict harm on people who had breached sacred taboos like the rules of kinship or social behaviour or where an individual had committed an offence against a member of another tribe. In traditional society there were three main ways to remove the curse, which could sometimes end in the death of an individual. The first was to pay compensation. The second was to seek the help of another medicine man who could perform stronger magic. The third, in the event of someone dying, was to avenge a death by a payback killing using a knife, axe or spear. Sorcery was so prevalent throughout PNG that the government enacted a Sorcery Act with severe penalties to try to curb it. Sorcery was known throughout PNG by a host of different names, including puri puri, mura mura, dikana, vada, mea mea, sanguma and malira. Bad sorcery attracted prison sentences, imposed under the law. Charges included pretending to be a sorcerer, attempting to use or procure sorcery, possessing the tools of sorcery, or even telling fortunes. Sorcery could even be used as a defence for wilful murder to get the charge reduced to just murder or manslaughter.

Petrus returned from the village with Leo in tow. Leo was limping badly and was obviously in a lot of pain. He leaned heavily on a makeshift crutch and approached Tony sheepishly. He was afraid Tony might order him to do something he did not want to do. Tony saw the grotesque gaping ulcerated wounds on Leo's leg and ordered Petrus to accompany Leo to Nonga Hospital immediately for treatment. He gave him money for transport and a note for the head surgeon of the Nonga Base Hospital. During the year, tennis team competitions were the main expat sporting activity and both Tony and Doctor Markus, a surgeon, belonged to a team called Chalkies and Choppers. Tony hoped Doctor Markus would look after Leo and give Tony updates on his progress each week on tennis night.

Tony went home and the "jungle telegraph" had already done its work and informed Tony's haus boi that his Masta was back from Australia. Sam was there waiting at the bottom of the stairs to his house, greeting him with a wide smile and a mouth and teeth stained red as if he had been rinsing them daily with mercurochrome. Sam followed him all around the house, asking about the family and peppering him with stories about all the things that happened while he was away.

Sam emptied his suitcase while Tony showered, and put everything neatly away except for the wrapped gift which he left on the double bed. When Tony entered the bedroom, Sam was still staring at it like a dog keeping watch over his bone.

"Presen bilong yu Sam. Opim em," Tony smiled.

Sam caressed it for a moment with his eyes and hands before opening it carefully. His huge black fingers were as dexterous as the points of knitting needles. He removed and then folded the wrapping paper neatly and cradled the box containing the gift. He shook it a little as if trying to guess the contents and cast furtive glances at Tony.

"Opim em," Tony repeated.

Sam opened the box and inside was a bright yellow transistor radio in a yellow leather case, complete with a set of yellow headphones. Sam's eyes lit up and he was gobsmacked. Tony inserted the batteries and loud clear music started pumping out of the "liklik wailis". Sam was ecstatic.

Tony packed a small suitcase with a few clothes, including a pair of swimming togs. The rest of the suitcase was packed with duty-free alcohol for him and the others to enjoy over the weekend – a bottle of Johnny Walker Black Label Scotch whisky, a bottle of Bundaberg Rum, two bottles of Baileys and a bottle of vodka.

The water on Simpson Harbour was as smooth as a sheet of glass as Rob hoisted the sail to catch the gentle westerly breeze that propelled his catamaran *The Flying Dutchman* on its course due east towards Ulu Island; the second largest island of the Duke of York Island group. The twenty mile journey took six hours. Groups of dolphins accompanied the boat in relays, as swarms of multi-coloured fish hitched a free ride in the slipstreams of both hulls. The two bottles of Baileys and plenty of ice ensured that nobody's throat had a chance to become parched. All Tony and Manfred had to do was to relax and enjoy the journey.

Rob and Jack stayed overnight with them at the small mission guest house on Ulu Island and left for Balangot plantation early the next morning. Balangot was about twenty-two miles east-south-east of Ulu and south of the settlement of Namatanai on the west coast of New Ireland. Tony and Manfred went in for an early morning swim near the small jetty a fair distance from the front of the guest house. The water glistened as though handfuls of coloured jewels were being cast into the refracted sunlight just under the surface. The jewels settled on the sandy bottom among a myriad of sea-urchins, starfish and bêche-de-mer. Schools of fish ventured closer to gawk at the two foreign bodies invading their aquatic environment.

They later exchanged one heaven surrounding the underwater reef for another of cool light sea breezes underneath a cluster of small coconut palms. Tony went back into the guest house and returned with two cold South Pacific "green" bottles of lager from the kerosene powered refrigerator.

"Good thing you thought to bring along a case of these little beauties," Tony said as he thrust one into Manfred's hand.

"Pub opened already has it?" asked Manfred. "I was worried it might be closed for the public holiday we just declared. You took long enough."

"Yeah, I thought I would bring back a couple of these as well." Tony showed Manfred the two cones he had in the cup of his hand, "To help bring back the memories of the good old days."

"Don't usually smoke that shit," Manfred said, looking at them. "The Yanks were forever puffing on the old hoochy cooch. The VC could smell them coming from a mile away." He thought about it and then accepted one. "There weren't any 'good old days' in Vietnam, Tony," he added. "Maybe we can skip that chapter in our lives and go back to our Happy Valley days; they were good days." He accepted a joint.

Tony lit it and then lit his own. They breathed in deeply to savour the delights that they knew were locked away in the fine textured weed and dreamed a while. Manfred was the first to speak as if his mind was beginning to unravel.

"Remember the story I told you when we were kids; about 'Wallaby Jack' Joe Black's heroic feat in the rescue of his mate, up in the scrub at the Boulders in Babinda? Well, as you know, he was my hero as a kid. I think he was almost everybody's hero, old Joe Black. Etched his name into the folklore of our district, Joe did." He waited for Tony to acknowledge it.

"Yeah, well how could I ever forget it? Every time we crossed the double-barrelled bridge on our way to Happy Valley, you reminded me of it," Tony said.

"Yeah, well, when I went over to Vietnam, I got told another ripper of a story." Manfred just stared at the stub of the joint pinned between his thumb and forefinger. "Like an angel pissing on your tongue this stuff, man. I feel like I'm twenty-one again, Tony me mate."

"Yeah, you're not wrong," Tony said. "So what story were you going to tell me? All I know is that while you were over there holed up in some bunker somewhere, us guys over in Oz were shacking up with a whole bunch of crazy love-struck sheilas, smoking this stuff. Then we got into the mushrooms up in Kuranda. I nearly died once from mushroom poisoning. Not a very nice trip, that one. It was the sort of trip you need to have if you're thinking of giving up the habit. Man, it was bad."

As they both kicked back a while, Tony sucked on the remnants of his joint. Eventually, the burn on his fingers left him in no doubt that there was not another draw left in it. He jettisoned it, flicking his fingers as if to shake off the hurt it had caused him. Manfred had lost his train of thought. He was happy just floating. Then, he sat up suddenly, as if he had just fallen off his magic carpet.

"Wow, I haven't known that feeling for a long while!" Manfred's eyes were wide. He started blinking repetitively as if he was trying to sight-test whether or not he was back to reality.

"I'm still here aren't I? I'm not in heaven or something am I?" he said as if needing reassurance.

"Nah, you're still here, mate. You were about to tell me a story that you heard in Vietnam. I need another good story. It's been a long time since 'Wallaby Jack' Joe Black," Tony fished.

"Oh, yes. Well, I was only in Vietnam a few weeks when this story came filtering through about this Yank sniper operating around Hill 55. His name was Carlos Norman Hathcock II would you believe."

It was a rhetorical question but Tony had to answer it.

"You'd have to believe it. I haven't ever known a Yank that didn't use his middle name and didn't have a number after his surname ... like royalty or something. Jeez, they'd grease him in North Queensland if he tried to call himself that up there," Tony remarked.

Manfred smiled. "Maybe, but this guy was better than royalty. This guy was a legend. He was so deadly as a sniper that the VC had a $30,000 bounty on his head. Dead-eye

Dick had nothing on this fella. Over ninety-three confirmed kills were accredited to Carlos and his personal tally was over 300."

"What's a confirmed kill?" Tony asked.

"A confirmed kill is where the kill has been confirmed by an active third party who has to be an officer, besides the sniper's spotter," Manfred explained.

"Anyhow, this guy starts making a name for himself. The VC called him 'Lông Trăng' because of the white feather he wore in the band of his hat. He was accredited with shooting an enemy sniper through the sniper's own scope, hitting him in the eye and killing him. That particular sniper was high profile, code-named 'Cobra' and had been recruited to Hill 55 with the express purpose of taking out Lông Trăng.

"Now his next kill was especially high profile. She was a Viet Cong sniper as well as a platoon commander and interrogator. She struck fear into the hearts of the troops around Hill 55. Her most notorious deed was when she cut off the eyelids of a captured twenty-year-old American soldier during his interrogation. Then she cut off his genitals and had him released back to his camp where he bled to death shortly after."

Manfred took a deep breath then continued. "She was known as 'Apache' by both the US Marines and the Army of the Republic of (South) Vietnam because of her methods of torturing the enemy.

"When Carlos took her out, it really shook the bees out of the hive. The enemy sent out a whole platoon of snipers to get Lông Trăng and avenge Apache's death. It was time for Carlos to remove the white feather. He was then deployed to take out an even greater trophy. He volunteered to crawl 1500 yards on his belly to take out an NVA Commanding General. It took four days and three nights of crawling to get himself into a position behind enemy lines where he could take out the general. Bang!" Manfred made the simultaneous gesture, representing a gun, with the thumb and index finger of his right hand extended towards Tony, who was wide-eyed with disbelief. "Right through the heart ... killed him stone dead."

"Wow, incredible bloke this Carlos. Did he learn to shoot in Vietnam?"

"No, he learned to shoot just like you and me; hunting in the bush with his dog and a .22 calibre single-shot rifle. Only difference was that in Vietnam he became a man hunter."

Tony thought for a moment. "I have read where Ernest Hemingway once claimed that there was no hunting like the hunting of man. He then went on to say that those who have hunted armed men long enough and liked it, never really cared for anything else thereafter. I guess Carlos was one of them; a hunter of man. Did he survive the war?"

"Yes, and I haven't even got to the really heroic part of the story yet. Snipers are loners. They operate independently of all the troops. They have the ability and the discipline to just lie in wait and remain in a state of utterly complete concentration. They are answerable to nobody but themselves, with no obligation towards anybody else; just do or die.

"Anyhow, after I had been in Vietnam for about eight or nine months, I hear about this LVT-5 Amtrak that struck an anti-tank mine and was immediately engulfed in flames. Carlos, who was riding on the vehicle at the time, pulled seven marines out and was himself severely burned in the process. As a lone-wolf sniper, he used to maintain that he killed to save the lives of marines. On that day, he proved that he really cared for them."

"Interesting hearing those stories, Manfred," Tony said. "Most people in Australia had no idea what you guys were going through and what you were prepared to do for your mates. We may have heard about the atrocities in My Lai and to a lesser extent My Khe, but the savagery of people like Apache against soldiers in the field was never reported. I believe the moratoriums held across Australia in 1970 to 1971 were held with a genuine desire to stop the war in Vietnam. However, I question in my heart the reasons why people in both Australia and America wanted to stop the war. Was it because of what was happening to you guys or was it because of what was happening to the Vietnamese? We knew you guys were being killed and wounded. We knew enemy soldiers were being killed and wounded in even greater numbers. That's part of the normal course of events in war.

"What we found out was that in Vietnam, women and children, the old and the sick, were also becoming the casualties of war and in great numbers. Villages were being razed to the ground, crops and food stores were destroyed and the whole infrastructure of the country was being decimated by 'search and destroy' missions and sustained bombing campaigns. Whole forests were being defoliated by Agent Orange. Families and future generations were being poisoned by dioxins, while farmers' fields were being sown with landmines that would claim the limbs and lives of innocents long after the war was over. We won't even talk about napalm.

"What we were never told, not once, was it ever reported what it was really like to walk in the shoes you guys had to walk in. What do you do when you are confronted by orders to carry out certain tasks that are anathema to anything you have ever done before? Orders are orders and need to be obeyed. In war the victims are not only among those who fought the war, but also those who stayed behind. Vietnam vets have been saddled with a conscience over deeds that were carried out under orders. Where does society draw the line between right and wrong, courage and cowardice, loyalty and treachery, obedience and mutiny or religious values and social values?

"Negligence in confronting these issues is what has caused our society to be divided in apportioning the blame, so that ultimately, the returned soldiers were condemned to be society's scapegoats and saddled with society's conscience." Tony went silent.

"Well, it's 1976 now. The war's over and not too many people have got around to thinking about it like you have Tony, my friend. It's all hatred out there. 'Baby killers', that's what they see us as and they actually called us that. Regardless of what anyone thinks, mud sticks. Those thoughts are not going to go away anytime soon," Manfred lamented.

"The government needs to take responsibility and to man up to the fact that they made a monumental blunder. That would be the least they could do to get you guys off the hook," Tony suggested.

He cracked open another two South Pacific stubbies of beer and took two more joints out of his pocket. He handed one of each to Manfred, who took a long hard swig and emptied half a stubby of beer in one gulp. Then he settled with his back against the trunk of a palm tree and lit the joint with the lighter that Tony had passed to him.

"When we were on a mission," Manfred resumed talking, "Sometimes they would go on for two to three days. Most of the time, everyone was on edge. The enemy's use of booby traps had a very negative psychological impact on us. The sheer fear of booby traps created such stress that it led to severe anxiety in both the commanders and individuals. The needle-sharp punji stake pits or the more sophisticated 'bear traps' and crossbow traps were all designed to cause maximum pain and inflict horrific wounds without necessarily killing the soldier. The punji stakes were fire-hardened to penetrate the soles of soldiers' boots and were coated with excrement or poison to cause blood infections.

"Trip wires tied to grenades, 'toe poppers' and anti-personnel mines like 'jumping jacks', 'bouncing betties' or Claymore mines created the most damage. Those guys were actually digging up our mines and using them against us. Again, they usually only severely maimed the soldiers and were another part of the terror campaign by the enemy. Anti-vehicle weapons like the B40 rocket-propelled grenade, concrete fragmentation mines, mortar-shell mines and oil drum mines were all lethal." Tony remained quiet. Manfred was on a roll and Tony knew that he would keep on talking, so interjecting wasn't going to do any good. He felt that talking about his experiences and having a good listener was probably helping Manfred come to terms with his demons. Tony had read about the healing attributes of this phenomenon, where disclosure often helped with the recovery process of people traumatised by war.

Manfred continued. "In all of these stressful situations, sometimes it was easier to just do as you were told. It saved you from having to think or justify your actions. If you created any delay in responding to instructions, you could be jeopardising the rest of the soldiers in your platoon.

"Often, we would come across people in the field who, for one reason or another, were acting suspiciously. They would be challenged and told to 'stop', 'halt', 'put your hands up' or 'don't move'. Someone would call out in Vietnamese 'dừng lai', 'tam dừng lai', 'giỏ tay'! or 'không cara chuyền'. If they didn't do as they were told, that was interpreted as suspicious.

"One farmer was walking across a ploughed paddy field with his buffalo. The animal was not pulling any implements and when the farmer saw us, he jerked the animal in another direction and started walking quickly towards the forested end of the field away from us. The commanding officer of our platoon instructed someone to call out to the man in Vietnamese. The peasant began to walk faster. The lieutenant was quick to make a decision. 'Moore, get ready to take him out. Comino, warn him again in Vietnamese.'

"Comino called out again, loudly, 'dừng lai ... tam dừng lai ... giỏ tay! ... không cara chuyền', but the man kept walking away with his back towards us.

"'Okay Moore, take him out!' the lieutenant said. The silence of the rice field was shattered by one single rifle-shot from Moore's SLR. In two neatly executed actions, the peasant fell to his knees and then face down into the water.

"The platoon immediately spread out and took up a defensive position. Moore and two others were sent off to confirm the kill. 'Silly bastard,' swore the lieutenant. 'All he had to do was stop.' He then added, as if to justify his decision, 'Probably had something strapped to that buffalo. Check all around for any sign of abandoned weaponry,' he shouted out to the three men.

"When Moore and the two grunts reached the buffalo and the dead man, Moore raised his thumb skyward. The other two began persuading the buffalo to turn around towards the platoon commander. There, strapped in a tight straw bundle to the beast's side were six rocket-propelled grenade launchers. The lieutenant had made a good call on that occasion.

"On the other hand, they often made bad calls as well. I guess bad calls just have to be lumped in with all the other collateral damage the war brought to Vietnam."

Manfred and Tony sat in silence, finishing off the stubbies and sucking deep mouthfuls of therapeutic smoke into their lungs.

"Then, one day, it was my turn." Manfred's face turned to a deathly pale, devoid of any colour.

Tony sensed some kind of confession coming on. The time was right for it, with both primed and Tony proving to be a good listener. He didn't ask stupid questions. In fact, he didn't ask anything at all. He just listened and that was precisely what Manfred needed.

"Same sort of situation. It was the same as fifty or more similar situations that the platoon came across on their many missions. This time, about sixty yards away, two girls stepped out of the forest from behind some shrubbery and started walking slowly and determinedly towards us. They were dressed in black 'pyjamas' similar to what the Viet Cong wore, and white cotton blouses. They each had on the traditional Vietnamese style conical rice-paper hat; the nón lá. The hat on the girl to the left seemed to be sitting towards the back of her head and was shading what seemed to be a baby in swaddling clothes strapped to her back. At that distance, they could easily have been just children.

"As they continued walking towards the platoon, the lieutenant called a halt. 'Tell them to stop,' he called out to Comino and Comino shouted, 'dừng lai ... tam dừng lai ... giỏ tay!... không cara chuyền', in Vietnamese. The leading girl extended her left hand out towards them. 'Uc dai loi, got chocolate?' she called out clearly in a childish voice as they kept coming forward.

"'Wright,' yelled the lieutenant, 'Get ready to take the front one out.' My SLR was up into the pit of my arm and firmly against my shoulder. My eye had the front girl planted firmly and clearly in the sights. 'Give them a last warning Comino,' he demanded a second time. Comino called out again, 'dừng lai ... tam dừng lai ... giỏ tay! ... không cara chuyền'.

"As they ignored the second set of commands in Vietnamese, it triggered a sort of paralysis in me. It was like that time I nearly drowned in Babinda Creek. The muscles in my arms went limp. I couldn't think. All I wanted to do was call out 'Help! Help!' and hope someone could come and rescue me. My mind kept telling me that they were only children for God's sake; girls just wanting Australian Army rations chocolate. Inside my head I could hear myself begging them, 'Please stop. Don't make me do this. Put your hands up.'

"'Take the front one out, Wright', was the lieutenant's call. Beads of sweat were rolling down my face, or maybe they were tears. Yet I could still see her clearly in my sights. All I had to do was pull the trigger and it would be over, for her and for me. 'Shoot, Wright ... shoot damn you!' shouted the lieutenant.

"As I watched, the girl at the front leaned forward and placed both hands firmly on her knees. The girl on the left immediately moved across and took up a position behind her. There, in the middle of my sights, I saw the whole situation unfold before me. A Soviet made RPD light machine gun, propped up on a bipod, had been strapped to the leader's back just above the shoulder blade and was now facing our whole platoon.

"I could still have fired, but the message from my brain was not coming through. The girl behind grasped the gun and began firing. The sound of rapid fire filled my ears as soldiers either side of me began falling. By the time I could get a second bead on the girl, the gunner had lifted another drum magazine from the 'swaddling' behind her back. She jettisoned the empty magazine and slammed the new one into the machine gun. That meant she had already pumped 100 7.6mm rounds into our troops and was ready to pump another 100 rounds into us in the next ten seconds.

"Then the gunner fell and so did her accomplice. I don't know who it was, but I certainly did not fire a single shot. Wounded soldiers were calling out all over the place. I couldn't tell who was hit, because they were all at the ready and had all gone to ground and started shooting as soon as the girl started firing. I was the only one standing; shell-shocked, in suspended animation it seemed. I just stood there gaping and wondering what I had done.

"'Dickhead, Wright! Why didn't you shoot when I told you to?' the lieutenant screamed at me. 'Now look what you've done!' I looked around me and all I could see was the blood on the uniforms of several of the soldiers. Two had been shot in the head and were stone dead. Others were writhing on the ground, while the medics were rushing around trying to stem the flow of blood.

"All I had to do was pull the trigger; obey the order. If I was so concerned about the two girls, I could have fired a warning shot. If they were innocent, that warning shot would have stopped them coming forward and they could have raised their hands. If only I could have had the presence of mind to do that, I would not have found myself with the blood of my mates on my hands. They were kids asking for chocolate. I was sure they were kids. I didn't want to kill kids. There was a baby as well. That's what I thought."

"Hey, hey, Manfred," Tony urged, trying to snap him out of that spiral of self despair. "Stop beating up on yourself. You can't help what happened. All the soldiers in that platoon knew the danger. They were all at the ready. You said so yourself. You don't know what happened. It all happened too fast. In that split second that the girl bent forward, the rest were already on to it. They took her out, didn't they? It all happened in the first ten seconds. What was done was done. Nothing is ever going to change that now. It was just a bad call on your part. You said so yourself. We all make bad calls. For that moment in time, you just happened to be Manfred, the warm-blooded God-fearing civilian. You couldn't let yourself become a cold-blooded assassin just on the whim of a bloody command from some lieutenant for God's sake. It's not as if you were a long-term professional soldier like a mercenary or something. You were just a glorified civilian dressed up in battle fatigues and co-opted into fighting a war. In your situation I would have done exactly the same thing. If I thought they were just children asking for chocolates, I could never have pulled the trigger to 'take them out'. What makes me so different from you, Manfred?

"If you're guilty of not pulling the trigger, then I'm guilty of not going to war. It wasn't me out there with my finger on the trigger having to make the decision and live with the consequences. It's taken a long time for me to realise this, but collectively, those of us who weren't over there have to be prepared to share the blame for the things that went wrong. War is a very busy street. It doesn't matter which side of the street you are on, you make a mistake and you can get hurt. You said so yourself. If someone else makes a mistake, you can get hurt. People who have nothing to do with the war get hurt. Shit happens, Manfred. People sitting on the fence back home, watching it all happen on TV or reading about it in the papers, don't know anything about war. I'm sorry this had to happen to you, Manfred."

Tony shook his head as he grasped a new perspective on how things could go pear-shaped so quickly. How else would he have found out if Manfred hadn't explained it to him and given him such a vivid example? It was a good thing that Rob and Jack returned the following morning to take the focus away from what had transpired the previous day. There was no alternative but to put all of those events behind them and shelve the past for a while to allow the body and soul to extricate themselves from the shock and horror of it all and begin to breathe again so that life could go on.

Chapter 11

In Rabaul, there was always the likelihood of a volcanic eruption or earthquake but the one event that eclipsed all else at the commencement of the school year in Rabaul turned out to be a natural event as well. Frangipani gave birth to a Brahman-Jersey cross heifer calf called Jimini. It was announced officially on morning assembly at the school, but the word had already passed around and it was old news for most of the students. There was an audible buzz of excitement around the school as students migrated to the cattle yard at the back of the school after the morning assembly to celebrate Jimini coming into their world. At one day old, the calf was already suckling on her mother's teat and with such determination that the students were quite astonished. It was Frangipani's first calf and she was not accustomed to this behaviour. Occasionally, she would lash out with a well placed kick to Jimini's body or even head, which left the gathered multitude aghast. Already, after just one day on this earth, Jimini was experiencing both the joys and the pain of living.

Soon there was a procession of pre-school and primary school children from all over Rabaul and the surrounding districts visiting the school to get a glimpse of Jimini. Many of the town's people dropped in daily to witness the progress of this golden coloured calf. Plantation workers from the Western, Southern and Eastern Highlands and the Enga District came at weekends to gawk at those strange "bulmakau" beasts that produced meat and yet looked nothing like the pigs they knew. They loved the taste of the meat that they called "skweamit" because it was used to make stew. Most of them had thought the meat came from tins of bully beef purchased at trade stores. It took an extra dozen eggs to take the furrow out of the health inspector Karl Schneider's brow. He had come to assess the community health implications of the birth of another potentially large animal. He also expressed the desire to sample some fresh milk on his next visit before giving his official nod of acceptance.

Tony was fortunate to have a staffer who was raised on a dairy farm in Australia. Kev was coerced into agreeing to train a few students to milk Frangipani as Jimini was too small to consume the large amounts of milk her mother was producing. The cow wasn't used to being milked, and on the first day kicked Kev in the jaw and nearly knocked him out. He yelled and he swore, claiming that the reason he had gone to Papua New Guinea was to get away from cows. After that, he showed them how to tie a leg-rope to stop Frangipani from kicking them or the milk bucket while they were milking.

Back in Australia, Cara was missing her man and the children were missing their father. Talking for long periods of time on the phone each night was proving expensive, while Tony was experiencing what it was like to be working away from his family. He began to feel the real pain of separation for the first time. He immersed himself in his work to keep his mind off those thoughts. He had been planning to expand his agricultural project by starting up agricultural business ventures in the field. Several village elders whose children had studied at Rabaul High School, had expressed an interest in setting up chicken projects in their village. However, Tony had already decided which village would be awarded the project. It was Pauline's village of Navunaram where a powerful Tolai clan ruled. They could make a substantial contribution to helping the project flourish. Pauline had the business acumen and bookkeeping skills and the practical experience to help establish the venture as a commercial enterprise. The chickens were housed in sheds made from bush materials and chicken wire with corrugated iron roofs. Instead of cages, they used deep litter, automatic feeding and drinking troughs for hygiene with laying boxes and roosting structures built-in. All the work on the village project had to be done on weekends as extra-curricular activities for students who travelled to Navunaram in the school truck. The villagers fed them and gave them small gifts of food such as yams, sweet potato, bananas and coconut to bring home to their parents at the end of the day's work.

Pauline's father was a village elder, and the family was quite wealthy in terms of the traditional wealth of shell money called "tambu". The shell money had intrinsic value because of the intensive labour that went into making it. First, the raw kina shell was harvested in West New Britain and laid out in the sun to dry. Once dry, a small hole was bored through the shell to enable it to be threaded onto long thin slivers of bamboo. The wealth of a family was gauged by the length of shell money the family had stored in their house, a custom handed down through each generation.

Once the project was underway, Tony invited Manfred to go up to the village with him to inspect it for himself. Navunaram was about a twenty minute drive from Rabaul along the picturesque Burma Road towards Kokopo. The road skirted the waters of Simpson Harbour on the left and then a sharp right turn started them on a gentle climb into the mountains towards Navunaram. A luxuriant stand of palms on both sides canopied the road, creating a tunnel of fronds that allowed only flickers of light to trickle through the dense foliage.

Japanese POWs had built the road after World War II as part of the post-war reconstruction in the area. Caves that the Japanese had dug out to protect themselves during bombing raids honeycombed both sides of the mountain. An eerie atmosphere of abandonment hovered over the entrances to those caves. Tony noticed that Manfred seemed apprehensive and tense as his body bounced around on the front seat. His hands were wrapped tightly around the handles above the door and on the dashboard, and his knuckles were white from the pressure being exerted on them. Tony could tell that Manfred was uneasy about something because the usual camaraderie he exhibited towards Tony had been replaced by silence and a stern expression that signified some inner turmoil. However, once they reached the village, he became more relaxed and seemed to enjoy the tour of inspection. Manfred liked building things, and the use of bush materials intrigued him. All of the villagers crowded around them, and the children were particularly inquisitive, edging their way in as closely as possible. Tony again noticed Manfred's discomfort. One explanation could have been something to do with the children but that did not explain his behaviour on the way up the mountain. Tony guessed it must have had something to do with Manfred associating present events and situations with past experiences. Much of the terrain, vegetation, smells, and sounds of the jungle in PNG were like Vietnam, and even the people and the way they lived in the villages had a lot in common with the Vietnamese. That explanation made sense to Tony and it was easy to empathise with him. In fact, Tony was beginning to feel that he could anticipate Manfred's moods and behaviour.

It wasn't until they were on their way back down the mountain that Manfred began to open up again, explaining to Tony that whenever he went into a jungle environment, he inadvertently became hyper alert and vigilant. He felt it in particular when he was travelling through the tunnel of palms and when he was confronted by the foreboding entrances to the caves. A feeling of claustrophobia enveloped him invading his psyche so that he felt as if he was entrapped in a coffin underground and couldn't breathe. His body felt as if it was in limbo, unable to respond physically to the situation, while his brain was short-circuiting continuously, urging him to break out and get into the fresh air while there was still time or he would surely die. Sometimes the urgency was so great that he "would lose it" for a period of time as he described it.

"It is times like that," Manfred explained, "that I begin to think I'm a pretty sick puppy; that maybe I should try and get help. It's abnormal and it's terrifying. There's no way I would have walked into one of those caves for quids. To my mind, they would have to be booby-trapped. Shit mate, something's stuffing with my head and I don't know how to deal with it. In the village, I figured those kids were going to climb all over me and suffocate me. How ridiculous is that?"

Tony didn't reply. He was pleased to be Manfred's confidante and he thought it was better to listen, giving Manfred the opportunity to change to another subject, which he finally did.

"Who would ever believe it possible that we should both meet up here in PNG and be looking at little villages together in the middle of the jungle?" Manfred marvelled.

"Yeah, who would believe that when you were lying in hospital with your wounds we were only a stone's throw away?" Tony replied. "I thought you were dead, would you believe?"

"What about the two special students working on your project who happen to be working for me now?"

"That's bizarre," Tony agreed. "Maybe you and I are linked together through some sort of kindred spirit."

"Well that's all I need to know. As if I haven't got enough bogeymen haunting me at this point in time," Manfred replied dismissively.

They both laughed and that set the tone for the rest of the journey back to Rabaul.

Manfred's principal job with New Guinea Engineering was to liaise with four major clients in the northern part of Papua New Guinea. He would troubleshoot problems at any location and then arrange for the work to be transported to the Port Moresby workshop. His biggest client was Steamships Trading Company. Since 1924, the Steamships Trading Company had been synonymous with the development of PNG and New Guinea Engineering was heavily involved with the logistics side of the company. Steamships Shipping and Consort Express Lines were the subsidiaries of the company that provided coastal shipping services, while the land freight division was called East West Transport. Most of the work with Steamships had to do with the refitting of ships and engine maintenance. Manfred would compile a scheme of work required for each individual refitting job and, after his quote was accepted, arrangements would be made to sail the boat to the workshop in Port Moresby for the refit to be carried out. Smaller jobs were transported overland to the nearest port and then shipped to Port Moresby for repairs. Some work required dismantling at the source which the local trade staff did under Manfred's guidance and supervision. Often, as an incentive to the local trade staff, Manfred would arrange for a two week stint of work experience for locals in the workshop in Port Moresby. This was also consistent with the ethos of localisation of industry and work staffing that was the newly independent government's initiative. Over time, those people from the outlying districts were given the opportunity to work and experience life in the capital.

The Papua New Guinea Electricity Commission (ELCOM) also provided much work. ELCOM was responsible for the generation, transmission, distribution and retailing of electricity in PNG as well as servicing individual electricity consumers. New Guinea Engineering for its part was commissioned to carry out all the work on their turbines, fixing bases and blades on a contract basis as well as providing ad hoc engineering services to their agents. Manfred soon found himself travelling the length and breadth of the northern section of PNG, as well as making short visits to the highlands of central PNG.

The third major customer was the PNG Defence Force. This involved mainly the refitting and repair of patrol boats that were all provided to the PNG Government through foreign aid from Australia. Manfred also looked after the requests of patrol officers from Provincial Affairs. These were usually smaller jobs such as repairing native runabouts – boats that were abandoned when they stopped working. New Guinea Engineering assessed the work at patrol officer outposts and either repaired or replaced them. This was also financed through foreign aid and thus proved to be a lucrative contract for the company. Meanwhile, Manfred was able to meet many real characters among the scores of patrol officers. He often commented to Tony how they all bordered on being troppo and how he often felt comfortable while in their company.

"It doesn't say much for the state of my mind," he admitted.

The other client, which required specific specialised services, was Bougainville Copper Limited, the world's largest open-cut copper mine at the time, situated on Bougainville Island. If the job was too difficult or too large for the company to handle, Manfred would have to fly over from Rabaul and oversee the removal and transport of the machinery or machinery parts to Port Moresby. Otherwise, New Guinea Engineering would only visit twice a year.

Because Manfred was so professionally involved with his clients, it was often necessary to travel to Port Moresby with the job and that was when he would take local staff with him to gain the workshop experience available in the capital. It was all progressing well. On one occasion, while in Port Moresby, he stayed with Ted Jantz. He liked Ted's company and he felt they had a lot in common.

"Why did you leave it to the last moment Ted to tell me that you were a Vietnam vet?" Manfred had been longing to ask him and finally did.

"Because I know that a lot of people don't want to talk about it," Ted replied. "It doesn't take a lot to push one of us guys over the edge. We have copped it from every angle for too long. Firstly, during our training, they conditioned us to behave like robots; do as you are told, ask no questions, do not think for yourself, show no compassion and fight 'til you die.

"Then in the battle field, survival strategies and other priorities changed the way we thought. Incessant patrols, being shot at by snipers, the fear of landmines and booby traps, being attacked or ambushed, experiencing the death of a comrade or witnessing horrendous wounding and mutilation ... civilian deaths; they all took their toll, Manfred, as you well know. Finally, you went home and the people who sent you there in the first place are waiting for you at the airport to spit on you and call you names. They didn't want to employ you. Even the RSL in many cities and towns didn't want to acknowledge you. Where I was, it became quite clear they didn't want us to march on Anzac Day. You lived in fear of what people were going to say to you and with shame. You lost your self-esteem and sense of belonging. There was no support out there to get you through the hard times, the bad memories, the flashbacks and nightmares and hallucinations.

"No-one wanted to even try to understand what you had been through; as if it was entirely your fault in the first place. How could they be expected to understand why we are always on edge or jumpy or nervous when they have never had to live the way we had to – hyper vigilant, minute after minute, day after day, week after week. How could they imagine the stench of dead bodies full of flies and floating in puddles of grey mud?

"They all wanted to hear stories of great courage and winning, but nobody wanted to hear about human weakness or losing; heroes not humans, that's what they were expecting. We can't all be heroes all of the time. Isn't it all just part and parcel of being human?"

"Exactly!" Manfred concurred. "Being human was knocked out of you very quickly and efficiently. From the first day you went into the army, they gave you a service number. That's all you were, a number … and 'never forget it' they told you. They dehumanised you to such an extent that you no longer even considered the enemy as a human being. They took away your right to exercise any emotions whatsoever in the battlefield and then, when you came home, people back there expected you to cry at funerals," Manfred recalled.

He felt he needed to talk about those things just as Ted did. At last he was talking to someone who knew where he was coming from and it felt good. Those were the exact sentiments Ted had uttered to him after he had given him the job and it had struck a chord.

"Well, I don't want to 'hard luck' you Manfred, but the day my wife left me and I lost the kids, that was the day I just wanted to die. Believe me, it was more my fault than hers. I couldn't live with myself, let alone expect her to live with me. I expected too much from her. She tried; believe me Manfred, she tried. She said she forgave me when I said I was sorry for abusing her. She said she forgave me when I said I was sorry for striking her in a fit of rage. She forgave me for being angry all the time and for being cold and heartless towards her. She even said she was sorry when she left me. No woman should have to go through what that poor woman went through.

"The children ... the children didn't have a father, not really. They had a depression junkie living with them. When I wasn't having an anxiety attack and hiding under the bed from the sounds of a helicopter or ducking for cover when a light bulb blew, it didn't take them long to work out they were living with a wreck yet they were supposed to pretend I was normal. All they ever wanted to do was avoid me and escape from my presence. All I ever wanted was for them to get out of my sight as well. What a great relationship that was.

"So what did I do? I did exactly what they taught me in the army. I ran and I went to ground. I ran to a place where nobody would want to follow me and I hid. Every now and then I would take a peek out there but the enemy had me outnumbered. They talk about 'the enemy within', which is far more daunting than any enemy at war. They spit at you and you duck just like when you are under fire from the enemy. Only the spit never goes away. It sticks to you up here." He tapped his head. "And it burns, just like napalm."

"Tell me about it," Manfred's face was deadpan as he prepared for the first time to talk about Angel's death.

"I lost my wife in an unfortunate car accident, but I know that she too suffered from her disappointments. Most of her disappointments were with the powers that be. She would never forgive them for abandoning the 'sons and daughters of our nation in their time of need', that's how she described it. She was forever trying to fight my battles the moment she realised the government and the people had turned their backs on Vietnam vets. She would never accept that and she was always there for those partners of Vietnam vets who needed to be given hope. She even started up a women and friends' action support group to offer each other some semblance of a lifeline to sanity. Their families had become dysfunctional and in various states of disarray. Many veterans weren't able to face society let alone hold a job.

"I'm one of them, Ted. In five years I've had five jobs. I'm a loner now. I'm doing what the war, not the army, taught me to do in order to survive; trust nobody but yourself. The 'new guy' in the platoon was dangerous because he was green. The short timers were dangerous because all they wanted to do was go home alive. We were the piggies in the middle surrounded by 'Charlie' and forever in danger of being killed by friendly fire from the Yanks.

"Sure, I lost my wife in a car accident; snuffed out just like that," Manfred clicked his fingers in front of Jantz's face. "You know what the real tragedy is Ted? We all lost our wives, our families and our friends to some extent, after our tour of duty. Some were divorced, others kept up a facade, and the rest simply walked away. When I came up here for the job interview with you, I sat next to this bloke on the plane called Jack Schultz. The first thing he asked me was 'What are you running away from?' I'm there thinking 'Is this guy a psychic or something?' because that was exactly what I was doing. I just wanted to start a new life in another country."

Jantz stood up and went to the refrigerator to take out another two stubbies. The kitchen table was littered with empty stubbies; 'dead marines' he called them, because they were green and empty, of no further use and lifeless.

"Let's have another drink before the ship goes down. That's what I say, as I echo the famous words uttered on the *Titanic* when all hope was gone," Jantz said. They clicked bottles and downed the stubbies slowly with neither yielding until both stubbies were empty.

"You have a plane to catch back to Rabaul tomorrow. Maybe we should think about getting a few hours sleep," he suggested, patting Manfred on the shoulder and bidding him goodnight.

* * *

No sooner had Manfred returned to the office in Rabaul when he received a phone call from Jantz informing him that the managing director of Bougainville Copper Limited (BCL) had put out an SOS to New Guinea Engineering in Port Moresby. The supply of electricity from the Loloho power plant on Anewa Bay on Bougainville was in jeopardy. Electricity was the lifeline to the Panguna mine site. Apparently, anti-mine pro-secessionist saboteurs had damaged some of the in-house machinery in the Loloho engineering workshop. The managing director was worried that in the event of the turbines breaking down, production at the mine would be brought to a halt. A contingency plan was urgently needed to avert such a scenario.

It was only a few months earlier in January when Manfred had just arrived in Rabaul that anti-National government riots in Bougainville had been stepped up. Prior to those riots, the situation with the mine had always been manageable, albeit on tenterhooks. Conzinc Rio Tinto Australia (CRA), the parent company of BCL, had made an agreement with the PNG administration to give the national government twenty per cent of the mine profits. The Bougainvillians were offered nothing. In protest, villagers around Panguna forced the suspension of drilling operations which were eventually resumed under police protection.

The site of the huge mine on Arawa plantation was acquired compulsorily from the natives for a pittance and the Australian High Court dismissed the villagers' objection to the granting of a special mining lease to BCL. Within a year, a meeting of 1500 villagers gave birth to another micro-nationalist movement called Napidakoe Navitu, demanding secession from PNG and that all royalties from the mine go to Bougainvilleans. In 1974, the Bougainville Provincial Council was formed by the PNG Government as a compromise, promising a bright future and more royalties from the mine but unfortunately for the Bougainvilleans, nothing eventuated in terms of royalties. The Bougainville Provincial Assembly took it upon themselves to declare the independence of the Republic of North Solomons; the new name for Bougainville. It was September 1, 1975, fifteen days before PNG's independence from Australia, and again, they demanded all royalties from the mine.

When Manfred arrived to take up his position at New Guinea Engineering in January 1976, the North Solomon Islanders had begun rioting in Bougainville. Landowners were receiving a paltry 1.3% of the mine profits which was a far cry from their request for all of the royalties. Government offices were attacked, the airstrip was torn up and the mine site of Panguna was invaded. Police and PNG paramilitary forces, the dreaded "riot squads", had to be brought in to quell the riots.

A couple of months later and Manfred had suddenly inherited a role in any contingency plan with BCL. He had to ensure that the Loloho power station in-house engineering workshop was functioning again as soon as possible and he would have to be available to supervise and carry out any hands-on repairs. Secondly, he had to be on call at the actual mine site in Panguna which had an emergency power generator on stand-by. Manfred was up to the task and he had Steven to help navigate any indigenous issues that might arise during that politically sensitive period.

On the coast away from the mine site, BCL built Arawa, the new capital of Bougainville, as a dormitory town halfway between Kieta, the original old German capital, and Loloho. It had a population of 40,000 people of whom 3000 were expatriates. It was locked in to a sandy stretch of beach by the rugged Crown Prince Mountain Range which hosted the huge open-cut Panguna mine. The town was a modern metropolis by PNG standards, with banks, schools, modern fully staffed hospitals and large shopping centres. AFL and rugby league teams drew massive crowds of spectators every weekend, and the waters off the beaches were a playground for sailing boats, speed boats and cruisers. The town had become a symbol of prosperity in PNG.

A welcoming party of Steven's family and wantoks surprised Manfred and Steven when they arrived at Arawa airport. It was arranged that after they had done their business at the Loloho power plant, they would go back to Steven's village for a traditional feast and some celebrations. At the power plant, Manfred assessed the damage to the machinery and he decided it would need to be shipped to Port Moresby for repairs, and at first light the next day, Manfred himself pitched in to help achieve that as quickly as possible.

In Arawa, they were booked in to a motel close to the beach. After a welcome shower and a few hours in the air-conditioned unit, they were ready to face the arduous journey up to Steven's village. Manfred wondered what Steven's perspective was of the whole BCL dilemma.

What he discovered in the time it took for them to reach Steven's village, was that from the people's standpoint it was the deceit factor that was the most despicable element in the whole sordid affair. The people were deceived about profit sharing in the revenue from the mine, jobs for Bougainvillians at the mine, pollution from the mine, the rights of landowners around the mine, and the right to self-determination promised to the people. None of those promises was kept. The people stood to lose all they had – their land, livelihood, self-respect and their culture, and in some cases their freedom and even their lives. That's the way Steven saw it, and Manfred was able to identify with their plight because he could see how fickle the political promises had been and how greed, the quest for power and deceit had been used as tools to subjugate them. They had been betrayed by their "god" BCL, just as he had been betrayed by the "god" he soldiered for in the war in Vietnam. BCL was offering them the crumbs that fell from the table and Manfred's government was offering the same, denying the Vietnam veterans the support they should have been entitled to after the war.

The village consisted of twelve low-set A-frame bush material huts arranged in a circle with a large communal area in the middle. The thatch on the roofs was folded kunai grass that had a sweet smell of crisp dried hay. Small black patches of ash remained where fires had burned out the night before, while the rest of the village had been swept out diligently with their straw brooms so that not a leaf littered the area.

That night, Manfred was treated to a colourful display of cultural splendour with food, dance, singing and music arranged for the evening. The villagers were hosting a "singsing kaur" with the traditional food being Tamatama. It was mixture of cassava, taro, banana, aromatic herbs and spices mashed into a pulp and then fashioned into small dim-sim size bites and served on a platter of green banana leaves. The villagers rubbed coconut milk mixed with Tamatama on Manfred's face as part of their welcome, which did not impress him. Then as the singsing kaur progressed, they performed the Solomon Dance to the beat of a bamboo band. Dressed in long grass skirts, tarpa cloth arm bands, head bands and breast bands and shell necklaces, the dancers mesmerised Manfred in the flickering firelight. The ritual of rubbing Tamatama on the faces of the people singing, dancing or playing music was repeated as well as rubbing cooking oil on their instruments and costumes. Finally, all the cooked food such as taro, banana, kaukau and yams was shared among the villagers. It was a feast and a sense of community that Manfred told Steven he would never forget.

Next day, back at the Loloho power plant, Manfred was in excellent humour. He put it down to the great time he had had the night before. The trade staff efficiently dismantled the equipment under his direction, and packed it all into crates. That evening he was able to phone Jantz and tell him that the cargo was on its way to Port Moresby. Jantz was impressed and hoped Manfred and Steven could take a day off to enjoy the beach at Arawa after sorting out Panguna, the site of the BCL copper mine.

His two days in Arawa and Loloho was the break he needed to prepare him for the nightmare he was about to witness on his journey with Steven up to the Panguna mine site. The absolute destruction, degradation and pollution of the land, river, sea and air was Vietnam all over again by another name. What the allies did to the environment in Vietnam with Agent Orange, incessant bombing and during search and destroy missions, BCL emulated in peacetime under the banner of economic development. Steven pointed out the heavy siltation on the banks of the river and how the highly polluted poisonous tailings had been dumped into it. The Jabu River and the Kawarung River were graveyards for every form of marine life. The bad river water, which was their only source for drinking and washing, was causing the locals to break out in sores, forcing them to move away from their traditional lands. But they had nowhere to go. What the company hadn't taken or polluted beyond use belonged to other tribes. Dispossessed, the villagers moved to shanty towns on the fringes of the larger settlements of Kieta and Arawa, forced to work for the company to earn money for food or face starvation. Unfortunately for them, the wages were a fraction of the wages paid to expatriates, and if they objected, there were plenty of "redskins" from the mainland and other islands happy to take their place.

Manfred had been in PNG for two-and-a-half months and BCL was the only client he had not done business with so far, mainly because the company had access to its own engineering workshop at the power plant. He was supposed to visit the mine in June as the first of two scheduled visits a year, so the environmental holocaust that stared him in the face during that unexpected visit was very confronting. Devastated by what he had seen and heard about the whole BCL saga, Manfred knew there was a "solution" to the Bougainville Copper conflict and it lay in the huge power pylons lined up all along Panguna Road. It was that simple; use the dynamite at the mine to blow up the power pylons and sever the artery that was the lifeline to Panguna.

* * *

Another unpredictable event for Manfred and Tony was the news about the impending marriage of Pauline. Neither of them had a clue that she was in a relationship, and if anyone should have known something, it should have been Tony because he knew Pauline and her family so well. Steven however was able to explain it all. The reason Pauline had never been in a relationship was because she had been betrothed to a Matupit boy when she was just 15 years old. Tony had always wondered why such a striking and intelligent woman had never shown any interest in boys at any stage during her stint at Rabaul High School. Steven discovered she had in fact been betrothed the year Tony came to teach in PNG. Pauline however would have none of it and was exercising her independence by declaring her love for a Sepik boy from the mainland. The bride price down payment would have to be refunded.

Tolais have always been very traditional, with every tribe consisting of two clans and marriages arranged across clans. Sometimes, marriages occurred across tribes within the same language group, which was a common practice and acceptable. Pauline's tribe spoke kuanua, and therefore she could have married someone from the Matupit or Raluana tribes who also spoke kuanua. Steven explained the plotting and intrigue that went into any marriage in Tolai society. In Pauline's case, she was marrying into uncharted territory. The marriage to someone from another district and a mainlander as well was breaking with the tradition of marriage and ceremony in Tolai society. Firstly, the Tolais were structured as a matrilineal society, and thus the system of inheritance and land stewardship was through the female line. Secondly, the rules of kinship were different in Tolai society compared to patrilineal societies on the mainland. For example, Pauline's first-born child had to come under the care of the father's family. The rest of her children had to live in her village.

There were ways around it and the best way was for a suitable Tolai family to "adopt" the groom according to tradition. The "adopting" family could then satisfy all of the demands of a traditional wedding ceremony. This was what the prospective groom did. A Matupit Island family whose son he had befriended at the Vudal Agricultural College "adopted him". It was then incumbent on the groom's family in Sepik district or the groom himself to provide the necessary shell money or tambu for the bride price to the adopting family. The bride price was measured in fathoms of tambu. The Matupit family kept some of the tambu to cover their expenses for the wedding. The remainder went to the father of the bride who used part of it to cover expenses and part of it went as a gift to the bride who would accumulate the shell money and eventually pass it on to her children.

Once the tambu was ready for distribution, everything was in readiness for the marriage ceremony. Representatives from both families met at the bride's village and faced each other with ceremonial spears that were ominously jabbed into the ground. Then, the groom's "adopted" family threw tambu onto the ground in front of the bride's family as a symbolic gesture, like a down payment. The bride's family, in response, picked up the tambu and threw it back on the ground in front of the groom's family, suggesting it was insufficient. The tambu was sent back and forth a number of times until the full amount previously agreed to was presented. They then exchanged betel nut, lime and pepper to seal the deal.

The drama continued as the bride hid in the village while the groom sought her with a group of his friends. When they "found" her, she was "stolen" from the village. The villagers from the bride's village retaliated in a ritual chase after the "thieves", throwing stones and hitting them with sticks. The groom's party escaped and carried her to their village where she lived with his family until the actual wedding ceremony. Everybody contributed to the feast at the ceremony. Traditional foods such as yams, taro, sweet potato, kaukau, pig meat, chicken meat, green vegetables and coconut sauces were all on offer and in generous portions. "Blood pudding" from the slaughtered pigs was mixed with ferns, wrapped in banana leaves and cooked in underground mumus. It wasn't until after copious consumption of betel nuts and alcoholic beverages that the wedding ceremony was supposed to be over.

However, ironically, a second Christian ceremony was then performed with the taking of vows before God. Manfred argued with Tony that it made a mockery of the majesty of the initial ceremony and felt like "Okay, you've had your fun, your child's play. Now, let's do it right".

"Tell me Tony," he questioned. "Why in the hell would you stuff up a really good traditional marriage ceremony by tacking on a Christian version at the end?"

Tony just shook his head.

"Come on now," Manfred insisted. "You've done all this study of anthropology, sociology and psychology. Give me one good reason."

Tony remained silent.

"You know what Tony, you should have studied criminology, that's what you should have studied, because that's what it is ... bloody criminal," Manfred said.

"I guess it all comes back to the 'superior' white man having to do things 'his way' in the end," Tony suggested. "We have always been the only ones with all the answers, despite these so called 'primitives' surviving quite well for thousands of years without us."

"Makes me want to puke," Manfred responded. "We always stick our noses in where they don't belong, just like we did in Vietnam. Look at how 'our way' turned out there. Only difference is that with Pauline, 'our way' was religious and economic whereas with Vietnam it was political ideology. How much does anyone really care about these people? How much does anyone really care about the Bougainville people? I'll tell you how much … about as much as they cared about us when we returned from Vietnam. They just kicked us in the guts and relegated us to the scrap heap because they had no further use for us. There was no 'sorry', no support, no 'thank you', no resettlement, no rehabilitation; only resentment, retribution and ridicule.

"Look at these poor buggers; all we ever did was exploit them. Our mob has always had this obsession with money. When a disciple like Judas can sell his soul for thirty pieces of silver, what does that say for our religion? Why couldn't we just leave these people alone? We kept telling them their culture was not worth a brass razoo until they eventually believed it," Manfred fumed.

"Unfortunately, that seems to be the way of the world, Manfred. The argument keeps coming back to 'if we didn't do it to them, then somebody else would have'," Tony said.

"Pretty shithouse argument isn't it!" Manfred growled. "I went to that singsing kaur thingy festival with Steven I told you about, when I was on Bougainville. It was totally traditional. The food, the dancing, the music, the costumes were all part of their society in its purest form. Nothing changed there, until the white man came with their bloody Bougainville Copper. Promises of a better life came thick and fast, with better health, an education and better living conditions and that ridiculous tinsel town of Arawa ... promises, promises. How did those promises all end up? They ended up with another tribe reduced to begging in the streets, dispossessed of their land, stripped of their pride, their self-respect, their right to live, their right to work and now, even their right to worship. What the shit ever happened to the International Charter of Human Rights? BCL was championed to these people as the intervention that was supposed to lift them out of the Stone Age and parachute them safely into the modern world.

"It was exactly the same as all that bullshit about World War I being supposedly the 'war to end all wars'. Then they tried the same story again with World War II. It was never going to happen. We just carry the can mate." He then turned on Tony. " 'All the way with LBJ', that's what you all chanted when Johnson went over to Oz. When our guys got back, you would have heard a pin drop if you could have filtered out all the abuse. There was no chant supporting our guys. It was all 'up your nose with a rubber hose' in sign language. What about those moratoriums and protest marches you guys held when you felt you wanted to be the good guys in the whole rotten saga? If you really wanted to bring the boys home, you would have welcomed them when they got there, not spat on them."

Manfred turned on his heels and stormed off towards his car. He started the engine and took off, leaving Tony abandoned in the village and shaking his head as to how

Manfred could lose control so hopelessly once he became wound up over an issue.

Thoughts about Manfred's rather callous but truthful outburst and the fact that he had walked out on him on the night of the wedding in Navunaram, remained with Tony for several days. It left him wondering what Manfred really thought of him. After all, he had made it obvious he believed that Tony was no different from the rest of them although Tony had made it clear to him that he was all the way *against* LBJ. What did worry Tony was where to draw the line between those who chanted 'All the way with LBJ' and those people who attended the moratoriums across Australia. Were they the same people? He had no reason to doubt that they were. Why? Was it because they had been told to do so? Were they just following a herd mentality and if so, what right did they have even being there? Was it just another one of their 'coats of many colours'? The more he thought about it, the more Tony realised that Manfred was never going to forget what Vietnam did to him. He would put it aside perhaps, appear to be readjusting to civilian life, appear to be happy in his work, appear to be at peace with himself and pretend that he might be able to forgive and forget, while his reality was that his anger and his disappointment would build up inside him like a pressure cooker until he had to let off steam like he did at the wedding.

The defence forces, especially in the United States, brought many diggers back home in the middle of the night after those moratoriums. Those who were repatriated with their units on the *HMAS Sydney* were better prepared for the homecoming than those who came back as individuals. The discharge papers of individuals returning were processed and they were told to find their own way home. That was exactly what had happened to Manfred, only his discharge papers were not completed by the time he left 1 Military Hospital Yeronga and he had to ask his mother to purchase his plane ticket in Babinda because he had no money to get home. It was no wonder he became unsure whether he should hold his head high or cower like a dog that had been beaten; not only at the hands of the enemy but by his own master. Why did some veterans feel compelled to change into civvies on their return home? Were they so ashamed of their uniforms? Why did some RSL members spurn them and make them feel unwelcome there? The stigma was such that many diggers were reticent to participate in the Anzac Day marches. Anzac Day was a significant, if not pivotal part of Australia's cultural heritage, and this denial was a cruel act of finality in making them feel that they had been ostracised from Australian society.

Tony pondered all of those unanswered questions. Perhaps the answer was to be found elsewhere in the Australian psyche. Had the Australian people done all of these things in order to expunge their own guilt for having sent those boys to war? Were they just shifting the blame? Did the soldiers go to Vietnam of their own accord or did the Australian people send them there with no choice? Did the actions of the Australian people against Vietnam vets equate to an atrocity committed against their own people?

When Tony was satisfied that he had reflected enough on most of the issues, he decided to go over and see Manfred at his house. It had been a week since the wedding and they needed to talk. Manfred was sitting in the lounge having a beer and staring at the wall. Tony knocked and Manfred yelled out to him to come in.

"It's me, Tony," Tony called out in case Manfred didn't want to see him. There was always a possibility that might be the case after what had transpired at Navunaram.

"Oh, great mate, I'll get you a cold beer." Manfred jumped up to go to the fridge. "Green or Brown?" He referred to the colours of the stubbies of South Pacific Lager.

"Green thanks," Tony said, relieved and pleasantly surprised.

Manfred handed him a stubby.

"Hey look, about the other night …" Tony started.

"What other night? I don't remember anything about the other night. Must have had too much to drink," Manfred interjected.

"That's great by me. I probably had too much to drink as well," Tony replied, happy to have been given the opportunity to make peace.

"So what's happening?" Manfred asked as he sat down.

"Well, I was thinking … it's Anzac Day this Sunday. I thought you might want to go along with me to the RSL club."

"Don't go to RSL clubs. Vietnam vets aren't welcome there … and I won't be marching either. They've made it pretty clear in the past that they don't want us around," he replied gruffly.

"I mean for the two-up game. It's in the afternoon and it's not a matter of being welcome. Everyone goes, even Father Frankie, the Catholic priest from Vunapope Mission. It's a ripper of an eye-opener. I have never seen or heard of a two-up game that could ever approach the scale of the one they have up here in Rabaul each year. It's big-time mate; all the bookies set up stalls at the venue and there's no limit on the bets. You gotta come along. Come on. What do you say?"

"Nah, I'm not much of a gambler," he countered.

"Aw, come on. It's only once a year. I need someone to keep an eye on me and to make sure I don't get into trouble," Tony begged.

"What sort of trouble might that be?" Manfred inquired.

"Well, like ... if anyone says one bad thing about Vietnam vets, I'm gonna punch them in the nose," he joked.

"Shit Tony, in that case, you can count me in. Anyone touches you, I take them out. Is that a deal?" Manfred put out his hand to shake on it.

"Don't think we need to take it that far. Just if I look like I'm losing, or if a couple of them come on to me, I'd appreciate a bit of help." He slapped the back of Manfred's hand with the back of his hand and that was as good as any handshake.

That Sunday, everything Tony said about the scale of the two-up game proved to be right. All the bookies and the tellers from the four banks were there, and the place was overflowing with expatriates. Father Frankie was in his black ankle-length smock to participate in the festivities. A lot of people had been drinking since early morning so there was a lot of noise and most people would be loose with their money. Many people were just there for the social outing and were happy to sit and chat or have a beer with their friends. There were women and children, but no locals ever went into the bar even though theoretically they were allowed. There were several mixed race people there as well, reflecting the old PNG maxim Manfred had heard from expats that "If you're white, you're right. If you're brown, stick around. If you're black, stand back".

When the game was about to begin, all the tables were moved away from the centre of the room. The players gravitated towards the outer edge of a "ring" delineated by a low circular wooden structure about twenty feet in diameter. The "boxer" took charge of the game and the "ringie" looked after all of the activities in the ring. The boxer asked for a "spinner" from outside of the circle who had to put up a certain amount of money as a wager that he could throw heads three times. There were two pennies. The sides with the head were polished and the sides with the tails were kept dark. They were placed tails up on a six inch length of thin flat wood marginally wider than the pennies, called a "kip". The idea of the game was for the spinner to toss the coins at least ten feet into the air, ensuring they spun in the process and landed on the ground within the circle. It was the ringie's job to make sure all of these things happened or else he would call "foul toss" and the spinner had to throw again. The coins either landed with the two heads showing, the boxer declaring "heads up" or with two tails showing, whereupon he called "tails up", or they landed head and tail showing, which he called "odds". Odds meant that nobody won and the spinner tossed again. If the spinner threw three sets of heads in a row, he could "toss the kip", which meant that he could withdraw from the game and collect seven times his initial stake from the boxer who would take a commission out and give him the balance of the monies. That commission money went to Legacy, which was the body that helped support the children of war casualties.

People placed bets against the "box" which contained the spinner's money. They hoped that the call was tails up, which meant they won and a new spinner was called in to carry on the game. If the call was heads up then the spinner won and prepared to toss again. Punters also bet on the side on heads or tails. The tails punters held the bets and matched the money outlaid. When all bets had been laid, the boxer called out "come in spinner" and the game began. Thousands of kina, the official PNG currency, were lost and won as the game rolled on. At one stage, Tony, who was betting tails and was holding bets on the side, was winning almost 1000 kina. Then he had a bad run and started to lose. The banks ran out of money by 10pm and declared that there was 30,000 kina in circulation.

The whole club was buzzing. Some people passed out from too much alcohol while other drunks became aggressive after losing their money. Nobody came near Tony who had the giant 6ft 2in tall bodyguard standing beside him with arms folded, just waiting for somebody to step out of line. When the game shut down at midnight, Father Frankie had been given 1000 kina in donations for the mission, Tony was ahead about 120 kina, Legacy made several thousand kina, and everyone else claimed they had lost.

Tony invested the winnings into cartons of beer and they drove off to continue celebrating at Manfred's place. Peter was there in the yard chewing betel nut with the haus boi he had trained for Manfred, and they helped bring the cartons into Manfred's house.

"Yu spak, bos?" he asked, wanting to know if Manfred was drunk.

"Mi tupela spak," confessed Tony as he handed him a six-pack of beer.

Manfred had to admit that he had had a most enjoyable night although he said it took a lot to get used to the crowds shoving and pushing.

"I was tempted to plant a few of those fairy-fingered bank teller guys," he said. "Half of them wouldn't have lasted a day in Vietnam." He thought for a moment. "Jeez Tony, I miss me mates in Vietnam. Wish they could have been there with us tonight. You would have really liked them. Old Gazza, he had his head half blown off in the Battle of Binh Ba in June 1969. You don't even get a chance to say goodbye mate. One minute you see him go down and the next minute he's being dusted off in a chopper. They don't even call time-out to bury the guy. It's just go, go, go. Then there were all the guys who were wounded and to think we have never even had a reunion and it's almost five years down the track already. Everyone just took to their foxholes and disappeared out of sight out of mind the moment they got back to Oz. It's not right, Tony."

"I'm sorry about those guys, Manfred. I wish they could have been here for you tonight. I would have loved to have met them and bought them a beer. It would have been the least I could have done for them … better than nothing," Tony said, sensing things were just going to get worse.

"I'm the one who should be sorry. I just took to my foxhole too. I should have found the families of the two guys who died because I made an error of judgment. They would have been alive now if it wasn't for me. Instead, they were machine-gunned down; shot through the head. I saw it with my own eyes Tony. What sort of a mate would you call that? It should have been me, not them that got shot. Why should I be the one that had to survive? Why should it have to be me that got to go to the two-up game and have fun while their bodies are six foot under out there rotting in some grave somewhere? Tony, I don't deserve to be here."

"Don't talk like that, Manfred. You gotta get help. I'll help you find help," Tony assured him.

"Help for what? There isn't any help for me out there. I tried to get help. When I went to the doctors in Australia, they told me I was just 'battle fatigued' as they called it. Another one told me I had 'post-war neuroses'. I went to a shrink and he told me I had 'survivor's syndrome'. Shit, I could have told him that. The first two told me to take painkillers and the psychiatrist told me my condition would eventually go away and to try not to think about it.

"Then they conned me into going to see a counsellor. When I came out of that meeting, I felt worse than when I went in, Tony. I was so ashamed when I confessed to the counsellor about those two guys who were shot in the head. I didn't even tell Angel about that day. I couldn't tell her I was responsible for two of my mates dying and several others getting wounded. I wake up in the middle of the night and they are there, just staring at me. That's it for sleep for the night. I sit up all night drinking piss because I'm too scared to go to sleep. I tell you, this problem is never going to go away. There's nothing you or anyone can do to help me."

Tony just sat there listening. He was so overwhelmed by the whole conversation he had to hear him out because he had nothing useful to say.

"Maybe you are helping a bit, Tony," Manfred conceded. "At least I can talk to you. I know you can't give me absolution but maybe the idea of absolution is bullshit anyway. Maybe just the ability to talk to someone like I can talk to you can help me. I feel better when I can talk to you."

"I'll go one step further than that," Tony said. "Let me carry some of your burden. Whenever you feel it's too much to carry, just will it over to me. Just imagine that I am there walking with you wherever you go and lean on me. I'll be there to help you get through it. We can get through this together."

Manfred looked at him as if it made some sense to him. "Thanks Tony." He stood up. "I want to go to bed now. You can let yourself out. Goodnight."

Tony returned home to an empty house. He showered and went to bed as it was 2am but he couldn't sleep. He put it down to the adrenalin from the two-up game the previous evening. It was a good opportunity to think about Manfred's dilemma and what he could do to help. The idea that he had even considered making Manfred's problem his problem seemed irrational at first. He had not gone to Vietnam. He did not have blood on his hands. He had not even voted for the government that sent Manfred to Vietnam because at that time the voting age was still 21 and he was too young. He had a wife and two children to think about. He had participated in the moratoriums and had helped organise them. If the moratoriums had incited people to hate Vietnam veterans then, as a former organiser, he had to take responsibility for that at least.

Then there was another way of looking at the problem of guilt. Maybe he should have felt guilty because he hadn't gone to war, because he had been lucky and his marble hadn't been drawn in the lottery. Maybe he should have felt guilty because he wasn't put in a position where he could have been killed or wounded. After all, Manfred felt guilty for having survived the war. Tony had never previously had any conscience in feeling compelled to share the blame for the war in Vietnam or for what happened to the veterans on their return home. He had just kept his head buried in the sand. Perhaps it was true that he had participated in moratoriums and played the hero, pretending that he was trying to bring the boys back home when really he was participating in a process that was demonising them. He felt guilty that he was not there for Manfred while he was feeling alone and abandoned in the military hospital in Brisbane, but the truth was that he really didn't know. Yet if he had really felt for the boys he wanted to bring home, surely he could have made an effort to visit the injured and disabled soldiers at the hospital. It had never occurred to him because it was never on his agenda. Admittedly, he was young and if he had known then what he knew today, he certainly would have gone to visit them.

He was at least guilty by association of all the terrible taunts and humiliation that the veterans suffered. The more he thought about it, the more everything Manfred said about him was probably true although he would never have come to that realisation if Manfred hadn't put it to him so bluntly. He kept asking himself what he would have done if he had been ordered to shoot the two girls asking for chocolates in cold blood in Vietnam field that day, as if the answer to that question would give him the answer to his dilemma. *"There but for the grace of God go I,"* he thought. Manfred had been asked to do the dirty work that could have well been asked of him.

He thought about any parallel situations that had already been played out in history that might help him respond to his predicament. He remembered reading about the weight of conscience that descended upon the German people after the Nazis committed so many atrocities against the Jews in World War II. Those who were innocent of any participation in any of the crimes still felt guilty by association. They felt guilty because they did not do anything to stop them. They had chosen to remain silent. The worst consequence was yet to unfold for them. Many of the descendants of those Germans soon began to feel guilty for what their parents had done. Tony remembered that after Israel proclaimed statehood in 1948, it became a place for survivors of the Holocaust. He had since read about how many young Germans volunteered to work in the Israeli Kibbutzim for periods of up to a year as a way to help expiate their sense of guilt.

He began to agonise over the thought of Manfred's pain and the state of his psychological wellbeing. He had already confessed that he was "a sick puppy". How could he help someone who has already tried and failed to help himself? Was he looking for an excuse out of having to help Manfred? Was he just pretending to want to help him? Was the time for pretending over? What could he do to try to make a difference? What could he do to try to help Manfred get his life back?

Maybe it was too late and all that had happened was predestined the moment conscription was introduced. Maybe Tony had to accept that those were the cards that had been dealt to Manfred. If he was realistic, what real avenue of support and eventual rehabilitation was there for Manfred? If, on the other hand, one of the main contributors to his condition had to do with being programmed during his basic training in the defence forces, then maybe he could be deprogrammed. In other words, if the desensitising and dehumanising could be reversed, there would be hope for him yet. He thought about it and despaired that the likelihood of that happening would be about as slim as trying to reverse a lobotomy. He could have been pensioned off and hidden away somewhere but that would have cost money and governments did not like committing themselves to paying out large sums of money over long periods. That would also have been tantamount to the government admitting liability for his condition. The simplest way was often to find some loophole or opportune behavioural breach that allowed them to lock him up, but that cost money too.

The Australian Defence Force had created its own Frankenstein in Manfred and he had become everyone's problem. Tony realised he would have to put his concerns about Manfred to one side as Cara and the children were coming up to PNG for the May school holidays in two weeks' time. Their arrival could legitimately take him away from all of the commitments he had made to support Manfred and give him more time to think. Maybe he was forgetting his priorities. Maybe he should be more concerned about his immediate family and let Manfred fend for himself for a while but that rationale was merely feeding his desire to opt out of the responsibility he had taken on with Manfred. What he really needed was to pull himself together.

Chapter 12

Jantz had come up to Rabaul to help sort out some issues regarding work with the management at the Panguna mine in Bougainville. Tony heard that Jantz had arrived in town and was staying at Manfred's house for a few days, and that provided him with some respite. On the morning after he arrived, a loud hammering on Tony's front door awakened him. It was Steven who told Tony that in the early hours of the morning, after a night of heavy drinking, a fight broke out between Jantz and Manfred.

"Fight? What sort of a fight? Was it a fist fight or an argument?" he asked.

"Both sir. First it started off as an argument and then it turned into a very bad fist fight. They broke furniture, they were swearing and they were both very drunk."

"Where are they now?" Tony asked.

"Mr Wright drove down to the wharf with a carton of beer and took off in the company speedboat."

"How do you know?' Tony asked.

"I followed him," Steven replied, and then added, "And he had a gun … a pistol."

"He had a pistol? Where did he get the pistol from?"

"He got it from his suitcase. He brought it from Australia."

"Where's Mr Jantz?"

"He's still at the house."

"Did you speak to him?"

"No. I thought it was best if you talked to him, sir. I have the car outside."

"All right, I'll come with you now and talk to Jantz. Just give me a minute while I get a couple of things."

Steven drove them to the office and Tony walked up to the house. Jantz was on the phone, but as soon as he saw Tony approaching, he gestured to him to go in. He had some severe bruising around his right eye.

"Take a seat, Tony," Jantz said after he put down the phone. "Manfred really flipped out this morning. We were talking about the mine at Panguna and he suddenly went off his brain about BCL and all the destruction it was causing to the island and its inhabitants. He kept calling it 'the other Vietnam' and he was visibly upset. He actually said to me that somebody should do something about closing the mine down. When I asked him what he meant by that statement, he said 'Someone ought to take out a few of those pylons carrying the transmission cables up to the mine. Take out the electricity and you take out the mine ... 'maximum chance of success and minimum chance of collateral damage'. That's how he described it."

"So how did it get to the fisticuffs?" Tony asked.

"I tried to talk him down at first but he has no way of coping with his anger. Then, the moment I placed my hands on his shoulders to try to coax him to sit down, he just let go with a barrage of punches that had me flat out on my backside before I even knew what hit me. He just told me to 'stick the job' and stormed out of the place."

"Look, Steven said he went down to the wharf and took off in the company boat with a carton of beer. I think he's probably going over to Ulu Island to have a few quiet beers and to cool down. He had a gun. Where would he get a pistol from?"

"Anyone can get a gun in Papua New Guinea. He could have bought it off someone at the yacht club or he could even have brought it from Australia."

"I'll take another boat and go looking for him. Maybe we should keep this quiet from the cops for now otherwise they'll be locking him away. If I'm not back by three o'clock tomorrow afternoon, then someone should come looking for me. Let's assess the situation first and make a decision later."

Jantz nodded. "He's a loose cannon at the moment, Tony. Don't imagine for one minute that there's a silver bullet that's going to fix all this. Most importantly, don't even dream that you might be that bullet. The problem with our condition is that it festers like a sore that won't go away. The germ can sit under the skin for years and then suddenly it erupts like a volcano and we become powerless. At best, it might have a half life, where over time the pain gets less and less. Most of the time, it goes the other way and gets worse as time passes."

That all made sense to Tony, but he refused to believe in his heart that there was nothing he could do for Manfred. Sometimes it was important to be prepared to go out on a limb if someone wanted to change things. People power was what had brought an end to the war in Vietnam and it was time for people power to get behind those guys and help lighten their burden. Tony's father used to tell him that God only put so much weight on any man's shoulders and never more than he could carry. After that, the humanity in man stepped up to the plate to pitch in and share the load. He had seen it himself where whole armies of volunteers and piles of food and medical supplies had been mobilised to help relieve the plight of communities struck down by disease, starvation and natural disasters.

Jantz arranged for Steven to take Tony down to the wharf and give him the keys to the second company speed boat. They checked that the boat had been fuelled up and the motor was running smoothly. It was a 17ft Haines Hunter with a 115hp Evinrude motor and Tony figured he would take an hour at most to get there. The journey across St George's Channel gave Tony time to think about what he was going to do once he arrived. The waters were smooth and the speedboat glided effortlessly on the glazed surface. Dolphins tried to keep pace with him, but they were no match for the power propelling the boat and soon dropped off, leaving other pods to take up the challenge along the way. The boat was called *Akuriap* which meant "dolphin" in kuanua. Dolphins hated sharks and Tony imagined he was *Akuriap* on a quest to save Manfred from being devoured by the "sharks" that were tormenting him.

The Duke of York Island towered over the horizon, making navigation easy. The main island to the east was so tall it shaded Ulu Island for the first hour of the early morning after dawn. He was certain Manfred would be there as he hadn't been anywhere else by boat and it was a place that was conducive to someone yearning for solitude; with water all around and "tides that took away the footprints in the sand and wiped the slate clean twice every day". Manfred had used those words himself when he had told Tony how he found it easier to escape demons like the "stalker" by being close to the sea on Magnetic Island off the coast of Townsville during his time in his rented hacienda after Angel died.

Upon arrival at Ulu Island, Tony noticed that the other company speedboat was tethered at the little jetty just out of sight of the mission guest house. He eased the throttle back, and edged his way towards the second pylon, pulling in just behind Manfred's boat. He hitched *Akuriap* to the wooden anchor post, and felt a little apprehensive as to what might transpire between him and Manfred. He climbed onto the jetty and scanned the beach and beyond the guest house, but could see no sign of Manfred. He stood on the beach just beyond the jetty with his hands on his hips watching and waiting a while. Then he called out.

"Manfred, it's me, Tony. I've come here to talk."

There was no reply. Tony approached the steps to the guest house and could see something had been scrawled on the flap of a cardboard beer carton. It read: "Seek and you shall find" in capital letters. It looked like Manfred wanted to play games. Tony was uncertain as to whether that was a good or a bad thing. He walked slowly up the short flight of stairs. There was an eerie silence about the place that Tony had never thought about before on Ulu Island. The door to the guest house was ajar and as he warily crossed the threshold, he pushed the door open and peered inside.

Suddenly, a tangle of human skin, hair and muscle came hurtling down upon him from the rafters above the door. The shock of it alone was almost enough to cause Tony to blackout and the sheer weight caused him to lose his balance and he fell heavily to the floor. Face-to-face with Manfred, he could see every vein swelling up around his neck and a death stare that was cold and calculating.

Manfred flipped him over onto his stomach and placed him in a headlock with his arm twisted behind his back. The side of Tony's face was pressed hard against the roughly hewn floorboards.

"Well, did you find me?" shouted Manfred as he shook Tony twice and rubbed his face against the boards. "Well, did you find me? Eh? Eh?" He repeated as he shook Tony again as if he was a rag doll that couldn't speak. "Did the 'word of God' come true for you? Eh, Tony, Eh?" he scowled.

"Shit Manfred, go easy. You're killing me, man," he spluttered through the half a mouth he was still able to get to function.

Manfred relaxed his grip a little, "'Seek and you shall find'; that's what your God promised you. Well you found me, so God's word came true for you," Manfred answered for him as he slowly shifted his body weight off Tony and squatted on the floor beside him.

Tony rolled over tentatively without wanting to appear too presumptuous about his freedom. "Great way to welcome your old mate, Manfred," he commented. "You almost broke my arm and scraped off half my face." He rubbed his arm and re-aligned his jaw.

"Aw, don't be such a pussy, Tony. You're lucky I wasn't in combat mode or I would have shot you. That's what we did in Vietnam – shoot first and asked questions later. What the hell are you doing here?"

Tony sat up and adjusted his shirt. "I'm looking for you ya mug. What do you think I'm doing?"

"Well, you've found me now. Seek and you will find. Remember God's promise?" He prodded Tony a few times and lowered his head to look into Tony's eyes.

"Oh, remind me, what's all this about God's promise?"

"It's about your God and my 'god'," Manfred said.

"When the army got their claws into me, they took your God away from me and replaced Him with their own 'god'. Their 'god' gave me the licence to kill and made me feel omnipotent. What chance did I have; I was young, I was impressionable, easily conditioned, adventurous and subservient to my commanders who were the high priests of the greater 'god', the 'god' of war. They replaced 'seek and you will find' with 'search and destroy' and that's all I did for the whole year of my tour of duty. You see Tony, that's where our two paths diverged. Yours wove its weary way into the woods where 'the deer and the antelope played'. You frolicked with the nymphs, swam with the fairies and floated on clouds of marijuana.

"As a soldier, on the other hand, I was crashing and bashing my way through the jungle in Vietnam, in the mud and the rain, being bitten by mozzies and sucked on by leeches. I kicked arse and had my arse kicked every day."

"Yeah," said Tony, looking for an opportunity to change the subject. "You've already told me all about that before, so when are you going to offer me a beer, Rambo?"

Manfred sprang to his feet and hoisted Tony up from the floor.

"What did Jantz have to say this morning? I bet he was really pissed off at me." Manfred dragged two stubbies out of the half empty carton on the kitchenette table.

"Well, what do you expect? First you give him a black eye, then you smash all the furniture, then you resign on the spot. Of course he's pissed."

"Yeah, well he shouldn't have put his hands on my shoulders. Everything I did after that was instinctive. He should know that."

"What's with the pistol there on the table?" Tony asked, pointing to the six-shooter behind the case of beer.

"That's my mate 'Charlie', the only one I'm certain I can trust; that is, until you came back into my life." He took the pistol and tucked it into his belt.

"Well, we've got a lot of important things we need to talk about. How about going for a bit of a walk around the island?" Tony asked. "There's a great little reef called Ulu Reef where we can swim, about half a mile to the south of here. I can grab some goggles and a couple of snorkels out of the Haines Hunter. Maybe you should put the rest of those beers in the fridge."

Manfred shrugged and nodded so Tony hurried off towards the boat. He figured the swim would serve as a distraction from the events of the last twenty-four hours as well as an ice-breaker for some idle chit-chat. When he returned, Manfred had stripped down to his shorts which he had rolled up to the crotch. He looked like the Tarzan of the North character with his arms folded and his tanned bristling muscles. The only difference was that Manfred had "Charlie" tucked into his belt in place of a hunting knife. Tony went inside to light up the kerosene fridge before they headed off to the beach. It was an easy walk and they were soon waist deep in the cool caressing waters of the channel between the sandy beach and the reef. Ripples of lemonade-like froth burst and plucked at their faces as the water deepened, and they pulled the goggles over their eyes. They dived in among the corals of the reef and immediately came across a pod of lobsters. They snuck up behind and caught two with their bare hands, which took care of lunch. The next hour was spent snorkelling across the shallow areas of the reef. Swarms of silver bait fish swept past their goggles. Angelfish with vivid stripes and speckled patterns dodged around the bright yellow butterfly fish with their thin elongated noses. Parrotfish with mouths resembling a parrot's beak flitted around in the shallower waters beside the cardinal fish with their large eyes and mouths staring down the two men through their goggles. Clownfish with their bright orange and glowing white markings or light blue bands contrasted with the bright blue surgeon fish with their yellow and black markings, spiked blade and venomous fins protruding from their bodies. Defensive damselfish in various shades of blue staked out their territory and guarded it with their lives, refusing to budge an inch. Tony signalled to Manfred to come over and catch a glimpse of one of the giants of the reef. Blended in beneath the coral was a huge groper over five feet long and probably weighing over 300 pounds. The sheer size of that fish was enough to convince them both to leave the water.

Tony collected some dry driftwood and soon had a small fire crackling on the beach. They decided to cook the lobsters there before going back to the guest house to finish off the beers.

"Did you ever see the movie called *They Shoot Horses, Don't They?*" Manfred asked as the delicate shellfish aroma of the lobsters began to break out from where they were cloistered in the hot coals.

"No. How long ago was it screened?"

"It was in 1970. I remember seeing it at one of the local cinemas around Yeronga somewhere on the rare occasion that they let us out of the military 'prison' hospital."

"It was probably either the Regal at Graceville or the El Dorado Cinema at Indooroopilly. They are the two closest to Yeronga," Tony said.

"That's the one – the Indooroopilly Cinema. Well in the movie, this couple, Robert and Gloria, enter a ridiculous 1930s marathon dancing competition in Los Angeles. They desperately needed the $1500 prize money and they desperately wanted to win so that they might become noticed and be able to break into the Hollywood film scene. After weeks of dancing, Gloria is so exhausted all she wants to do is die. On top of that, they suddenly find out that the cost of the marathon will be deducted from the prize money, leaving virtually no money for the eventual winners.

"Gloria is totally devastated by the promoters reneging on their promise. She feels betrayed and empty inside and broken down both mentally and physically by the marathon. She takes out a gun and points it at herself ..." Manfred takes his pistol from his belt and points it at his own temple.

Tony panics and pushes it away.

"What the hell are you doing, Manfred, you silly bugger. Don't play those games!"

"No, let me finish. This isn't a game. Let me finish the story. She points the gun at herself ... but finds she can't pull the trigger."

He took the gun away and Tony breathed a deep sigh of relief. Manfred handed the pistol to Tony who accepted it without thinking, then continued.

"'Help me,' she begs Robert, handing him the gun. Robert takes the gun and shoots her."

"What the hell!" Tony threw the gun on the sand. "What the hell are you on about, Manfred?"

"It's simple. In his youth, Robert saw a horse break its leg. Horses don't recover from a broken leg so it was shot to put it out of its misery. So he shot her. When asked why he did it, he replied, 'They shoot horses, don't they?' That's where the title of the movie came from."

* * *

While Tony tried to deal with the turn of events on Ulu Island, swashbuckler Rob De Werter was under full sail and skipping through the silvery tips of the waters of Saint George's Channel travelling west-north-west towards the Duke of Yorks. He was returning from another trip to Balangot plantation on New Ireland. It was late afternoon and he had been on the water for five hours and loving every minute of his buccaneering lifestyle. He knew that he would never be able to make it back to Rabaul that night under sail, so he headed for the southern tip of Duke of York Island. It was then only a matter of skirting past Mioko Island and Utan Island and sailing about another half hour to the mission guest house on Ulu Island. He was planning to stay the night there and leave the following morning for Rabaul.

Tony and Manfred enjoyed their lobster meal, relaxed on the beach for a few hours in the warm sunshine, had a couple more swims and eventually headed back towards the guest house to finish off the beer. Upon arrival, Manfred grabbed what was left of the carton from the fridge and gestured to Tony to go outside.

"Come on, we'll drink these over there under those palms where we smoked those joints last time."

They sat down shoulder to shoulder at the base of a coconut tree and Manfred handed him a stubby of beer.

"We'll have to leave pretty soon to make sure we get back to Rabaul before dark," Tony reminded him. "That is unless you want to live on green coconuts for a day once the beer has run out."

"That's okay, I'm used to having to live off the land," Manfred laughed. "I'm forever looking for death-defying situations to feed the guilt of my diagnosed condition of 'survivor's syndrome'."

"Yeah, well I've got to be honest with you Manfred," Tony confessed. "I really thought you were going to do yourself in or something this morning. Especially when I found out you had that pistol. Then you jumped on me from the rafters and I was certain it was going to be curtains for me as well. Then you go and pull that one on me about shooting horses on the beach. Shit mate that was serious stuff back there."

"Nah, I only came here because I had to get away from Jantz and all the shit that was going on in my head in Rabaul. I left Australia because I had to get away from all that was happening in Australia. There aren't many places left where I can go to anymore, matey. Here, on Ulu Island, as it turned out, we snorkelled a bit, we swam, we caught a few lobsters and now we are having few beers. It's just like being with my old mates in Babinda again. You don't happen to have any more of that 'hoochy cooch' by any chance, do you?" he asked, without waiting for an answer. "Maybe it was the 'hoochy cooch' or maybe it was the bit of Babinda in you, but something reminded me of the good old days of my childhood and the good old God that I once knew. Now I can feel it again ... that calm ... so deep. Well, there's no 'hoochy cooch' this time, so it must be the bit of Babinda in you that has brought it all back to me. The bike rides out to the double-barrelled bridge, the spear-fishing and swimming in Babinda Creek at Happy Valley, the old folk in the little house in Church Street, the mill, the school ...

"Hey ..." He sat forward as he broke out of his reverie. "Now here's something you never knew about me. I bet you never knew that I wasn't christened Manfred. I was christened Everyman ... Everyman Wright. Would you believe it?"

"Nah, you're kidding me?" Tony said.

"Nope, Everyman Wright. My father named me after the main character in a medieval street theatre play called *Everyman*. In it, Everyman represents all of mankind. At the start of the play, God sent 'Death' to summon Everyman to meet his maker, and 'Death' told him that if he wanted to enter the kingdom of Heaven, he had to make a good account of himself in relation to his time spent on Earth. He even suggested Everyman should take along some friend who could vouch for him; like a sort of referee, I guess. Of course, when it came to the crunch, even his best friends deserted him, because none of them wanted to go that far to help."

Tony sat with his mouth agape, trying to digest it all. "Well I'll be blowed. How come you never got Everyman at school?"

"By the time I had to go to school, a zillion people must have suggested to my parents that the name Everyman Wright was not a name any child should have to carry into an Australian classroom. How'd you be getting stuck with a yoke like that around your neck? Anyhow, when it came time for my enrolment, it was the principal who finally convinced the old man to rename me. He explained how Manfred was a proper name, yet it was also a blended word of both Everyman and my father's name Wilfred. That must have been what did it in the end."

"So the boy who was christened Everyman was enrolled in the school as Manfred Wright, on the stroke of midnight so to speak." Tony was still shaking his head in disbelief.

"That's correct, and on my very first day at school, Wilfred and Ella went down to the Clerk of the Court at the Babinda police station and had my name changed officially by deed poll."

"So ... so." Tony was still trying to take it all in.

Manfred nudged him and laughed. "So, just last week, I filled out the papers to change my name back to Everyman again. That's it, one problem solved."

"Maybe that's a bit drastic but you have to do what you have to do. Just don't try and explain it to me. It all goes to prove that nothing has to be forever, Manfred, not even your name." Tony leaned back and gave him a pat on the back and thought for a moment to try to match Manfred's story with one of his own.

"It still leaves me with my 'survivor' problem, but I've worked out how to beat that as well," Manfred added, before Tony had a chance to speak.

"You know Manfred, there was something I once did when we were kids that I never told you about. Remember when we caught those day-old crocs down on the sandbank on the Russell River? The next day you brought them into class in Grade One for Show and Tell in a shoebox."

"Yeah, I got caned for that."

"Well, I felt really bad about that because I was there when we caught them and I was there when you said you were going to bring them to school. We both thought it was a good idea. We thought it was a much better thing to show the kids then the rubbish all the other kids talked about. I felt so bad, I went up to the headmaster after school and told him he shouldn't have caned you for that, because you were just a kid."

"Tell me about it. You had guts, matey."

"I told him Show and Tell wasn't your idea, yet you got punished for doing what you were told to do." Tony hung his head down as he could not look at Manfred.

"You're not wrong. He caned me – one on each hand," Manfred reminded him.

"Well, I told him he was wrong and that we should all share the blame."

"You're kidding me," Manfred playfully ruffled the hair on the back of Tony's head. "You told Chrome Dome he was wrong? What did he say?"

"He caned me – one on each hand."

Manfred shuffled his bulk towards Tony a little and put his left arm over his shoulder.

"I reckon what you did was what 'Wallaby Jack' Joe Black would have done. He had guts too, just like you. Talk about injustice. We are surrounded by injustice and cover-up. 'If something isn't right, then it isn't right and no amount of lying, pretending or cover-up is ever going to make it right'; that's what Angel always said. Someone has to be prepared to stand up and be counted."

"So who is that someone supposed to be?" Tony asked.

"It's up to everyman to stand up and be counted." Manfred clenched his fist and pressed it against his chest.

Tony looked around and saw the sadness in Manfred's eyes which glistened as he drew Tony across to him with his left arm and pulled him up tightly against his chest. Tony could feel the pistol tucked into Manfred's belt pressing against him.

"I'm Everyman now, the medieval character in the morality play who is about to meet his maker, and I have to prepare a good account of myself in relation to my journey here on this Earth. After what I have done, who would want to vouch for me, Tony?"

It was as if both had become frozen in that embrace at those words, but it was only for a few seconds. Tony reached for Manfred's clenched fist, prised his fingers open and grasped his hand in a handshake with his own.

"I'll vouch for you, Manfred. I'll vouch for you."

A gentle breeze began to rustle the leaves in the palm fronds, resonating the faintest drum roll above them. The pistol was ceremoniously raised and the barrel placed against his temple.

"Vietnam ...Viet-Bloody-Nam," were the last words spoken before he pulled the trigger. The loud explosion so close to his brain, catapulted Tony into the air. It felt as though he had done a complete double somersault and then landed on his feet. He stood there stooped, covered in blood, in shock and shaking uncontrollably.

Rob De Werter had just pulled into the jetty at Ulu Island for the night, when he heard a shot. He looked up and then in the direction of the sound. He calmly looped the anchor rope over the pylon closest to the other two boats and climbed onto the jetty. As he hurried along the jetty in the direction of the shot, he heard a second shot and all he could remember was wondering what went wrong.

* * *

Postscript

Vietnam War Veterans finally had a long-awaited *Welcome Home March for Vietnam Veterans* on 3rd October 1987. There were 35000 marchers including 25000 veterans and an estimated 100,000 people lined the Sydney streets. In 1992, a *National Memorial for the Vietnam War* was unveiled in Canberra and these gestures finally gave Vietnam Veterans recognition for their sacrifices during the controversial war.

1987 was twelve years after the Vietnam War ended and 1992 was seventeen years after the Vietnam War ended. Nevertheless, those two things meant so much to so many, even though it was too little, too late, for too many.

A lot of help has been forthcoming from and the Returned and Services League of Australia and since 1979 from the Vietnam Veterans Association of Australia and the Vietnam Veterans Federation of Australia whose sole interest is the welfare of veterans and the families of veterans.

If any reader is still feeling invaded by the "stalker" or has a loved one so suffering, help can be obtained through the following help lines and websites:

Help Lines:
- Lifeline - 13 11 14
- Men's Line Australia - 1300 78 99 78
- Salvo Care Line - 1300 36 36 22
- Salvo Youth Line - (02) 8736 3293 (Sydney local call)
- Suicide Call Back Service - 1300 659 467
- Carers Australia – 1800 242 636
- Headspace – 1800 650 890
- MindSpot Clinic – 1800 61 44 34
- Relationships Australia – 1300 364 277
- Sane Australia Helpline – 1800 18 7263

Websites:
- Lifeline Australia: www.lifeline.org.au
- beyondblue: www.beyondblue.org.au
- Black Dog Institute: www.blackdoginstitute.org.au